Prologue

Madeline woke to the sound of a howl. The horrible cry trailed off and died out. Coughs racked her body, and her raw throat throbbed. The terrible noise had ripped its way out of her own chest. She struggled to breathe. The howl had been too big and too rough for her throat. It had ripped through her throat so that every breath that followed was a harsh rasp.

Seconds later, terror caused even those shallow breaths to catch. She forgot the rude awakening and the raw pain in her throat.

The baby was gone.

Trevor. Was. Gone.

She struggled to open her eyes. The world that met her was blurry and vague. She could feel the loss of the baby better than she could see her empty arms. His weight against her chest was missing.

She'd held him for such a long time.

But another familiar weight was still beside her.

Madeline reached for the ruby sword. The gem in its hilt flickered weakly, oddly illuminating her blurred surroundings. When her fingers closed around it, its red light flared. She could suddenly make out her strange crystalline bed. Someone or something had shattered the enclosure and taken her child.

The sword vibrated with power, but she held it easily, from practice and skill. The scarlet light grew and became an aura around her whole body as she rose.

She wasn't dressed for battle. Her gown and kirtle were much more cumbersome than the leggings and tunic she would have worn for fighting. But it didn't matter. There was no time to search for more practical clothes. Trevor was gone, and she could sense a great and horrible danger bearing down on her.

Crystal shards fell away from her as she stood. Madeline could barely make out the tangle of bushes around her, though the scent of roses filled the air. But none of those sensations mattered. She was pulled out of the garden as if by an invisible hand toward the threat she sensed.

She was a warrior. Every instinct she possessed drove her forward. Her vision was still blurry; her heart pounded painfully beneath her breast. Her throat felt as if it had been torn apart by her howling scream. But she brandished her ruby sword and made her way to the battle that waited for her.

"Lev, no!" someone shouted.

The meaning of the shout didn't penetrate her understanding. Her attention was focused on a great and terrible beast on the edge of a cliff as she climbed up a steep rise above the garden where she'd been sleeping. Everything else was indistinct to her perceptions ex-

LEGENDARY BEAST

BARBARA J. HANCOCK

MILLS & BOON

First Published in Great Britain 2018
by Mills & Boon, an imprint of HarperCollins*Publishers*
1 London Bridge Street, London, SE1 9GF

Legendary Beast © 2018 Barbara J. Hancock

ISBN: 978-0-263-26689-4

1018

MIX
Paper from
responsible sources
FSC® C007454

This book is produced from independently certified FSC™ paper to ensure responsible forest management.

For more information visit: www.harpercollins.co.uk/green

Printed and bound in Spain
by CPI, Barcelona

For the lovers who mean it
when they pledge their hearts "forever."

cept the massive figure of a monstrous white wolf that snarled and growled and threatened the people nearby.

Rain began to fall. It plastered the wolf's hair against his giant body, and even though the red aura of her ruby sword deflected much of the moisture from her face, her vision was even more obscured as the rain hit the barrier of energy and became rivulets of water in front of her eyes.

The tempestuous storm and the creature's sudden loud and long howl seemed to echo the tumult in her own chest. She had to clamp her jaw against the urge to howl again along with the beast, as his sound made the very ground on which she stood vibrate.

Madeline raised her blade against the monster and against the fury that threatened to tear her body apart because she couldn't contain the enormity of it all.

But then the white wolf was gone.

Her anger didn't disappear, but a pain so intense it overshadowed any she had felt before joined it. Her sword arm weakened beneath the onslaught of emotion, and she lowered it until the tip of her blade met the ground so that the mighty ruby blade became more cane than weapon. It was the only thing keeping her on her feet.

Until a warm body braced against hers on the other side.

Trevor was gone. The white wolf was gone. Her numb fingers no longer held the ruby blade. The same person who helped her to stay on her feet had taken the blade from her and tossed it aside. It was lying on the ground, several feet away. The protection of its red aura was gone. Rain pelted her face and soaked through her hair and her dress.

And then a cold, calm, powerful presence was also

there. All the terrible, overwhelming pain was soothed away by a cool psychic touch inside her mind. Her legs gave out beneath her, but it didn't matter. The cool presence approached and took her weight from the smaller, warmer one.

Vasilisa and her daughter, Anna. The knowledge of their names was placed in her mind by the cool presence. Her thoughts were as hazy as her vision and as impossible to process, but the explanation calmed her slightly. She should trust her queen. Her instincts were screaming other things, but they were rusty from disuse, and the psychic touch chilled them into silence.

Madeline accepted the coolness in her mind. It came from the woman who held her on her feet, Vasilisa. She exuded an aura that numbed all else. Vasilisa turned Madeline, and they walked away together. But Madeline wasn't entirely soothed. She had failed. She hadn't killed the white wolf. The monstrous beast must have been the terrible threat that had woken her.

And now he had escaped.

Her mind was able to hold on to only one clear thought: wherever Trevor had gone, he wouldn't be safe until the white wolf was destroyed.

Chapter 1

Madeline's fingers were smudged with charcoal from the hundredth pencil she'd worn down to a nub. She used her thumb and forefinger to blend the shadows around the figure of the white wolf she'd drawn. He was large on the page. Much bigger than a natural wolf. As always, he loomed, ready to pounce. She'd lost count of how many times she'd committed her memory of him to paper. No matter how many pages she filled with his savage likeness, she never exorcised him from her mind.

Good. She needed to remember so she would be prepared to protect Trevor if the white wolf should ever return.

That stormy day she'd first woken after hundreds of years, it had been Vasilisa who had broken the crystal chamber that had been her bed for so long. The queen had taken Trevor from her arms to keep him safe while Madeline confronted the threat of the white wolf. It had been horrible to wake up and find her baby gone, but she was glad the queen had protected him from harm.

Vasilisa had been the cool presence that had helped her. Madeline's body had woken from a long illness, but her mind hadn't. Every sight that met her eyes had dazzled and confused her.

The queen encouraged her drawings. She said the sketches came from the recesses of her mind that were still sleeping. Besides the wolf, there were sketches of a life she'd forgotten—a life very unlike the world she had woken to on Vasilisa's island, Krajina.

Vasilisa was the Light *Volkhvy* queen, and Madeline had trusted her from the moment she realized it had been the queen who protected Trevor from the white wolf. *Her queen. Her beloved liege.* Vasilisa had rushed to break the crystal and take the baby from Madeline's arms when the white wolf appeared on the island. His appearance had woken Madeline too harshly from her long sleep. She had risen to face his attack, but she hadn't been strong enough. Vasilisa had explained everything as she helped Madeline recover. Healthy food and exercise seemed to clear her head a little more each day. As her health improved, Vasilisa gently tried to help Madeline recover the memories she'd lost.

But, most of all, the queen had continued to take care of Madeline's infant son, who was still sleeping. She'd explained that Trevor needed to wake up slowly, and that soon he would be smiling, gurgling and grasping Madeline's finger once more.

Madeline had forgotten a great many things, but she hadn't forgotten her baby.

Trevor, the white wolf and her ruby sword—everything else in this strange new world she had to relearn, but not those things. Knowledge of them flashed behind her eyes with every blink and pounded in her chest with every beat of her heart.

Madeline finished the sketch and pulled her blackened fingers away from the page. The white wolf's snarl was threatening, even though she'd created it herself with charcoal and paper. She calmly looked into the beast's eyes for a few moments. Remembering his savagery made her stronger.

She had quickly come to love Vasilisa, who treated her as a daughter and Trevor as a beloved grandchild. But she wouldn't depend on the queen to keep Trevor safe. Madeline was his mother. Facing the threat of the white wolf was her responsibility, and she was determined to be ready.

She closed the sketchbook and placed it on the window ledge that overlooked the ocean below.

Vasilisa was walking on the beach. She held a tiny bundle in her arms—Trevor. Even far away from her breast, Madeline could feel the tug of the invisible heartstrings that held her and her baby together. Yet she trusted the queen with him; Vasilisa visited with him every day, often taking him on walks beneath the Mediterranean sun.

The queen's footsteps took her and the baby closer and closer to the cliff where the white wolf had appeared. Though Madeline trusted Vasilisa entirely, her breath still came quicker and her pulse leaped in her throat.

Vasilisa said the white wolf had once been her champion, but he had become a wild and savage monster that couldn't be trusted any longer.

Madeline looked from the empty cliff down to the kind queen, who crooned to the sleeping baby she held against her chest. Queen Vasilisa's enemies were Madeline's enemies. It was a truth she felt to her bones.

She stepped back from the window and stretched before dropping down to the floor. She caught her weight with her hands and then pressed up and down until her shoulders protested from the effort. Then she pressed up and down a dozen times more.

When she'd woken up, her vision had been blurry and weak, but her instincts had driven her to rise and climb to the top of a cliff, where she'd found the white wolf. His presence had drawn her like a magnet—a terrifying magnet with vicious teeth and glowing red eyes.

She'd confronted the wolf with the ruby sword in her hands, but she hadn't killed him. When he'd shifted into his human form, she'd been taken by surprise. Then Vasilisa had appeared to bring her back to the palace, along with Trevor. The white wolf's brother had taken the beast back to his home.

Letting them go had been a mistake.

But her weakness that morning had only guaranteed she would work hard to heal so she could fight the white wolf another day.

Madeline brought her legs up beneath her and used them to lift her body back to a standing position with her arms outstretched. She exercised in secret because she didn't want Vasilisa to worry she was overexerting herself. She grew stronger every day. Her arms, back and legs were responding to her efforts. Madeline straightened her shirt and stepped back to the window. She smoothed her hair back from her face.

The queen was heading back to the palace. As she came nearer, Madeline turned to go outside and meet them. In midmorning, she always sang to Trevor and watched his little face for signs of waking.

A sudden quaking of the earth beneath Madeline's feet shook the entire palace and sent her to her knees. It was a testament to her persistence in recovering that she was able to leap back up again within seconds. As soon as she was back on her feet, she raced to the window, but the beach was empty, as was the stone stairway that led from the sand up to the palace portico.

Vasilisa and Trevor were gone.

Her gaze flew up from the sand to the cliff, but it was also deserted.

If the white wolf had returned, he hadn't appeared in the same place as last time.

Madeline abandoned the window, but before she could make it to the door of her room, the screams had already begun. She wrenched open the door anyway and headed toward the noise of battle. She didn't have the ruby sword by her side, and she was far from as strong as she could be, but she'd fight for Trevor with her bare hands if she had to.

He was all she had left of a life she couldn't remember.

The palace was under attack, but it wasn't the white wolf. Madeline searched for Trevor as witches all around her battled each other with bolts of energy from their hands. The transformation of the beautiful Mediterranean palace into a battlefield jarred her already tender senses, but she didn't allow the shock to slow her down. She wasn't *Volkhvy*, and her sword was gone, but she was quicker on her feet than she would have been because of her secret exercise regimen. She used that quickness to dodge and weave and make her way around the fighting witches.

As she ran, she noted that the witches who had attacked Vasilisa's palace had black marks on their foreheads. Were all Dark *Volkhvy* marked? She couldn't remember.

She only knew Vasilisa's enemies were her enemies. She memorized the mark for later reference, but for now, she had to find Trevor and keep her baby from harm.

"This way," a voice whispered from one of Vasilisa's sitting rooms. Madeline reacted just in time, sliding inside the narrowly opened door before a contingent of marked *Volkhvy* could see her. She blinked when the door clicked shut, enveloping her in darkness. The marked *Volkhvy* ran by, their booted feet ringing down the hall.

"I'm looking for Trevor," Madeline said into the darkness.

"They've taken him. And the queen. Her last order was that I should keep you safe," the voice explained.

Madeline could finally make out one of Vasilisa's older servants. The woman allowed the energy in her fingers to glow only slightly, lighting up the room enough to illuminate her face.

"No," Madeline said. "I can help them."

The servant reached out and touched Madeline's cheek with her cold fingers. The violet glow of energy felt tingly on Madeline's skin.

"You can't help them alone," the servant said. "Sleep now. Then you can seek the white wolf's help."

Madeline had slept over a thousand years during her illness. She resisted the sudden cool fog that claimed her mind with the servant's touch to no avail. She slipped into an unconsciousness that was as dark and deep as before, but it wasn't as silent. As her body crumpled, the last thing she felt was the servant lowering her to the floor and the last thing she heard was the white wolf's howl. His cry echoed through her soul in an endless protest against losing loved ones to the evil *Volkhvy*.

Her journey from the Light *Volkhvy* island of Krajina had been long. Without the use of Vasilisa's more powerful abilities, Madeline had been dependent on Vasilia's followers and their help in procuring human modes of transportation. There had been a boat and a stormy, rough passage by sea. Following that, she had flown in a plane that seemed to her as magical as Vasilisa herself. But the length of her travels had caused her body to ache nearly as much as her heart. The soreness reached all the way to her bones and deeper still. The jarring movement of the final leg on a train that carried her closer and closer to her destination didn't help. Not nearly as quiet as the plane's flight, the constant metallic screeches of the train strained her ears.

Only her sketches soothed her.

She finished a particularly menacing charcoal drawing of the white wolf, and then she closed her sketchbook and pushed it into the backpack that sat beside her in an empty seat. She put the pencil in a side pocket of her pack, even though it was probably spent. It rattled against a handful of others that had been used up. She had a few good ones left—soon she would sharpen another and sketch some more.

Soon.

Trevor and Vasilisa had been ruthlessly ripped from her life by an attack that had taken even the queen of all Light witches by surprise because it had been perpetuated by a traitorous Light *Volkhvy* who had turned to the Dark. Vasilisa had told her that long ago she'd been a warrior for the Light. Madeline felt that truth in her heart, but it wasn't echoed by any sort of ability in her muscles and mind. She hadn't been prepared for the old servant who had knocked her out and hidden her from the fight.

She'd failed to protect her son. She'd failed to help the witch queen who had done so much for her.

"Care for some tea, miss?" an older woman sitting across from her asked. She poured herself a cup from a steaming metal container as Madeline shook her head. Her stomach was too knotted to keep the liquid down.

She'd put her sketchbook away and zipped her backpack closed, but the white wolf's snarl was still vivid in her memory as the train took her closer and closer to the monster himself.

Lev Romanov.

She didn't know him. She couldn't remember him at all. But Vasilisa had told her the legend of the Romanov wolves. The Light *Volkhvy* queen had created champion shape-shifters to help her stand against the Dark. She had forged three enchanted swords to be wielded by their warrior mates.

Madeline's heart beat too quickly in her chest, and her breathing was shallow. As usual, when she wasn't sketching, she wasn't sure what to do with the adrenaline that urged her to some vague action. She had forgotten too much for too long. Vasilisa had encouraged her to take her time. She'd told her to remember how to live first. The simple mundane tasks of daily life that so many took for granted had challenged Madeline for months.

But now she must do so much more.

She had to save Trevor.

Her secret exercises seemed silly now, poor preparation for what lay ahead. She was physically stronger, but her memory loss left her vulnerable.

Her arms were empty. She needed to sketch or she would go mad. She clenched her smudged fingers into fists and placed them on her lap. She only had a few pencils left, and she needed to ration out the precious charcoal as a starving man would his last crumbs of bread.

Vasilisa had urged her to take her time to recover all she had lost, but her time had run out.

"Here. You look like you could use a hot drink more than I could," the old woman insisted.

Now that her sketchbook was tucked away, Madeline really looked at the woman across from her for the first time. She raised her hand to accept the proffered cup as the older passenger nodded in approval.

But something was wrong. The woman wasn't as old as she had seemed. Her hair wasn't gray. It was white like Vasilisa's, and her eyes were sharp, not elderly and vague as they focused keenly on the cup in Madeline's hands.

Steam rose from the hot tea, but as she brought the cup closer to her face, its wafting fragrance wasn't the aromatic scent of strong tea she expected. Instead, an unpleasant bitter scent assailed her. Madeline's nose crinkled, and she lowered the cup without sipping.

"There's something bad in your tea," she gasped as her eyes watered.

The woman grabbed the cup from Madeline's fingers before she could drop it. She raised it to her own face and sniffed.

"I only smell tea. Nothing else. You can't possibly smell the poison. Not unless…" The woman's eyes widened, and she rose so quickly that the bad tea slopped on the floor. "They told me it was safe to approach you alone. They said you'd lost your connection to the wolf."

Madeline sat frozen as the woman's movements caused a black mark on her forehead to be revealed. She'd seen the same mark on the foreheads of the corrupt *Volkhvy* who had attacked Vasilisa's island. She'd sketched the ashy flower all around the wolf drawings in her pad.

"My son. Where is my son?" Madeline asked. Her sharp demand caused the other passengers to shuffle and murmur. She and the witch who had apparently tried to poison her were now the objects of everyone's attention.

But the *Volkhvy* was already backing away. Her eyes were round with fear.

"It doesn't matter. Your connection to the wolf won't stop us. I'll be back, and next time I won't be alone," the marked witch threatened. She continued to back away toward the door, her gaze spinning wildly around the passenger car as if she expected the savage white wolf to suddenly spring from thin air.

Madeline knew there was no wolf connection coming to her rescue, but before she could rise and go after the witch, armed with nothing but a sketchbook, the train entered a tunnel. The darkness wasn't complete, but it was enough cover for the *Volkhvy* assassin to disappear.

When the train exited the tunnel and daylight streamed through its windows once more, the sun found Madeline clutching her backpack to her chest as if it was the baby she'd lost.

Her uncertainty in her abilities didn't matter. The assassin's fear meant she was on the right path. The white wolf was her only hope.

The savage wolf was a shape-shifter, and at one time he had been her husband. In this whole wide world she navigated alone, there was only one other who might be able to help her save Trevor from the marked *Volkhvy* who had stolen him away.

His father.

Vasilisa said he was wild and he couldn't be trusted, but Madeline had no one else to turn to for help.

Chapter 2

Lev had thrown most of the furniture out of the tower room. Niceties enraged him. He was currently dissatisfied with the shredded bed he'd kept in the middle of the room. The gemlike stained-glass windows he'd shattered with his fists lay all around the floor in glittering shards, while the biting wind howled through the ramparts and into the room he'd opened to the elements outside. The cold air didn't bother him. He welcomed it. He craved discomfort. In fact, he wanted to run away from the care and concern of everyone around him, but reduced to two legs and two feet cut by the glass he'd walked over as he paced back and forth for days, how far could he possibly go?

Not far enough. Never far enough.

On four legs, he'd finally found her. She had greeted him as an enemy. She had raised the ruby sword against him…and he'd wanted its blade to fall. He'd stood on the edge of the cliff as the white wolf, and then he'd kneeled there as a broken man. He deserved her hatred. He should have thrown himself into the raging sea far below the cliff's edge.

But Soren had brought him home.

Bronwal. The Carpathian castle Vasilisa had built for her enchanted warriors so long ago. It still stood. Only now it remained ever-manifest in an isolated mountain pass where once it had come from the Ether because of Vasilisa's curse.

His twin brother wouldn't give up on him. He never had. As the red wolf, Soren had been relentless in his pursuit. If Lev could have shifted back into his wolf form in those moments, he would have fought Soren tooth and nail to remain at Madeline's mercy.

But the shift wouldn't come to him no matter how hard he tried to summon it.

He was still a man. He'd been trapped in his human form since the day he'd found Madeline on Vasilisa's island. His human body was unrecognizable to him. He'd been a battle-hardened warrior in long-ago days he could barely remember. He'd lived a demanding life in the saddle and on the battlefield, even when he wasn't a wolf. But none of that had compared to the relentless life he'd lived for hundreds of years as the white wolf. That life was written on his scarred skin and ruthlessly toned physique. Only now could he look back and realize he'd been as relentless as Soren. The red wolf had hunted him. The white wolf had hunted for his lost wife and child even after he'd forgotten their faces and names.

Witches had done this to him. They had tortured him for centuries by taking his family and leaving him with a mad hunger for his wife and son that couldn't be satiated no matter how much blood he spilled. He'd thought them dead. He'd searched anyway.

Never resting. Never stopping. Never giving up.

Only to discover his long-lost love hated him when he finally found her. It was a suitable end to his legendary tale. The only one he deserved. He hadn't protected Madeline or Trevor from Vasilisa. He had howled and howled against the *Volkhvy* queen, but he had never been able to find the family she'd stolen from him. And still he howled. He couldn't shift and he couldn't leave Bronwal, not while Madeline, Trevor, Soren and his entire family were at the mercy of witches.

Lev jumped up from the bed and wrenched one of its solid posters free from its frame. His long years as the white wolf had given him incredible strength. His muscles were lean and firm and roped with veins. They bulged as he tore apart the bed and flung its pieces down the winding stairs.

He had felt her fear. It had been a part of him. It had driven him back into the human form he'd shunned for hundreds of years.

Servants would come. They would clear the busted wood away. They would bring him food and drink. They would bring him clothes to replace the shirts and trousers he tore from his skin. They would try to bathe him and bandage the wounds on his feet.

But his rage always won in the end. They always ran away and left him alone. Even his devoted brother, Soren, when he came to check on Lev like clockwork every night, would eventually leave him to howl alone at the too-distant moon.

He'd lived with torment for many years, but it was far worse now that he had felt Madeline's fear.

* * *

Without the help of some of Vasilisa's loyal servants, who had also survived the attack, Madeline never would have found Bronwal. The servants had given her the money she would need and explained how to use it. In spite of her illness, she was quick-witted and only needed to see or hear something once to understand how to do it herself. They explained that at one time, there had been a mirror portal between Krajina and the Romanovs' castle, but it had been destroyed.

Madeline was desperate to save Trevor, but she was also terrified to see the white wolf again. The long journey helped to prepare her for what she might have to face. Still, once she hiked to the protected pass where the castle the world had forgotten stood, she stared up at its towered heights with trepidation.

The sword seemed like a dream. Her ability to wield it seemed like a joke. Her hands seemed much more suited to charcoal pencils than deadlier things. But she no longer had the luxury of taking the time to rediscover herself. It was time to decide who she would be. Right here. Right now.

Madeline decided she would be the person who saved her son.

She had dreaded seeing the white wolf again. She hadn't stopped to imagine what it would be like for all the other citizens of Bronwal to welcome her "home." She recognized no one. For her, it was exactly as if she'd approached the castle for the first time. She wondered at its breadth and depth. She marveled at its immensity. Only *Volkhvy* enchantments could have kept it hidden from the outside world for so long.

But by far, it was the whispers and exclamations and

expressions on people's faces that seemed like the greatest barrier between her and the shape-shifter she sought.

"Please, ma'am. Wait here," an elderly servant advised.

The great hall she entered was cavernous, but its details were swallowed up in shadows.

When someone came to meet her, Madeline finally saw her first familiar face. It was one of the people the white wolf had threatened on the cliff during the storm when she'd woken up to confront him—the warm presence that had taken the sword from her numb fingers.

This was Anna, the Light *Volkhvy* princess, and Vasilisa's daughter.

"We didn't expect you so soon," the curvy, dark-haired woman said. Her hair tumbled around her face in a chestnut cap of curls. And her lush figure was enhanced by the obvious swell of pregnancy that rounded out the loose tunic she wore. In her arms, she carried a long bundle wrapped in scarlet cloth. The cloth was embroidered with thorny vines. For some reason, the design made Madeline's heartbeat quicken.

"I'm surprised you expected me at all, but I have no choice. Marked *Volkhvy* attacked Krajina. They've taken Trevor and Vasilisa," Madeline said. The other woman's eyes widened and her face blanched. Madeline's urgency for her son had caused her to be inconsiderate. She should have been gentler when she told Anna about her mother's kidnapping.

"I marked them. They're worse than Dark *Volkhvy*. They were once Light, but they've been corrupted by their thirst for power," Anna said. "You've come for Lev's help," she continued in a softer tone. She had frozen several steps away. She held the scarlet bundle with one hand while the other had fallen on her stomach as if she was protecting her own baby from harm. "He hasn't recovered. He might never recover. He is still...lost," Anna warned.

It hadn't been concern for her mother that made Anna Romanov go suddenly pale. It had been the very idea that Madeline was here to seek out the white wolf's help.

She didn't need the other woman's fear to remind her of the white wolf's ferocity. She had sketched his snarl a thousand times from her memories of that day on the cliff. Anna's fears put hers in perspective. She was more afraid for Trevor than she was of the wolf. She was ready to face him. She had to be.

"I'm also lost. I can't remember my former life. Vasilisa said my recovery would take time, but I no longer have that luxury. I'm here because I can't rescue my baby alone," Madeline said.

"Soren can help. And Ivan. They can help you," Anna said. "Elena and I—"

"No. The black wolf and the red wolf have to protect their own families. You're ready to have a baby yourself, and Vasilisa told me that Elena has a newborn," Madeline said.

"I don't think Lev will help you," Anna said. "I don't think he can." Her grip on the scarlet bundle was white-knuckled as she spoke, and she took another step toward Madeline, as if she would try to persuade her to go away.

"I'm not here to *ask* for his help," Madeline said. "I'm here to demand it."

Anna paused again. She was shorter than Madeline by half a dozen inches, but even though she was forced to tilt her chin to meet Madeline's eyes, her direct green gaze still seemed formidable. It took all of Madeline's will not to back down. For Trevor she stood. For Trevor she didn't resist when Anna raised the bundle between them and held it horizontally supported on her forearms. The scarlet cloth fell aside to reveal what had been nestled carefully in its soft folds.

Madeline recognized the ruby sword. She reached for it automatically as if she could do nothing else, but when her fingers brushed over the large ruby in the sword's hilt, nothing happened. It didn't wake to greet her. It was dark and dull, more grayish black than red, as if it was tarnished by shadows.

Her hands dropped away from the one thing she remembered besides her baby and the white wolf. Its darkness seemed like a rejection. She wasn't the woman she used to be, and the sword knew it. She wasn't a brave warrior who had fought for the Light *Volkhvy* and Queen Vasilisa. She was a confused woman weakened by her long illness and her memory loss.

But she didn't back away.

"I wondered at its dormancy. I thought maybe it would wake in your presence," Anna said. She didn't wrap the cloth back around the sword. She still seemed to watch and wait for some sign that the ruby wasn't dead.

"I didn't come for the sword. I came for the white wolf," Madeline said. Her concerns over her memory loss had risen with her frantic heartbeat to fill her chest and then her throat with a tight heat she could barely speak around. But she wouldn't allow it to stop her.

"Lev is in the tower room," Anna replied. "Or what's left of it. I'll take you to the stairs. That's as far as I'm able to go. He rages at the sight of me. Or any *Volkhvy*. Maybe you'll receive a better welcome."

Her tone didn't sound hopeful. Madeline swallowed

against the knot of fear that had solidified at the back of her throat.

Anna turned. She led the way out of the room and toward the back of the castle. Madeline took a deep breath to try to dispel the tightness in her chest and followed. When they came to a large archway that framed the beginning of a spiral staircase, the pregnant woman paused and then stepped aside to make way for Madeline. The stone stairway twisted up and around until its treads curved out of sight.

Anna still held the sword out in front of her as if it was an offering for Madeline. Madeline refused it as she stepped forward.

"Whatever you find at the top of the stairs, you should know that he never stopped searching for you," Anna said. "He never rested in all the years you were sleeping."

Madeline paused for a moment. Her back was turned to Anna, but she heard. She also doubted. Vasilisa had warned her that the white wolf was feral. She'd woken to his rage. If he had looked for her and Trevor, he hadn't had benevolent intentions.

Madeline climbed the stairs. This time, she wouldn't raise a sword against the white wolf as she had done on the edge of Krajina's sea cliff. The sword was as closed off and dead to her as her past was to her mind and heart. She only had her love for Trevor to guide her and strengthen her as she climbed up toward the tower room. Her maternal feelings offset her fear. She didn't know what she would find at the top of the stairs, but she knew she had to try.

Soft electric torches glowed from the soot-blackened walls where flaming torches used to be. Madeline could almost see them flickering. She could almost remem-

ber the scent of scorched tallow-soaked cloth as she
forced herself to take step after step toward her greatest nightmare.

But any gentler memories were overwhelmed in her
mind by visions of the white wolf's snarl and his red
glowing eyes. He was a massive monster with long fear-
some fangs and bloodstained fur. She had been filled
with the absolute certainty that a dangerous presence
had threatened her and Trevor and everyone else there
that day. Madeline's response had been visceral, from
the howl that had woken her up as it ripped itself from
her body, to the intent that had claimed her to lash out
with her sword and kill the beast that seemed to be the
only threat she could see.

Anna had stopped her. The white wolf's shift had
stopped her. For some reason, she hadn't been able to
strike at the man as the rain fell and the wind whipped
around them. She'd been racked by an internal storm
as fierce as the one that tossed the ocean and the atmosphere around Krajina.

The ferocity of her emotion had seemed too big for
her body to contain, until Vasilisa had soothed it away
with her cool magic.

As she neared the top of the stairs, Madeline had to
step around and over the busted-up debris and shredded
remains of furniture and clothes. Feathers from pillows
that had been torn apart swirled up and floated down
around her feet like snow. Ripped-up pages of books
joined this feather "snow" to cover the stairs.

And still she climbed.

Her body was heavy. The uncertainty in her chest
and throat had expanded until it seemed to flow through
her veins to every part of her. Her legs felt weighted
down, but she moved them anyway. Her heightened

anxiety pressed against her shoulders as if it tried to hold her back. She ignored the pressure. Once again, it seemed as if her body could barely contain the emotions it tried to feel.

But her discomfort and the danger she faced didn't matter.

Trevor, Trevor, Trevor, Trevor.

He was all that mattered.

Each ringing step of her boots on the stone staircase seemed to echo with her baby's name. She only paused when she came to the top and found a door torn from its hinges and lying to the side. The door had been crafted with heavy wood on its bottom half and scrolled iron bars on its top half, but for all its sturdy artisan construction, it had been busted loose and practically splintered by whatever force had shoved it aside.

"Go away. I want nothing. I need nothing. How many times do I have to tell you to allow me to bleed?"

Every ounce of trepidation that had filled Madeline's body drained away when she heard the ragged rough voice ring out and echo down the stairs. Its deep reverberations flowed through her like rushing waters, leaving her hollowed out in their wake. For long seconds, she wasn't afraid. She wasn't anything. She was only an empty husk that might float down to settle with the feathers and torn papers on the stairs.

And then a basket whizzed past her head. Bandages and tape spilled from it, and the whole mess bounced down the stairs and out of sight. Silence fell, broken only by Madeline's own respiration. Her breathing was quicker than it should have been. She'd thought the fear was gone, but she found it again, a more silent, calmer disquiet than the overwhelming emotion of before.

She was certain that she was in trouble. She was

also certain she would face any trouble imaginable to save her son.

This time it was easier to take the last few steps that brought her into the tower room. She only had to reach up and hold the straps of her backpack and put one foot in front of the other.

And then she saw him again. For the first time in six months.

The trash on the stairs should have prepared her for what she would find, but her breath caught in her throat in a gasp when she saw Lev Romanov. Her fingers went numb on the straps of her bag, and her knees wobbled. She willed her joints to turn to steel, and she managed to stay on her feet.

She'd seen him on the cliff, completely nude and kneeling in the rain. According to Queen Vasilisa, she'd known and loved him, and if that was so, she'd certainly seen him thousands of times before.

Yet she was certain the man before her would have been a stranger even to the warrior she used to be.

He was braced for battle in the middle of the room, with his feet planted wide and his fists clenched at his sides. He wore only torn and bloody trousers low on lean hips. The rest of him was bare. And every inch of his exposed flesh was tensed and hard with ropy muscles that seemed to scream from past exertions she couldn't imagine. He also had fine white scars etched all over his arms, chest and abdomen. The marks seemed impossible because his flesh appeared too hard to brand. He was stone, a living, breathing statue to commemorate where a man used to be.

He glared at her with intense blue eyes that blazed from behind a shocking white streak of hair. The rest of his hair was blond. It fell in wild locks all around his face and shoulders. His beard was as untamed as his hair.

She couldn't read his expression. The set of his features was hidden. But the set of his body was not. He stood as if he was in midbattle, always in midbattle, prepared for the next blow and the one after that.

The meaning of his words, the bandages and the blood finally hit her, and Madeline breathed out a long shaky sigh. He was hurt. The blood on his ripped trousers was his own. His feet were crimson, and the flagstones on the floor were marked by his bloodied footsteps. A cold breeze filled the room, and there was glass from the broken windows all over the floor.

"No. I will not allow you to bleed. Nor will I go away and leave you alone. Trevor needs the white wolf to save him," Madeline said. Her voice sounded almost as rough as his had sounded. As if she hadn't spoken in an age. But at least it didn't tremble. She was shaken to her core by Lev Romanov's appearance, but her voice was firm.

She wasn't prepared for the savage man in the middle of the room to approach her right away, though she should have been. He was obviously racked by adrenaline and fully committed to waging a war only he could see.

He moved too quickly. Between one stunned blink and the next, he had crossed to her and taken her shoulders in his hands. His grip was too fierce. His fingers pressed into her flesh to hold her in place as he intently examined her face. And it wasn't only his hardness or his hold that was intimidating. He was well over six feet tall, and she was too used to being the tallest person in the room.

Suddenly, she was small and soft in comparison to him. She was also not nearly as braced for anything as she'd thought she was. He was midbattle. Her fight had just begun.

"Madeline," he said, and it sounded like a secret they would share, but she couldn't grasp its meaning. The intensity of his gaze was suddenly fully focused on her face. He scanned her features as if he would memorize them. She was caught and held by his blue eyes, just as he held her with his hands as if he would never let her go.

For weeks, she'd been handled with care by Vasilisa and the entire palace of *Volkhvy*. She'd been given time and space and consideration as she'd tried to understand the world around her.

Lev Romanov met her with an urgency that stunned her. He was wild with some need she couldn't begin to understand, when all else was confusion. He fought something with every rise and fall of his broad chest. His fight showed in the grip of his hands and the tension in his entire body.

He pulled her closer, the better to look deep into her eyes, but the move also brought her nearer to his large body. She had seen him nude in the rain, but her vision had been blurred. Here, now, only inches from her, she saw him clearly—every scar, every angle, every plane—and it was all too sudden and intimate for her senses, which had been sleeping for a very long time.

Her breathing had gone shallow, but the scent of the wind trapped in his hair still filled her nose. The room was chilly, but his masculine body heat enveloped her where they stood.

This man had thrown everyone and everything out of his room, but now he grabbed her and pulled her close. He looked deeply into her eyes as if he was preparing to…

Her insecurity over her memory loss flared back to life and resonated all the way to her bones.

"I don't remember you at all," Madeline said. "I'm not here for you. I'm here for Trevor. He needs the white wolf."

Her heart pounded, and the fear crowded out all else that might have been long ago and far away. She needed this savage stranger to help her. She didn't need to remember him or what they had shared.

His hands tightened for a split second and then released just before she cried out in pain. The sudden squeeze had been reflexive. He noted her pain and let her go as suddenly as the spasm had begun. She thought she saw regret flash in his eyes, but then he dipped his head, and his hair was in the way. Did he use his wild mane as a shield between them? If so, it was only somewhat effective, considering the rest of him was exposed.

"The white wolf is gone," Lev said. "I can't shift. I can't help you. This human body has me again, and it won't let me go."

Chapter 3

Madeline shivered as he stepped away, taking all his feral body heat with him. This was the fight she'd sensed in him. He battled the hold of his human form second by second, minute by minute. He fought to shift, and he'd been fighting since she'd seen him on Krajina. But the white wolf was close beneath the surface of his scarred skin. She could feel its ferocity, and she had seen the glimmer of wildness in Lev's eyes. She could sense the potential beast, barely contained.

The wolf was still there in him. She was certain of it. But *needing* the white wolf's help and *wanting* him to appear were two very different things.

"It doesn't matter. You are the white wolf. Whether you have four legs or two. And Trevor needs you," Madeline said.

"You know who the babe is to me? Who you once were to me?" Lev asked. His stance had gone deceptively distant. He'd taken several steps back. She could still see his tension. She could still feel his attention on her face, even though his hair hid his eyes.

"Vasilisa told me everything. That we were together once, but that the Romanovs betrayed her. She protected Trevor and me during a long illness," Madeline said.

"An illness? You think the *Volkhvy* queen saved you," Lev said hoarsely. He stepped toward her once more, without even seeming to realize he moved. "It isn't only our son you want to save. You want me to help you save the *witch*."

The tension in his body had gone so tight and so still that he had truly become a living statue. It seemed as if his scars were cracks in a marbleized form, and he might shatter into a million pieces if she said the wrong thing. Anna had said he hated all *Volkhvy*, but surely he would be grateful to the queen who had saved his former wife and his son?

"The ruby sword is dead and I don't remember how to wield it, but I'm awake now and I'm going after the *Volkhvy* that took my son," Madeline said. "I want you to go with me, but if you refuse, I'll go alone."

Her bag had been knocked crooked on her shoulders by Lev's strong grip on her arms. When she tried to straighten it, the zipper of its main compartment gaped open and her sketchbook fell on the floor. Before Madeline could stoop to retrieve it, Lev moved to scoop it up himself.

Madeline bit her lip against the cry of distress that rose to her lips, as if her prize possession had been stolen right before her eyes. Only Lev wasn't stealing it. He wasn't ripping it up to fling down the stairs. He was flipping through it. He turned and examined page after page of the sketches she'd drawn of the white wolf.

Her every charcoal stroke had been infused with the overwhelming feeling of danger and the threat she'd woken to that day.

His attention was riveted on the sketches. She allowed the hand that had reflexively risen to retrieve the sketchbook from him to fall back to her side.

She'd tried to be brave, but now he knew her deepest fears. They were displayed in drawing after drawing. He had searched her eyes for the warrior he had known. But here was evidence that the warrior was gone. In her place was someone mired in doubt and confusion, along with a deep, abiding helplessness she didn't know how to dispel. She could only press her way through it and hope to come out on the other side triumphant. For Trevor.

"You came anyway," Lev said after he had flipped to the last page. He slowly and carefully handed the book back to her, and Madeline took it from him. If possible, his calmness made her more nervous than his tension. She tucked the sketchbook back into her bag. "You came in spite of your fear."

"Vasilisa told me that witches fear only one thing— the Romanov wolves," Madeline said. "There's only one thing I fear as well—failing to save my child."

I'm awake now.

Every word she uttered pierced his gut with relentless blades of guilt. She didn't remember him. She didn't remember the life they'd lived. It had been so long ago. Even for him, running and fighting and searching, always searching, seemed much more immediate in his memories.

But he could see fear in her eyes, and that was the most cutting observation of all. Her fear stabbed into him, and its sharpness sliced away all other concerns. Her eyes no longer glimmered with the scarlet power of the enchanted ruby. Instead, they shimmered with unshed tears. She had come back to Bronwal. She had climbed the stairs that most were afraid to tread. She had trembled in his hands, and he had felt her fragility beneath his rough fingers.

He flexed those fingers now, as if he could force them to forget the warmth of her when they'd just been reminded after centuries of loss.

Her body was different. Her muscles had weakened during the long, enchanted sleep. But her body's weakness wasn't reflected in her eyes in spite of her fear. It also wasn't reflected in her actions. She was afraid of the beast that lived beneath his skin, but that hadn't stopped her from seeking his help.

Madeline was still a warrior.

She wasn't his warrior. She wasn't the ruby warrior. But she was prepared to fight. Her fear didn't diminish her determination or her bravery. It only complicated what must be done. He'd barely contained the howl that wanted to rip from his depths when she mentioned Vasilisa. Only the knowledge that Madeline was confused and vulnerable kept him from raging against the evil queen. That Madeline might never understand what the witch had done to them was another stinging cut against his scarred skin.

He deserved the pain.

He hadn't saved them. He had failed Madeline and Trevor, but he wouldn't fail them again. He would help her go after the *Volkhvy* that had kidnapped the baby. He would help Madeline save Trevor.

But he wouldn't save Vasilisa.

His family had to be protected from the evil queen.

Yet seeing Madeline again revealed a deeper, darker truth he had to face. She had filled an entire book with sketches of his monstrous snarl, and yet she had still sought him out. She had undertaken an epic journey for a woman out of her own time and place, and she had faced him as he stood, bloody and savage, to "greet" her. He would never forget the fear in her eyes. Paired with the fear he'd felt that morning on the cliff, it was a truth he could no longer fight. He would help her save Trevor. He would kill Vasilisa, and then he would leave.

He would never forget the feel of her arms and the way he had made her flinch with the tightness of his grip.

Even if he could never shift again, he needed to protect his family from the savagery of the white wolf that had settled in to live beneath his scarred skin.

Madeline watched as he decided to help her. She saw him soften and then harden once more. His shoulders slumped for only a moment before they were again stiff and straight and seemingly made of stone.

"I will find him," Lev said. His certainty was as solid as his lean, strong body. His scars stood out against his flexed muscles as his fists clenched.

Suddenly, adrenaline flowed in a cool rush beneath her skin. She gripped the straps of her backpack to hide the trembling in her hands. She'd made the white wolf a part of her life again, if only for a short time. That frightened her, mainly because she hadn't reclaimed the memories she needed to be strong enough to face him, but now she had to be concerned over something else: the way Lev Romanov made her feel.

His vivid blue irises blazed from behind the shock of white in his hair. His gaze was full of secrets about the woman she'd been. Those secrets called to her, but she had to ignore them. She had to ignore the tingling in her arms where this stranger had grabbed her, a tingling that had nothing to do with adrenaline and everything to do with his feral warmth.

He was a beast. The trashed room declared it. The sketches in her backpack were further evidence. As were the bruises he'd no doubt left on her skin with his urgency.

He vowed to find their son and help her save him, but she could only wonder, who would save Lev Romanov? He said he could no longer shift, but it was obvious that the white wolf would never let him go.

Madeline set her jaw and firmed her spine. She pressed her mouth into a hard, thin line to keep from betraying her nerves by nibbling her bottom lip. The move was a mistake. His attention fell from her eyes to her lips and lingered there. This should have meant nothing to her, but her heartbeat stuttered and the nerves in the pit of her stomach whirled out of control.

Because he didn't look at her lips like a stranger would. He looked as if he remembered the taste of her kisses from long ago, and parts of her had suddenly leaped to life, longing to remember, too.

Anna Romanov was waiting when Madeline came back down the stairs. She stood at the ready at the base of the spiraling stone stairway, as if she'd been prepared to do battle should the beast in Bronwal's tower choose to attack her guest. The sword she'd offered to Madeline in outstretched arms was now held by its hilt at Anna's side, but its ruby stone was still dark and gray.

"I thought maybe it would wake when you spoke with Lev, but it still sleeps. Not so much as a flicker,"

Anna informed her. "It gleamed when you wielded it on Krajina with a fierce ruby light."

"I remember. That moment on the cliff is all I recall. Nothing more," Madeline said. "But I will take the sword. The white wolf has agreed to help me save my son. I won't travel with him unarmed."

She reached for the hilt of the ruby blade, and Anna released it into her hands. Unlike before, it was heavy and awkward in her grip. She held it vertically with both hands at her waist and the blade extended in front of her breasts and face until the tip stretched beyond the top of her head. She looked from the hilt in her hands up to the sword's sharp point, and then she lowered her gaze to meet Anna's on either side of the sharp blade. Anna reached to place her hands over Madeline's on the hilt. The dark ruby stayed gray above their fingers, but Madeline's heart fluttered when the other woman squeezed her hands.

She felt…something. A kinship. A connection. To Anna Romanov, if not to the ruby or the blade or the scarred man in the tower above them.

"I am the red wolf's mate. I am Soren Romanov's wife. We are sisters, but we are also part of a sisterhood of warriors. The blade will wake in time. Trust it. Trust yourself and the warrior you're meant to be," Anna said solemnly, as if she recited a pledge.

"It isn't myself or the blade I distrust," Madeline replied. Although that wasn't entirely true. She remembered nothing of how to wield a blade. Her hands seemed to be made for charcoal pencils, not for legendary weapons. It was only that her self-doubt took second place to her doubt of the man who was supposed to be her mate. She accepted the sword as a practical tool, not its Calling. Anna must have sensed her reservations.

"He never forgot you and Trevor. Not even after he'd forgotten how to be a man. His search carried on until he found you," Anna said softly.

Madeline noted the woman's persuasive tone. No one would be able to negate her memory of the white wolf on the stormy cliff. He'd been prepared to attack. Only the arrival of Vasilisa had seemed to prevent it. Madeline took the sword with her as she moved, and Anna let her go. The other woman's hands fell to her sides.

"You are in as much turmoil as Lev. Please. Give him time. Take time to heal before you reject the connection you once embraced," Anna said.

"We don't have time to waste on healing or on each other. Trevor is in danger. We must find him and Queen Vasilisa," Madeline said. Her hands tightened on the hilt of the sword.

"There's a portal that will take us to Vasilisa," Lev Romanov said.

Anna's reaction to his sudden appearance caused Madeline's chest to constrict and her breath to catch. Anna Romanov stiffened from head to toe, and she raised her hands from her sides.

Her fingers glowed with emerald light, as if she'd summoned power to meet an attack head-on.

Madeline had allowed the tip of the sword to droop, but she raised it again now in response to Anna's defensive stance.

Lev paused on the last stone step above them. He was already much taller than Anna Romanov. On the rise, he towered over them both, in spite of Madeline's height. He had changed his clothes. The shredded pants were gone, and he'd replaced them with black leather leggings that fitted his hard muscles like a second skin. He'd also donned a gray long-sleeved undershirt that looked like it had been made for a smaller man—as if it might burst at the seams should he decide to take a deep breath. Over the tightly stretched T-shirt was a black vest, similar to a jerkin but with more modern features, and on his feet were tall black boots. Like hers, his clothing was a mix of old and new.

Although he was lean—almost starved-looking—his frame was broad-shouldered and his muscles had been built with centuries of strenuous activity. He filled the vestibule in which they all stood with the wild presence she'd already seen in the tower room. Truly, her sword and Anna's hands seemed like scant defense against the man or the beast he might become at any time.

But the scarred man didn't attack. He glanced at Anna, and then his attention was all for Madeline. His gaze settled on her face as it had in the tower room, as if he would memorize her features before she left him again. When he spoke, he looked at Madeline, but his words were for Anna Romanov.

"The white wolf attacked you once. I remember. His memories are my memories. I won't apologize. You're a witch. I was trying to protect my brother. But know this—Soren has married you. You are a witch, but you are also his wife. I would die before I harmed you now," Lev said.

"There was a time when I promised not to harm you as well, brother. But know this—I am pregnant, and I will protect my child," Anna warned.

Madeline only saw Anna's glow brighten out of the corner of her eye. She faced Lev without lowering her sword. *The white wolf had attacked Anna?* She couldn't imagine the petite woman surviving the white wolf's ferocious bite. She'd drawn his teeth in her sketchbook many times. Each had easily been as long as her hand.

Only at that revelation did Lev look from Madeline to his sister-in-law. Her obvious pregnancy must have escaped his notice since he'd returned to the castle.

"Rest assured, I'm leaving. The baby will be safe when I'm gone," Lev replied.

His voice was as gruff as it had been before, his vocal cords roughened by centuries of howls. But the glow in Anna's fingers faded until it was gone. The other woman lowered her hands before Madeline lowered her sword.

And the white wolf noticed, even though he was a man. Lev's attention seemed to be on Anna, but his spine didn't soften until Madeline lowered the ruby blade down to her side.

"Ivan destroyed the mirror portal when he found out Elena was going to have a baby. There is no longer a portal in Bronwal," Anna said.

Lev came off the stairs and into the vestibule in several long strides. His physicality was startling. Madeline had been awake for a while, but she had yet to encounter another human being with such grace and speed. If he had decided to attack, her sword would have been useless even if she hadn't lowered its tip to the floor. He might be on two legs instead of four. He might look hollow and hungry. But Lev Romanov was still dangerous. Along with the hunger in his appearance, there was also a deep, dark Carpathian wilderness behind his eyes.

"There is another," Lev said. He spoke to Madeline, as if to reassure her rather than to inform. But he couldn't be sensitive to the sudden clenching in her gut just above the womb, where Trevor had been carried so long ago.

"Yes. The fountain at Straluci. The fortress is in

ruin, but the portal should still be there. It will take you to my mother in the blink of an eye, wherever she is being held. The portals are connected to her," Anna said. "There are no roads. Only narrow game trails. You'll have to take horses instead of all-terrain vehicles. It will take more than a week to reach the pass."

The last was said for her benefit. Anna hadn't taken her eyes off the white wolf in his human form, but she turned to look at Madeline now. Her green eyes flickered with the power she'd previously called to her hands.

"Then the sooner we leave, the better," Madeline proclaimed. She wasn't wearing a scabbard for the ruby blade, and her arm was already tired. The sword was heavy. She felt like a pretender as she stood with it gripped tightly in her hand, but even though her body hadn't recovered its strength following her illness, her heart was filled with resolve.

"I could cover the distance in a quarter of that time on four legs," Lev said. He had fisted his hands, and as he spoke he stepped closer to Madeline. One pace. Then two. He stopped and closed his eyes. His head fell back as if he would howl at the moon. The tendons on either side of his neck stood out in sharp relief as his body tensed. He braced his long legs wide apart, and veins bulged on his muscular arms…but nothing happened. The earth didn't quake. His human form remained as imposing yet somehow vulnerable in all its scarred hardness, as it had been before.

Amazingly, his tight shirt hadn't given way at the seams. It had only stretched with his flexed muscles as he strained.

"It's probably best for us all that you can't," Anna responded. Madeline didn't argue. She wouldn't regret seeking help from Bronwal now that help had been found, even if Anna looked pale and troubled as the giant man beside them sought the shift that still eluded him.

She would face the threat of the white wolf for Trevor just as Anna had faced Lev for her unborn child. It didn't matter that she had no *Volkhvy* power to back up her determination. Her determination alone would have to be enough. She would get stronger. She would get wiser. She would navigate this strange modern world with a deadly beast by her side in order to save her son.

But she couldn't help the tightness in her chest, or the way the sword weighed too heavily in her hand. The witch on the train had tried to poison her. If the marked *Volkhvy* who had kidnapped the queen and her son wanted her dead, she faced more than the white-wolf threat by her side. She had to guard herself from magical stalkers as well. A longer journey would give the marked witches time to make another attempt on her life.

"The marked *Volkhvy* might have followed me here. They may try to stop us before we reach the portal," Madeline warned. She allowed the sword's tip to rest against the ground, and her arm sighed in relief.

Nothing escaped Lev Romanov's notice. He had a wolf's senses even in his human form. His intense glance went from the ruby blade up her arm to her face. Once again, she felt he must find her wanting compared to his memories of the warrior she'd been. Sketching didn't require strength. Battling those witches who might try to kill her would, as would protecting herself should the shift come to the man who so desperately summoned it. If the white wolf proved to be the foe of the stormy cliff rather than the ally she sought...

Her thoughts were interrupted by the tight smile that

claimed Lev's angular face. He had the Romanov nose and sculpted jaw. His beard didn't hide the perfection of his bone structure, nor did his scars detract from his symmetric features. He was many things—large, muscular and intimidating; scarred, wild and uncivilized—but he was also handsome. The smile startled her. It was a surprising punch to the tightness in her gut. The one-sided upward curve of his lips stole her breath and made her own lips go numb.

"I welcome them to try," Lev said. His husky voice was pitched even lower than it had been before. His lids had lowered over his vivid blue eyes, his thick lashes creating dusky shadows on his cheeks. Though Anna was only a few feet away from them, the moment was suddenly intimate, and it was as though no one besides Madeline and Lev was there.

It was a promise to help her and Trevor. An uttered contract between them. Madeline forced her lungs to expand. She moistened her lips and nibbled the numbness away.

Lev didn't blink or look away. He crossed his arms over his broad chest and met her eyes boldly, watching her soak in the promise he'd made.

She might not know if the white wolf was her friend or her foe, but at that moment, she knew Lev Romanov had been born a champion, and a champion he remained. After all he'd been through in his long, harsh life, he might no longer be her mate, but, shifted or not, he was still a Romanov wolf.

He would stand against the marked *Volkhvy* who stalked her, and he would help her rescue their son.

Chapter 4

Lev had ridden horses almost from the day he was born. He could ride as easily as he could walk. The question was whether the horses could handle being ridden by a man who had been a wolf for a very long time now.

As Lev approached, it took several men to settle the two large destriers Ivan Romanov had ordered prepared for his younger brother and the woman who had been his wife. Madeline had already been placed in her saddle on the smaller white gelding. She held on admirably well for someone who had been asleep for centuries. He noted the white-knuckled grip she had on the reins. He also noted the ruby sword in a scabbard that hung from the pommel of her saddle within easy reach should she need it.

He'd already seen how poorly she held the blade. Her grip had been uncertain, as if she'd never wielded a sword before. Somehow during their journey, he would have to help her remember her prowess with the blade in spite of the fact that she obviously thought he might be the one she would need to wield it against.

The second horse was an impressive dun stallion. Its polished black hooves stood out sharply from the fringes of long white hair. These were warhorses bred to carry armored warriors into battle. They, too, had been caught up in Vasilisa's curse. Her spell had prolonged the lives of everyone at Bronwal merely to torture them. The horses looked as out of place in this century as Lev felt.

"You frighten them," Soren said as he and Anna came out of the castle behind him. "Ivan does as well. They will calm down once they realize you're not going to eat them."

Although they were twin brothers, Soren had flaming red hair instead of blond. His beard and hair were also neatly trimmed save for a long bang that threatened to flop over his eyes. Lev was conscious of his own overgrown hair and beard. He'd pulled back the unruly waves into a thick queue at the nape of his neck. That was all. He'd refused to try to improve his appearance any more than that. If he looked uncivilized, it was only the God's honest truth. He was a savage. His years as the white wolf had left him with that legacy.

Better for everyone to see and acknowledge the wildness inside him, while Soren had embraced more than a witch. His trimmed hair and beard proclaimed his mastery over the red wolf.

Then again, Soren had always been more man than beast.

So unlike himself.

Anna and Soren held hands. Lev watched his brother

gently hold his pregnant wife as if she was a treasure he'd found. He'd once treated a pregnant Madeline the same way. He had to close his eyes and swallow against the ghost of tenderness that assailed him. He pushed the unwelcome memory away. Then he opened his eyes to watch Anna Romanov warily. Not as his sister-in-law, but as a threat. As always, the witch made his hair follicles tighten as if she brought with her a charge that fueled the very air around them.

Soren patted the dun horse on the rump. It did prance at his touch and snort, but then it settled into place without further fuss…until Lev reached for the reins. The side of his hand brushed along the dun's neck, and the horse whickered in fear. It sidestepped away from his touch, and its front hooves came up off the ground.

"Okay. Maybe they're a little more afraid of you than they are of me and Ivan," Soren said.

The white gelding's nostrils flared, and Madeline had to tighten her legs and speak calming words to her mount as Lev hoisted himself up into the saddle of the frightened dun. He pounced as he would have if he'd been hunting instead of riding. He settled gracefully into the saddle even though it was a moving target, and masterfully brought the horse back under control with his strong hands and thighs—but more so with his aura of authority and strength of will.

Ivan was the alpha of the Romanov pack, but only because Lev had never vied for the position.

The horse trembled beneath him, but it stopped trying to rear up on its hind legs.

"Show-off," Soren said. He'd come to stand beside Lev's leg. With one hand, he held the bridle of the dun and placed the other on Lev's knee. "Come back to us, brother. I searched for you too long and too hard for you to run away now that I've seen your face again."

"To Straluci," Lev said, giving his brother no reply. With a deft thump of his heel, he urged his mount to depart. Soren's hand fell away.

The dun leaped forward, and Madeline's horse followed at her direction. Lev refused to glance back at Bronwal or his twin brother. He couldn't allow his brother's love for his new wife to cloud his judgment. Her mother was an evil queen who must be destroyed. It was the only way.

As was his decision to never return. The brotherly connection he felt for his twin tugged at the very marrow of his bones as he rode away, but the wildness that haunted his soul was a stronger force. It propelled him away with the certainty that he could only protect those he loved by reclaiming the shift and leaving them far behind.

Madeline had seen an ATV in the stables. It was a mechanically propelled vehicle with cushioned seats. It wasn't quite midmorning when she began to obsess about those cushions and regret the necessity of horses on the narrow trails they followed.

The deep, evergreen Carpathian forest had devoured them shortly after they left Bronwal. Meager spring sunshine barely penetrated the canopy above them as the horses stepped carefully on the path that was frequented by sure-footed deer and wolves and bears, more than domesticated animals.

What began as a hum to soothe the skittish horse beneath her became a nostalgic song softly murmured below her breath. She didn't remember it exactly. The words came from somewhere inside her that was more warmth than memory. More feeling than thought. Tears sprang into her eyes and burned her nose when she realized she softly sang a lullaby. It was tentative, but it was there. More in her heart than in her mind.

"We'll water the horses here," Lev said, suddenly breaking off the trail and heading toward a stream that had been unobtrusively gurgling beside their route.

Needing to stretch and being able to stretch were two different things, Madeline thought, but her horse followed Lev's and she didn't attempt to stop it. There was no obvious clearing. Only a slight break in the trees allowed them to make their way toward a patch of moss above the water.

The white gelding came to a stop beside the larger dun, and she was somehow able to swing her leg over the pommel of her saddle. She hopped to the ground without moaning out loud. Lev seemed to ignore her. He didn't make conversation, didn't directly look her way, but she felt him. When he stood and tilted his head to drink, she could imagine his pleasure at the fresh, cold hydration. From a tingling awareness along her spine to the heat that rose in her cheeks, her problem was that she couldn't ignore him. His presence was too noticeable to dismiss.

She jumped when he turned at her approach to hand her the container. She had been right. His attention was on her the whole time. Her every step was noticed, even when he didn't look her way. She took the container and gulped too quickly. She ended up awkwardly coughing and gasping for air as she recovered from choking.

Lev still didn't speak. He didn't meet her eyes. She was glad. Her glances flicked over him constantly without settling. He made her nervous. It wasn't fear of the wolf in him so much as fear of being caught watching him. She didn't want her awareness of him to show. She didn't want him to know that she couldn't look away for long.

Suddenly, he broke away from the invisible awareness that seemed to draw them together in spite of forced disinterest on both their parts. Still unused to the scent of the white wolf in their midst, the horses snorted and pawed against their tethers as Lev approached. Madeline turned to see what he intended to do. When Lev pulled the ruby sword from its sheath on her saddle, the water container dropped from her fingers to the mossy ground.

She was supposed to become stronger and wiser. Instead, she'd left her sword half a dozen feet away.

Madeline took several steps toward the man who easily held the long warrior's blade in one hand, but she froze when Lev came around the horses toward her. He effortlessly spun the sword in an arc of graceful but deadly movement around his large frame. He might have been a wolf for centuries, but his physicality as a man had only been enhanced by his time as a beast. His muscles bulged and relaxed and bulged again with his moves, as he seemed to test and then savor the heft of the blade as it arced around and around.

"You don't remember the weight of it in your hand? Its power at your fingertips?" Lev asked.

A flush of heat spread from Madeline's cheeks down to her throat and chest. She swallowed, suddenly very aware of the pulse at the base of her neck. If he looked, he would see her heartbeat throb, and it would no longer be throbbing simply from fear.

He continued to approach, effortlessly testing the blade as if he had no idea his words would call up a vision of him in her head, his power at her fingertips. In her imagination, she combined the blade with the man. Both powerful. Both intriguing. Both obvious omissions in her hollow memories. What he was asking was "How could she have forgotten such a sword?" What she thought was "How could she have forgotten such a man?"

And then she pushed such impossible thoughts away.

It didn't matter what he'd once meant to her. For now, he was a necessary companion and also a potential danger to herself and to her child. She needed him. She also needed to be wary of the way he made her feel. He had said he couldn't shift, but how long would his inability to call the white wolf last? She had to behave as if the threat of the wolf was with her every moment.

"I can't reclaim the past I've lost. I can only move forward from here," Madeline said.

Lev lowered the blade. He had approached until he was facing her, and he stood too close to continue to test the sword. Instead, he held it outstretched beside them. It wasn't a threatening display, however—it was a pause. Whatever his intention, he'd been interrupted by his sudden awareness of her nearness. The sword was forgotten. He looked down into her eyes, and his whole powerful body stilled. His wide chest didn't rise and fall. He didn't move forward or back. He didn't so much as blink as their gazes locked.

Madeline took in enough oxygen for both of them. Her respiration was shallow and quick. Too quick. She couldn't look away. Instead, she searched his blue eyes for some indication of his intent. The blade was still in his hand, but his lids were low and his cheeks were flushed. His lips were slightly open and soft against the hardness of his angular face.

Her fingers flexed with the sudden desire to shave

the wild growth that prevented her from fully appreciating his cheeks and jaw and chin. His beard was darker
and more burnished gold than his blond hair, with no
trace of the white streak that was more of a nod to the
white wolf's fur than to Lev Romanov's age. The centuries showed more in Lev's muscular hardness than
they did in his general appearance. He looked as if he'd
been born twenty-five or thirty years ago. Not in the
Middle Ages.

She'd stared at herself in the mirror. Her age wasn't
apparent at all. She looked as if she'd fallen asleep at
twenty and woken up the next morning. Except for the
absence of light in her eyes. She was missing…some-
thing. The brown of her irises wasn't as liquid as it
should be. She needed to move forward, but the past
she couldn't remember might remain an emptiness in
her for the rest of her days.

"Moving forward will help you recall. Whether or
not you reclaim your memories will be your decision,"
Lev said. He leaned slightly toward her, his face tilted
down. Strands of thick, wavy hair fell forward, released from the binding at the nape of his neck by his
movement. She clenched her fingers into fists to keep
from reaching out to touch the startling white locks
that sprang free.

"This sword was made for your hand. Your body
will remember if you expect it to." His eyes gleamed a
brighter blue behind the white. She was relieved when
he moved back to bring the sword up between them.
He held it as Anna had held it, horizontally, as an offering for her to take.

"I'm not the woman I was before," Madeline said
softly. She'd seen him looking for the warrior she'd
been. He searched for her now in between one blink

and the next. His intense gaze burned its way deep into her soul, but he must have felt that his search came up empty because there were still no memories for her to recall. There was nothing but the weight of Trevor against her breast. "I can only remember the baby. I held him forever as I slept. I protected him in my arms for centuries. That's the only knowledge of the past that I have."

Now her fisted hands weren't to keep from touching Lev's hair. Her fists were for the witches who had kidnapped her child. She didn't need any memories of being a warrior to know that she would fight to save the baby they'd stolen.

"Take this blade to save our child. Remember it, and it will remember you," Lev said.

Madeline's fingers opened, and she lifted her hands to accept the blade. Lev laid it across her outstretched hands. For a stunning moment, the sunlight shone through the trees and onto the ruby. It seemed to flicker to life. But then the leaves whispered with the wind, and shadows fell once more.

The ruby was as gray and dull as it had been before.

Chapter 5

Take this blade to save our child. Remember it, and it will remember you.

He'd wanted to say "Remember me." The words had risen from his heart to his lips, but he'd stopped them just in time. He'd hardened his mouth against them. He was here to help Madeline save Trevor. He was here to find and kill Queen Vasilisa. That was all. As she'd said, the past couldn't be reclaimed. But not for the reason she thought. She was still a warrior. She would always be a warrior. She'd been a warrior while she was sleeping, protecting their baby against her breast. Her eyes were troubled and wounded, but they still gleamed with determination and fury, even if they didn't gleam with ruby fire.

He was the one who couldn't reclaim what had been lost. Even as he'd reclaimed his human form, he'd known it. It wasn't only his skin that had been scarred by the years of ceaseless wandering and torment. The white wolf's rage continued to live beneath his skin like a never-ending howl only he could hear, and its claws had dug away his humanity too deeply for him to ever fully find it again.

His body was a sham, his desire for Madeline only an echo of what had been when he was a civilized man. When he'd released the sword into her hands, he ignored the spark caused by the phantom ghost of their previous connection.

And then he'd stepped back, prepared to be the cool and impersonal instructor she needed to help her remember the sword. Only the sword.

Him, she could and should forget.

The training session lasted only an hour, but when they were finished, Madeline's arm was trembling and rubbery, and she was panting with exertion. Sweat had dampened her hair, even though the mountain forest was cold.

Lev didn't pant or sweat. He had shown her every thrust and twist and parry, often with his hands over hers to demonstrate technique, but other than a wind-kissed flush on his cheeks above his golden beard, he seemed wholly unaffected.

"Our lives consisted of battle and training for battle. Your muscles will remember even if your mind doesn't," Lev said.

"There must have been other things. Like singing…" Madeline thought of the lullaby. Then she tried not to think of how Trevor had been conceived. "Um, dancing?"

They had walked back to the horses. This time the dun didn't prance at all, and the white merely snorted at Lev's approach. It was Madeline who tried to prance away when Lev reached to help her tired body onto the back of the gelding. He caught her easily, but in deference to her avoidance, he deposited her quickly into the saddle and stepped away.

Her waist still burned from the memory of his short-lived grasp—so strong and sure—even after they headed back onto the trail. Her exhaustion was as much from resisting the effects of his touch during her training session as from the exercise itself. He had taken no liberties. Each time he'd positioned her hands on the hilt or her shoulders and hips, he'd released her the moment the demonstration was finished. Yet her body still became flushed and sensitive. By the time the session was over, she ached for his touch to become more personal.

She had counted the seconds each brush of his hands had lasted.

"We sang and danced. Of course. In between our battles with the Dark *Volkhvy*. And all the while we didn't realize we were kept in Vasilisa's gilded cage. We were her most treasured champions. Until we were not," Lev said.

"Did the Dark *Volkhvy* cause my long illness?" Madeline asked.

Lev pulled the large dun to a sudden stop. He turned in his saddle to face her. Madeline's horse stopped at the dun's hip because the trail was too narrow for him to pass.

"Is that what the witch told you?" he asked. She was suddenly on alert again after being lulled by the gelding's steady hoof beats beneath her. Lev was deceptively quiet. She could feel a new tension in the air. She could see his stiff shoulders and his white-knuckled grip on the reins.

"She only said I'd been ill. Not how or why," Madeline said.

"Queen Vasilisa spelled you into an enchanted sleep. One so deep and so long that it clouded your memories. Your past wasn't stolen by an illness or the Dark *Volkhvy*. There is no Dark and Light. All *Volkhvy* are evil. Vasilisa most of all. She wasn't your savior, Madeline. She was your tormentor. She stole you and Trevor away from Bronwal before she cursed us all," Lev said. The howl was present in his voice again. More than ever. His words were husky rasps in the shadowed forest. The sun had entirely disappeared. The canopy was dense, but clouds must have rolled in high above them in a sky they couldn't quite see.

Madeline's body no longer ached from physical exertion or burgeoning sensual need. She'd gone numb from her forehead to her toes. Her fingers had gone slack on the reins, and the gelding shuffled aimlessly in its tracks with no guidance except for the dun's broad hips ahead.

"She was helping me recover. She was making sure Trevor woke slowly so he wouldn't be affected the way I'd been. She tried to protect him from the marked *Volkhvy* when they attacked," Madeline said.

"Whatever she does, she does for herself. For her own ends. She isn't human—never forget it. Long ago she took my father from his family and manipulated his genes to create a supernatural champion. He helped her. He provided an entire family of supernatural beasts to fight her enemies. We married and brought our warrior mates into her service. And she repaid us with a horrible curse. The Ether ate us, again and again. Once every hundred years we materialized. She wanted to watch our slow demise," Lev said.

He kicked the dun and it leaped forward into a trot in spite of the rough path. The white gelding followed, and Madeline's hands were too numb to pull it back. Was everything she'd learned since she woke up a lie? The *Volkhvy* on Krajina had been kind to her. Very unlike the marked *Volkhvy* who had attacked the island. And she'd felt Anna's warmth. She'd instinctively trusted one of the other women who wielded a Romanov blade.

Lev had to be wrong about the Light *Volkhvy*. And if he was wrong about the Light, then he was wrong about Vasilisa, too. She was Anna's mother. Madeline's sanity was currently being saved by the idea that wherever Trevor had been taken, he at least hadn't been taken there alone. Vasilisa would take care of him until Madeline could get there. She had to believe that, in spite of what Lev believed.

Queen Vasilisa had created the Romanov wolves, and she'd forged the enchanted blades for their mates. That much was true. The rest? Madeline's mind seemed shrouded in fog. She had woken too quickly, Vasilisa had said. She'd risen from her long sleep too fast and left her memories behind.

It had been the white wolf's howl that had woken her up. She'd echoed it. His howl had ripped from her throat and passed her lips as it sprang from her own chest. The crystal bed she'd slept in had been shattered, Trevor gone.

But as her horse followed after the dun that had already disappeared down the curving trail, Madeline wondered who had shattered the crystal and taken the sleeping baby from her breast. She'd blamed the white wolf for waking her too soon, but perhaps the blame didn't lie entirely with him alone.

* * *

Her skin was as soft as the petals of a flower. The faint scent of roses was tangled in the auburn strands of her hair. As he'd tried to focus on reminding her of her prowess with a blade, he was distracted again and again by observations he couldn't ignore.

The forest canopy above them was dense. The majestic spruce surrounding the mossy bank were lined up in seemingly never-ending rows of bitter bark and evergreen bows. But sunlight still peeked through and found its way in beams down to the top of Madeline's head. The rays of light turned the waves of her hair to fire. The strands were a myriad of colors, from light gold to the deep red of tarnished copper. He'd grown up with a ginger twin, but Soren had ordinary red hair. Madeline had flames.

He forced himself to only touch her when necessary. He corrected her hold on the hilt of her weapon, and his fingers burned where they touched hers. He nudged her feet farther apart with the toe of his boot against her foot, and he hated himself for remembering his bare leg welcomed between her naked thighs. He pressed a hand against the small of her back to urge her to straighten her spine, and he quickly pulled it away rather than allowing himself to press her body against his.

It was an hour of the worst torture he'd ever experienced, but he endured it because in spite of all the observations that hurt him, he also noticed her shoulders begin to line up with her blade the way they should, directing the sword. He noticed that the sweat on her brow didn't stop her from going through the forms he suggested over and over again.

She would be prepared to wield the blade against the

Volkhvy even if it killed her. She possessed the same determination as ever. She didn't need memories to drive who she was at heart.

Of course, he also noticed her breath catch and her body go still when he leaned in close behind her to position her elbows. For only a moment their bodies had been touching, from her back to his chest all the way down to hips and legs. The swell of her bottom encased in tight fawn leggings had been pressed against the tops of his thighs. He had paused for only a second, allowed himself to savor the touch but only for the blink of an eye, and then he had stepped back before his response to their mutual stillness could betray itself against the small of her back.

He had ended the session soon after, no longer trusting himself or his focus. She had seemed as glad to back away and return to the horses as he had been.

And then Madeline had brought up her enchanted sleep. She'd reminded him of why they were undertaking this journey in the first place.

Vasilisa must be stopped.

She had endangered his family for the last time.

He would lose them for good when it was all said and done, but they would be safe. That was all that mattered.

The problem with travel on horseback down a narrow trail where she was required to do nothing but let her horse follow the one leading was that she had hours to think. Since she couldn't ponder memories, she was left reliving every second of her time with Lev on the mossy bank by the stream.

His body was inhuman in its hardness, but instead of being repelled by his steely arms and legs or the solid rock of his chest, she was drawn to him as if her soft body could soothe away the centuries of hardship that had caused his to turn to stone. She could tell he tried to keep his touch impersonal. She could also feel him fail each time he brushed his hand against hers. He leaned into her as if he was freezing and she was the flame.

She tried to keep the image of the white wolf in her mind, but even though she'd sketched the monster a thousand times, she failed. Lev Romanov was intimidating. He was tall and broad and as lean as any hungry hunter could be. But he didn't act like a predator. Oh, he noticed her every move. He sensed every time she reacted to his touch. But he didn't exploit her weakness.

Not even when, God forgive her, she'd hoped that he would.

He had held her from behind, and she'd felt every inch of his hard body against hers, including his obvious reaction to holding the small of her back to him.

Then he had stepped away.

She had quaked like a leaf afterward. Perhaps he had thought she had overexerted herself. He had ended their practice. He'd headed back to the horses. She'd been left to mull over the impossible: the white wolf she'd been told to distrust had refused to devour willing prey.

Chapter 6

They were being followed. As the forest darkened around them, Lev could detect the scent of wolves on the breeze. He was well used to wild wolves. He'd run with them for over a hundred years. They naturally bowed down to his giant white-wolf form. In his supernatural body, he was easily the apex predator of the mountain. *Volkhvy* power might be evil, but it had given him the power he'd needed to survive when Vasilisa cursed Bronwal.

Now his ability to shift was gone.

For whatever reason, he couldn't set the white wolf free. It was as if his human body was unwilling to risk disappearing for another hundred years or more. He was drenched with sweat by the time the sun set, but he was still a man. He'd asked Madeline to ride in front when he first scented the wolves. She hadn't looked back at him since then. If she had, she might have drawn the ruby sword from the scabbard at her knee. She would have seen his tension. She would have anticipated the arrival of the white wolf she feared.

Now she might have to draw her sword to fend off natural wolves instead.

"We'll stop here for the night," Lev said. He directed his horse toward the side of the trail, where a large spruce had fallen following a heavy snowstorm several months before. The branches were still filled with green needles, although they were dry and rustled with a sharp skeletal rush when the wind blew through them. He liked the fallen tree because it would form a barrier wall between the shadows of the forest and the open trail. It would be a line of defense against any wolves that might come from the trees. They would camp against it, and he could build a large fire between the massive trunk and the trail.

"We should keep going. I have flashlights in my pack," Madeline said. She'd turned her horse around, but she didn't dismount.

"We're being followed by a pack of wolves. A sizable one. If they choose to attack, it will be under the cover of darkness. We need a fire and a defensible position," Lev said.

Madeline didn't argue further. She jumped off her horse and led the animal to where Lev had dismounted. The white gelding seemed ghostly, and Madeline's face was indistinct in the shadows, even to his eyes—and his vision was enhanced by the wolf that lived beneath his skin.

"We'll need to keep the horses near the fire, which means they'll have to be near me. They won't like it, but it can't be helped," Lev said.

"They're not as skittish as they were. The dun hasn't reared once today," Madeline said.

"The wolves will have them prancing if they come much closer," Lev said. He raised his nose into the air and breathed in to try to gauge the position of the pack. Madeline watched him with wary eyes. She dreaded his shift. He lowered his nose and met her serious gaze. He stepped toward her without thinking. One pace and then two, stopping only a foot away from where she had frozen at his advance.

Once Madeline's eyes had shimmered with ruby highlights. Now they were dark and brown. Lev reached and placed one crooked finger under her chin. Gently, with the slightest pressure, he urged her face to tilt upward so he could get a better look at her eyes. It was a mistake to touch her. It was a mistake to get too close. Because no matter how close he got, it would never be close enough. "I've told you I can't shift, Maddy. Be wary of the wolves that stalk us, but don't be afraid of me."

"You are the wolf. I see him in your eyes. I see him in the way you move. So quick. So graceful. Your intensity is his intensity. You aren't afraid of the wolves. You're as ready for their challenge as the white wolf would be," Madeline whispered.

She didn't pull away. She didn't move back. Her willingness to stay close to him even though she saw him as the white wolf seared him to his core. She was right. He was ready for the wolves' challenge. It was her he couldn't face. Or the memory of what they had been to each other. Not now, when empty desire rose in affection's place. He wouldn't take advantage of her attraction for him. He wouldn't indulge the pull between them. Not even after centuries of being apart.

He looked at her lips as he made the decision not to taste them again for what she would perceive as the first time. They parted beneath his attention as she breathed a soft gasp of awareness. He wasn't ashamed of the tremble in his hand on her skin or how it betrayed the amount of control he had to use not to dip down and suck on her full, sweet lower lip.

"Bring your sword with you and bed down by the fire. I'm going to find our stalkers and ascertain their intent," Lev said. In truth, he simply needed to run away. From the soft flick of Madeline's tongue as she moistened her unkissed mouth, and from his desire to lick her lips himself. He would be a fool to try to sleep beside her, enveloped by the fire's heat.

He was the one who dropped his hand. Stepped back from her upturned face. Turned away.

Madeline went for her sword while he gathered the necessary kindling. With the modern lighter from his pack, it took no time to start a fire. It was roaring by the time Madeline returned with her sword and a roll of padded bedding.

"Keep the fire going through the night. I'll find the wolves and keep an eye on their movements until sunrise," Lev said. He saw a dawning wisdom in the depths of her eyes as he turned away. She knew he was avoiding being near her. He had confessed it with his touch on her chin and with his eyes on her mouth.

"I need your help to save my son," Madeline said.

"I'll be back in the morning," Lev said. "We will save our son together."

She didn't remember Lev's kiss of the past, but there was nothing wrong with her imagination. He was an intense man. His touch stayed on her skin long after he'd disappeared into the forest shadows. The heat he'd left on her face transferred itself to the mouth he hadn't touched with anything other than his gaze.

The white wolf was a monster—that was a truth she knew from her sketches and her vivid memories of the stormy cliff. And she wanted the monster's kiss. She ached to remember what it had been like to press her lips to Lev Romanov's mouth. She must have been far bolder than she was now. Far less cautious and afraid. Her heart pounded in her chest, and her breath came fast as she merely imagined what it would have been like earlier if she had narrowed the gap between them herself. She'd wanted to. She'd wanted to claim the only softness on his hard, scarred face. His lips were indulgent in an otherwise forbidding mien. They begged for kisses even as everything else warned her away.

Kissing him would be a mistake. It was wrong to even imagine flicking her tongue into his mouth and tasting him…again. The idea that she already had, that they had been mates once upon a time, was driving her crazy. Her body told her they would be good together, because it already knew they were.

That the white wolf was the one with enough control to walk away made her feel like the beast. She'd been awake for such a short time. The world was sudden and new. She had no memories to anchor her. Only the drive to save Trevor and help Vasilisa. Only the need to relearn the swordsmanship she'd forgotten.

And now this.

The desire to remember Lev Romanov's kiss.

A wolf howled far in the distance. It was a thready sound, small and wavering. Nothing to fear with a roaring fire beside her and a sword near her fingertips. The horses didn't even dance in their tethers.

Yet somewhere out in the forest, Lev ran alone on two legs instead of four, and even though they were no longer connected, Madeline couldn't put him from her mind as she lay by the fire. Invisible strings seemed to run from her consciousness out into the night as if they connected her to him, seeking to knit them together.

Madeline turned toward the fire. The ruby sword was within reach. The dancing flames illuminated the dull gray gem, seemingly bringing it to life. She couldn't reclaim the connection she'd once had with Lev Romanov. Not when she knew the beast that hid beneath his skin. She'd seen his wicked maw. She'd seen the blaze of fury in his eyes. The control he'd displayed today was a lie.

Madeline opened the backpack that sat beside the sword. She took out her sketchbook and flipped through its familiar pages. The firelight illuminated the ferocity and anger of the white wolf. His savagery. His menace.

Much better for Trevor that she focus on this truth: Lev Romanov couldn't be trusted. He was a monster waiting to happen. Her son had been through enough. Once he was back in her arms, she would protect him from all harm, including the threat posed by his own father.

The sword was waiting. It didn't have to glow with ruby light to be a weapon. Madeline reached for its hilt and stood up. This time, her fingers settled into the slight grooves of use that were invisible to the naked eye. Something in her knew where each digit should rest, where they had rested long ago.

Illuminated by simple firelight in the absence of *Volkhvy* power, Madeline went through the practice motions Lev had shown her. The ruby didn't glow. There was no connection between her and the blade and the white Romanov wolf. But there was muscle memory, just as Lev had said there would be. The moves came more smoothly with each repetition. Her body knew which way to bend and flow, so she allowed it to take control.

The night was long, but it was also familiar. Although he didn't have fur to warm him or giant paws to eat up the ground over which he traversed, running through the Carpathian woods had been his life for so long that it was anything but a hardship now. Within minutes, he had found his rhythm with two feet instead of four paws. He loped more easily than any other man could through the game trails that ran through the trees in a nearly invisible network of lines.

After a time, he found the pack, far enough away from Madeline and the horses to soothe his mind. He settled in to watch them from an upwind vantage point high in a tree he had easily scaled with his strong arms and legs. With his back braced against the trunk, he counted the wolves as they milled around. If their aimless wandering hadn't clued him in to an abnormality, their numbers would have. He'd been right. The pack was large. Too large. And as he watched, more wolves came from all directions to join the others already amassing beneath him.

He and Madeline wouldn't make it to Straluci without a fight.

But Madeline had also been right.

He would be prepared for the challenge, shifted or not. The white wolf inside him raised its head and howled with a ferocity unmatched by the natural wolves below him.

Chapter 7

Madeline slept fitfully, always waking in time to re-fuel the fire when it died down. It was nearly morning when she woke to discover that Lev had stoked the fire. He was wrapped in another sleeping roll that had come from a pack on the dun horse's back. He faced away from her toward the trees on the other side of the fire. The dancing flames painted his broad back with shadows and light.

He wasn't asleep.

She watched his breathing rise and fall, and some-how she knew he had sensed her waking. Neither of them spoke. The silence stretched, straining the strings she imagined between them, but just as she thought she would ask him about the wolves, another howl sounded. It was as far away as the last one she'd heard.

"I couldn't find the *Volkhvy* that are influencing them, but they aren't acting alone," Lev said. He didn't roll toward her. His back looked stiff.

"Will they try to prevent us from reaching Straluci?" Madeline asked. Her hand had gone for the hilt of her sword. The move was instinctive, driven by memories she couldn't recall.

"They won't succeed," Lev replied.

It was the answer she expected because it was the one she felt deep in her bones. She would save her son, come witches or wolves. The only other option was death.

He didn't sleep. He waited. Finally, when the night mist began to rise toward a hint of pink sky, he rose from his bedding. Madeline had been restless throughout the night, but she'd fallen into an exhausted slumber less than an hour ago. He'd sensed when she no longer watched his back. He knew when her eyes closed.

Before he left their campsite to check on the wolves again, he made sure the fire still had enough fuel to burn until the sun fully came up. Then he stepped lightly to his companion's side. She murmured indistinctly in her sleep. He couldn't be certain if her sounds were ones of protest or appeal. The firelight danced on her pale cheeks. The ruby sword was forgotten beside her.

But it was the position of her hands that stabbed him with invisible blades, cleaving his heart in two.

Her arms were crooked over her chest, and her hands were cupped as if her palms supported a baby's head and bottom. Trevor was in danger somewhere out in the world. Only Vasilisa and the marked witches knew where, but Madeline still tried to hold him safely to her breast.

Madeline murmured again and her fingers twitched as if her body knew something was wrong, even if her sleeping mind did not. It would be doubly cruel to wake to empty arms if her dreams were filled with lullabies and the powder scent of Trevor's sweet curls.

Lev's chest constricted. He knew that cruelty from personal experience. He fisted his hands at his sides and kept his spine straight and tall. She wouldn't welcome him leaning over and smoothing the waves of her fiery hair back from her forehead. She wouldn't want him bending down and holding her empty hands.

He had failed to protect his wife and child for centuries. He couldn't undo the harm that had been done to them. He could only try to protect them now. The pack of wolves he'd seen would be tired this morning. With the sunrise, they would probably collapse from their frenzy of the night before.

He still couldn't shift, but he was far from an ordinary man. He would go to the alpha wolf and try to overcome the unnatural influence he suspected the wolf was under. He would try to disband the pack and send them on their way before the *Volkhvy* could use them to try to stop Madeline from reaching their child.

It was a risky move. The alpha had the power of the pack behind him, and somewhere, the Dark power drawn from the Ether by the marked *Volkhvy* was also at work. Lev could almost scent the smell of Darkness caught and held in the ozone of the morning mist.

He turned away from Madeline's prone form and headed into the forest. He couldn't shift, but he had decided he would still try to challenge the alpha wolf with the ferocity of the white Romanov wolf that lived in his heart.

Aleksandr worried the raised skin of the brand on his forehead. His fingers had long since grown used to the roughened shape of the bellflower that Anna, the

Light *Volkhvy* princess, had emblazoned on him, on all her enemies, when they tried to send her red wolf into the Ether for the last time.

The amount of power it had taken for her to instantly sear the mark on all of them had been prodigious. Habit sent his fingers to the brand, but no matter how often he traced its design, he was surprised all over again. Anna's abilities had been magnified by the emerald in the hilt of the Romanov blade she had taken from him. It had come to life for her because her mother had forged it for the red wolf's mate. At that time, she hadn't consciously accepted the connection, but her heart had known.

She had literally glowed in defense of the red wolf she loved, and the energy she expelled had left a lasting testament to Anna's love for Soren Romanov on the skin of both Aleksandr and his followers.

When Aleksandr closed his eyes, he could still see the flash of emerald light that had imprinted itself on his corneas with its brilliance. He could smell scorched flesh and hear the screams of his followers. They had been rogues, not born to Darkness, but seduced by its promise of power. Anna had marked their foreheads so that their treachery against her mother, the queen, would be obvious for all to see.

They had been punished for their uprising.

Fortunately for Aleksandr, the mark accomplished something else as well. While it was a constant reminder of Anna's power and his failure, it was also a reminder of what had slipped through his fingers and what he could still achieve if he refused to let his initial failure stop him.

He could still defeat the Romanov wolves and their

mates. Vasilisa's powerful triumvirate of champions hadn't managed to reassemble yet. The black wolf and his sapphire warrior were connected once more, as was the red wolf and the emerald witch, but the white wolf and his former mate had been rent asunder by Queen Vasilisa herself. His spies had relayed to him all that had occurred since Madeline Romanov woke from her enchanted slumber.

She did not accept the white wolf as her mate. Her connection to the ruby blade wasn't complete. Therefore, her connection to the Romanov wolf was also incomplete. And Lev Romanov hadn't shifted for months. Perhaps he was so glad to be back in his human form he would reject his shift forevermore.

Just in case, Aleksandr had taken steps to ensure that Madeline and the scarred man who would no longer shift into his white wolf form would never come together again. He had invaded Krajina, intent on killing the former ruby warrior and her baby. He planned to destroy any possibility of the youngest Romanov reclaiming his wife and son.

His plan hadn't failed. It was merely taking more effort than he had expected. Queen Vasilisa was supposed to have been traveling that day. Her presence had caused a last-minute alteration of his plans. But Lev and Madeline were obviously broken. It was up to Aleksandr to ensure that their damage was permanent. Then he would claim Vasilisa's throne while the Romanov wolves grieved.

Eventually, he would make sure that the Romanovs' abilities died out. There would be no one to stand in his way.

Marked or not.

His fingers slid over and over the raised skin on his brow, but not in an attempt to wipe it away. He and his followers would wear the blackened petals on their foreheads with pride.

And the flower on his temple would be framed by a crown.

Chapter 8

Lev found the alpha wolf in a cave above a clearing where the amassed wolves had collapsed as the sun rose. They didn't behave as they should. The morning light revealed that they waited like puppets on the end of lax strings. He couldn't see their masters or even smell them on the breeze, but the *Volkhvy* had to be behind the wolves' odd behavior. Every wolf from old to young lay with their noses on their paws, as if they waited for instructions.

Only the alpha moved when Lev approached. He came from his shallow den on unsteady legs as though his natural protective instincts overcame the control imposed by the witches, but only with a fight. The tawny wolf's barrel chest heaved harshly, and Lev felt a pang of empathy. He might have to fight the alpha. He might even have to kill him, if to be killed was the only alternative. But he didn't like it. He knew what it was like to be manipulated by *Volkhvy* tricks and treachery.

He hardened his heart and stepped to meet the alpha wolf. He was less than half the size Lev would have been if he had been able to shift into his white-wolf form. But compared to Lev's human form, the wolf was formidable. Especially if Lev was forced to meet the wolf's large teeth with nothing but his fists.

They met eye-to-eye on the edge of the rise above the clearing. The wolves below remained on their bellies—a further indication that they were not in their right minds. Dominant wolves might fight for control of a pack, but an intruder would normally be met and driven away if a pack was sound.

"Leave this place. Resist. Don't allow yourselves to be used by witches who aren't even strong enough to fight their own battles," Lev said. His words might be meaningless to the alpha wolf, but his stance and his intentions were not. The full might of the white wolf was in his voice and his gaze.

But more than that, he was here to defend his family. After years of searching for them, he wasn't about ready to back down from a fight once they'd been found. He wouldn't allow sympathy for these wolves to get in the way of protecting Madeline and rescuing Trevor.

The tawny leader of the pack whined. If he'd been free, he might have sprung for Lev's throat or turned to run away from his challenge. Instead, he collapsed onto his belly, and his nose slowly descended to lie on his outstretched paws.

He definitely wasn't normally submissive. The tawny wolf's whines confirmed that the position at the feet of an adversary wasn't his choice. He was being forced to wait. Lev turned to look down on the clearing. Several more wolves had arrived to join those waiting below. There were at least twenty prime adults now. The

Volkhvy weren't going to settle for a large pack. They were calling an army of wolves. And he couldn't kill them where they lay. He couldn't fight them until they attacked. Right now they were innocent. How could he harm them without provocation? He might be a savage monster, but he wasn't going to exterminate these wolves when they had done nothing wrong.

"They're going to wait until there are too many of you for me to fight, aren't they?" Lev asked. He didn't expect a reply. If he fell before an army of wolf fangs, it would be ironic. He'd always thought the wolf gnawing inside his own breast would devour him. Now he wasn't so sure.

The tawny alpha dragged himself to his feet. Lev's heart leaped, but the wolf didn't attack. He only stretched his nose out to touch Lev's loosened fist. In spite of the witch's manipulations, the wolf acknowledged Lev's dominance. For a second, hope rose, but the powerful creature fell back down on his belly after the exertion of briefly disobeying his witch masters.

"We are only pawns to the *Volkhvy*, my wild brother. I will remember that you tried," Lev promised.

Madeline woke to an adrenaline rush. She scrambled to her feet to face an invisible threat. Lev was gone. The fire had burned itself out. A pile of smoking ash was all that was left as the sun dried the mountain mist that rose from the ground.

The forest was preternaturally silent. No birds sang. No rodents scurried through the trees. Something was very wrong. She felt her empty arms keenly, but she'd already known Trevor was gone. Waking to that truth wasn't a surprise, although there was still a sharp pain and a hollow in her heart that echoed in the silence.

The rush of fear she'd experienced still caused her skin to prickle and her breathing to be shallow and quick. In fact, she felt suddenly as if she was running even though her feet were still. Madeline pressed her empty hands to her stomach, but only for a second before she bent to pick up her sword off the ground. She had to obey her instincts and the signals her body was giving her even if she didn't understand: there was a threat. It was urgent that she face it. She just wasn't sure what or why.

When Lev silently erupted from the trees, his body powerfully intent on his destination—*her*. Madeline's sword was already raised in defense. He appeared between one blink and the next, and as he came to a stop only inches from her, she lowered her blade. He wasn't shifting. He was still a man. His broad chest rose and fell, and it only took a few inhales and exhales in unison for Madeline to know that their breathing was in sync.

His exertion was her exertion.

Her gaze tracked over the hard face tilted toward hers to the hollow of Lev's throat, where his pulse throbbed. As she watched, she felt the same beat—strong and steady—beneath her rib cage. The same rhythm. It wasn't only their breathing that had synced.

They hadn't touched since the training session by the creek, but somehow, she'd woken in tune with him in a way she hadn't been before.

Her attention rose back to his eyes. They glimmered blue beneath thick sooty lashes as he met the shock she could feel widening her eyes.

Madeline held her breath as Lev's breathing slowed. If she hadn't, she was certain hers would have slowed as well. At least until the man facing her raised his hand to touch one calloused finger to the hollow of her throat. She didn't pull away, even though she knew he felt the throbbing pulse point that was exactly in tune with his own.

"This was often the case when we faced adversity in the past. Don't worry. It means nothing now. The ruby is dead," Lev said. But he looked from his finger back into her eyes as if he thought it meant something in spite of his assurances. There were secrets she'd once understood in his irises. The sword didn't glow. Lev couldn't shift. But their heartbeats said those absent signs of connection were the lie.

"The alpha has lost control of the pack. He would have turned away if he could, but his body is no longer his," Lev said. "He and his pack will do whatever the *Volkhvy* order them to do. For now, they wait, but it's only a matter of time."

His finger was warm on her throat. She waited for him to draw it away, but instead he allowed that one gentle digit to stay. The pad of his forefinger lingered on her skin. He looked from her eyes to the place where his finger rested and back. Was he gauging her reaction? Measuring her response? When she breathed again, the rhythm of her respiration was her own, but it betrayed the shortness of breath she felt, not from exertion, but from other things. Impossible things. Like the pleasure of his slightest touch. Like the intrigue of him seeming to enjoy the flush of heat that spread from his finger outward.

She didn't have to look down. She was pale. She was certain that the heat she felt was obvious to him. His keen notice was as much a caress as his touch. Her shirt was unbuttoned only enough to allow the slightest hint of cleavage where the fabric parted, but she was certain her skin was flushed pink above the white cotton.

He said he couldn't shift, but surely he would become the white wolf when the wolves attacked. She reminded herself of that monster—his teeth, his howl, his savage red eyes. But it was hard to remember the beast when she was made breathless by the man. He towered over her, but his touch was gentle and light. He didn't grab or take. He tested the waters of her desire. He watched her face and studied her eyes.

Madeline licked her lips and regretted the move instantly when Lev's blue gaze fell to her mouth. It was his turn to flush. She watched the color rise above his golden beard and could have sworn that her temperature rose along with his.

"You're afraid I'll shift even though I've said I can't," Lev mused. He saw everything, always, even the fear she tried to fight.

"I came to Bronwal to find the white wolf. I need him to save our son," Madeline said. Her hand tightened on the sword. She'd nearly forgotten it. Talk of the white wolf reminded her why she had accepted the blade from Anna—to protect herself from the threat that would ride by her side.

"You're very brave. You always have been. But bravery doesn't negate fear. Or ignore it. Bravery makes plans. Bravery prepares," Lev said. He suddenly lifted his finger to softly trace the line of her jaw from the lobe of her ear to her chin. Madeline trembled. She was afraid. He was right. But fear wasn't all she felt for him, and that was the scariest sensation of all.

"You want to remember your skill with the blade so you can protect yourself from me…from the white wolf," Lev said. His voice was husky and low. Its rough tone was a pleasant burr against the skin he caressed.

But his finger had paused as if he didn't give it permission to continue.

The man respected her fear of the wolf.

"You say I'm a warrior. You say I've always been brave," Madeline said. "But all I know about myself is that I want to be prepared to face any danger I have to face to save Trevor."

Lev's hand fell away from her face. He stepped back so suddenly that she was left cold by the rush of morning air that filled his place. Madeline shivered, but the distance accomplished one thing. Her heartbeat was her own. The organ in her chest pounded slowly as it established its own rhythm separate from his.

"I'm sorry I am one of the dangers. I can only promise to protect you—from *all* wolves, including the one that lives in me," Lev said.

"I'll protect myself," Madeline said. She raised the sword to show how it fit in her hand. She rolled her shoulders. She'd made the preparatory move a hundred times before. She didn't remember, but her body did.

Lev's eyes widened. She thought she detected appreciation in the small, tight smile that curved his lips.

"You're remembering," he said.

"My mind grasps for memories I can't reach, but my body never forgot," Madeline said.

When Lev's lips softened, Madeline looked away from his smile. Yes. She thought maybe there were other things her body remembered, but she would never be free to indulge them. She might be brave, but she wasn't reckless. She couldn't be. Not when Trevor's future depended upon her decisions.

Chapter 9

The horses were skittish again. They had to be tied to trees as they packed up camp, and both the dun and the white horse pranced and pawed and danced away from their riders. This time it wasn't Lev. Although her companion didn't tilt his nose to the sky, the horses snorted with wide nostrils and worried their bits with nervous teeth.

The scent of the giant wolf pack was on the morning breeze.

It must be her imagination, but even she could detect a hint of predator in the air. The evergreen scent of the spruce trees was joined with a muskiness that made her think of damp fur and creatures used to sleeping in dens. She stilled the panic the scent instinctively caused. Her heart fluttered and she couldn't fill her lungs, but she ignored the unpleasant sensation of being hunted as best she could.

"We'll continue to Straluci. I don't think we'll get that far, but we'll try. It was built in a good, defensible position. We would do better to have stone walls instead of forest at our backs," Lev said.

He mounted, and then turned to wait for her. Madeline's fingers fumbled under her task. He watched as she adjusted the ruby sword's scabbard. Something about its angle suddenly seemed wrong to her. It wasn't something she could ignore. Guided by instinct more than memory, she positioned the hilt of the sword where she wanted—no, needed—it to be.

Lev didn't speak, but his eyes spoke volumes even as his lips stayed still. They gleamed a darker blue in the shadows of the trees. His eyelids narrowed speculatively at the edges. He thought the warrior he'd loved was waking, and maybe she was. Madeline moved with more certainty than she had before. But if she became the best swordsperson in the modern world, it wouldn't change things between her and the white wolf.

She would never be the woman she'd been even if the warrior inside her woke. Too much had changed while she was sleeping. Lev had been molded into something more fierce and fabled than he'd been before. It wasn't safe to desire the legendary beast he'd become. She had to keep her focus on Trevor.

Madeline pulled herself into the saddle. Her muscles were strengthening, day by day. She felt the stretch and release of fluidity in her limbs. Her fitness seemed right as if it was a return to the way she should be even though she didn't remember. Once she settled into the saddle, Lev kneed his horse around and onto the trail with an inhuman grace that mocked her pleasure in her movements. He didn't sit in the saddle. He held his weight in the stirrups as if he wanted to be ready to leap off the back of his horse should he need to. His muscular body moved with the horse's gait, and the big, powerful dun seemed soft in comparison to the hardened man on his back.

There was no reason to notice the bulging of Lev's arms as they directed the reins in his hands. The stretchy cotton of his long-sleeved shirt displayed more of his biceps and forearms than it covered. And his black leggings did the same for his long legs and strong thighs.

Madeline murmured to her horse about not being afraid of the wolves that stalked them, but her attention was far too focused on the wolf that led her down the trail. When she tried not to notice the grace and strength displayed in his horsemanship, her gaze skittered away from his legs and arms, only to land on his hair. He hadn't tied his wild mane back into its queue this morning. Long blond waves blew around his face and shoulders, and in the occasional sunbeam that penetrated the thick forest canopy, the lone white streak was stark testimony to the life he'd once lived.

"You never liked my beard. You preferred when I was clean-shaven," Lev suddenly said, and only then did Madeline know she'd been staring. They had come to a broader passage on the trail, and her horse had caught up with his. He released the reins with one hand to raise his fingers to the thick growth of golden hair on his chin. He smoothed it thoughtfully, as if reminiscing on memories she probably shared but couldn't call up.

She only knew she would like to free him from some of the wildness that had claimed him, but that was a desire she wouldn't reveal out loud. She didn't have the right to want to smooth his hair back or see his face. He was a stranger to her now. He always would be. Shaved or not. And yet, as another ray of sun fell on his head, she could almost feel the heat of the golden halo it created around his face.

Was it memories between them or something more? The sword was dead. The ruby didn't glow. There was no aura of power when she wielded it, no fire from her eyes or his. But there was a fire between them. It burned inside her and set her skin to flames, and it was kindled by his slightest touch. As their horses scraped the ground from lack of direction, Madeline's attention fell, not to Lev's beard but to his lips.

"You don't remember," Lev said.

"It's been so long. Surely you don't remember, either. In all the years, you must have forgotten," Madeline said.

Lev edged the dun closer to the white one. The horses were more skittish than they'd been before. They nodded and worried at their bits while ignoring the greenery on the side of the trail. The dun stomped his large hooves and kicked out as if the wolves were already at his heels. Madeline kept her knees tight to hold her seat, but she wasn't thinking about wolves, not natural ones or the white one she most feared. She closed her eyes at Lev's searching gaze and the urge to remember his kiss. His soft, sensual mouth was so intriguing against his harder face and the angles of his cheeks. She closed her eyes so she wouldn't stare. But when he spoke again, the mesmerizing quality of his voice on her other senses was heady.

"I remember every second of our time together. Every laugh. Every sigh. Every tear. Every taste. It was all written on my soul even when I was the white wolf. It drove me ever onward, year by year, through all the endless Ether nights," Lev said hoarsely.

The meaning of his words soaked into her and

warmed her as the sun had before. She blamed the warmth on a blush. His voice was low. His proclamation intimate. *Every taste. Every sigh.*

She remembered nothing, but it wasn't hard to imagine his hard body pressed against her curves. She also couldn't deny she'd been staring at his lips. She could easily fantasize how Lev's soft, sensual mouth had felt on her skin.

But when she opened her eyes again, his mouth had hardened. His whole demeanor had changed. His stony visage surveyed the thick trees around them as if he could penetrate the shadows her eyes could not. Then she noted the rise and fall of his chest and knew he was testing the scents on the air as well as observing with his glittering eyes.

"They have circled around us. We're riding into the pack, not away from it," Lev said.

Madeline went for her sword, but Lev reached to stay her hand.

"No. Release the scabbard from the saddle instead. It's time for us to send the horses to safety," Lev said.

His hand was calloused and warm on hers. He allowed his fingers to linger for only a moment before he let her go. In the tension-filled atmosphere of frightened horses and looming threat, his desire to touch her made her breath catch. Still, she quickly unknotted the leather holding the scabbard in place while Lev dismounted.

His dismount was an athletic leap onto the trail.

"We'll remove their tack and send them back the way we came. They'll be more than happy to leave the wolf pack behind for the safe stalls waiting for them at Bronwal," Lev said.

He was already loosening the dun's saddle when Madeline's feet hit the ground. She looped the scabbard's strap around one shoulder so that the sword fell across her back, out of the way of the tasks ahead. The gelding's saddle joined the dun's on the side of the trail. The bridles followed. Madeline held the gelding's mane in one hand to keep him steady. She firmly patted the side of his neck with the other. Then she released her hold.

Both horses needed no urging to fly. They had also caught wind of the wolf pack and had known they were being ridden into danger. Thundering hooves against packed earth filled the air with dust as the destriers eagerly headed toward home.

"Here. Let me help you," Lev said. He came toward her and reached for the leather strap on her left shoulder. He tightened it, arranging the sword diagonally so that its hilt extended above her left shoulder, where she could easily reach across and draw the blade with her right hand. He tied the scabbard firmly against her back, wrapping more leather strapping around her waist to hold the lower end of the scabbard in place. "This will enable you to run if you need to. Or leap without a long sword bumping your legs."

His movements were hurried, his hands all business and no flirtation. But his nearness still made her breath shallow and her pulse skip. Once the sword was settled, he stepped away to survey his handiwork. Only then did she feel the familiarity of the blade's position. She hadn't been satisfied with its position on the saddle even after she'd rearranged it multiple times. But this was different. The scabbard seemed to fit against her back as if the curves and contours of her muscles welcomed it.

"This is how I carried the ruby blade long ago. Not at my hip, but on my back," Madeline said softly. She reached for the hilt and drew the blade. It was a prac-

ticed move. An action of habit. One that flowed easily
from neck to shoulders to wrist. She was tall; her arms
were long. She realized that her move was nearly as
athletic as Lev's dismount moments before.

"Yes. Just so," Lev said hoarsely. She looked from
the dull ruby along the extension of the tarnished blade
all the way to the tip, and then her gaze lifted to meet
Lev's eyes. Appreciation seemed to glow in his irises.
His lips had softened again, and one corner of his mouth
tilted up into a half smile. Perhaps there was more of
the warrior left in her than she'd thought, even if the
wife had to be banished to the past.

"I might remember how to handle a sword, but I'm
not going to be able to outrun or outleap a wolf pack,"
Madeline warned. She sheathed her weapon, for once
regretting its lack of enchanted power in her hand.

"You won't have to," Lev replied.

He stepped to her side and bent to scoop her up
into his arms before she understood his intentions. His
powerful arms cradled under her knees and around her
back, scabbard and all.

"We only have to take the *Volkhvy* by surprise.
They're expecting a slaughter on the trail up ahead.
They aren't expecting us to take an alternate route.
We're lucky it's the witches and not the wolves that are
in control. Left to their own devices, the wolves would
have flanked and surrounded their prey. Their witch
masters aren't used to hunting. We'll use their igno-
rance against them," Lev said.

Madeline tried to follow his logic, but it was hard to
think clearly with her arms wrapped around Lev Romanov's neck. He was such a formidable man. His impossibly muscular body had intimidated her from the
start, even as the contrast between his muscles and his

scars had also fascinated her. How horrible must his adversaries have been if they'd been able to mark his steely flesh? And now her body was pressed intimately against his. Her softness conformed to his hard chest. Lev's body heat radiated out to envelop her in his masculine aura.

And then he started to run.

She was not a small woman. She was as tall as many men, and her build wasn't lithe. She had a solidity that she now realized had come from years of training and fighting with a sword. Her arms and legs were strong and her hips were sturdy. Lev carried her effortlessly as if she was no burden at all. And there was no argument that he ran faster than she could have.

They came to a fork in the trail she hadn't seen from horseback, and Lev veered toward the left. The trail was barely a path. It would have been too narrow for the horses, and it was almost too narrow for Lev's broad shoulders and the length of her body, even curled as it was into his arms. Branches caught at her hair, but she didn't complain. Not when Lev managed to duck and weave and gracefully avoid most of the obstacles they came upon in a blur of movement she could hardly observe.

He was a Romanov wolf even when he wasn't shifted.

He was legendary on two legs, as if phantom paws propelled him over the rough, overgrown ground he traversed.

Madeline held on. They moved faster than she would have been carried on galloping horseback. But there were howls in the distance, and they were coming closer. One was louder than all the rest, just shy of sounding like the white wolf's howl. The ferocious cry shivered from her ears down her spine, sending a wash of fear in its wake. She'd left her backpack tied to the saddle. For a second, it seemed as if her sketches might have sprung to life and crawled from the abandoned book to hunt her.

But no, the predators chasing them weren't supernatural. They were merely the apex predators of the Carpathian Mountains. Even an experienced swordswoman would have no chance of defeating an ordinary pack of wolves, much less a massive horde brought together by *Volkhvy* magic.

If that experienced swordswoman also had a supernatural ally…then maybe she would have a chance.

Suddenly, the forest opened up to the gape of a deep and wide ravine. Far below, water rushed in a rocky river. Madeline had heard the roar in the distance for a long time as they'd traveled. It had become such a part of their environment that she hadn't separated it from the gurgle of the smaller creek they'd ridden beside. In fact, now that she was near the rush, she couldn't believe she'd heard it at all, but she had. For days. Lev must have as well.

Lev stopped in the lee of a large hollowed oak tree. His breathing wasn't labored, but it was heavy. His exertion must be extreme, even for an enchanted shapeshifter. His form was human even if his heart was not. His heat and the woodsy scent of the forest radiated off his skin in visible steam.

"They know what we've done. They've set the wolves on us now. I don't want to kill them. They're innocent wild beasts caught in the witches' plot," Lev said. He breathed deeply in between sentences. Madeline understood he was oxygenating his system for another push. Where? Where could they run now that the trail came to an end?

"We have to save Trevor," Madeline said. Her sympathy for the wolves was tempered by maternal instinct. It would be horrible to have to kill wolves that were being forced to attack them, but she would. For Trevor. Just as she had traveled from Krajina to Bronwal to face the white wolf.

"We will," Lev promised. He must feel empathy for the wolves, having once been a wild beast caught in a witch's plot himself. He met her eyes in the forest shadows. His breathing had slowed. "But we can also defeat these witches who hunt us. They want us to fight because we might be injured or killed. Even if we take out dozens of wolves, there are dozens more to rise and take their place. I have a better plan."

His hands loosened on Madeline, and she slid until her feet met the ground. She thought to let her arms slide away from him, too, but he had other ideas. His hands came up quicker than she could blink and held her forearms so that her palms were still against the sides of his warm neck. Without thinking, her fingers caressed the skin there, hidden beneath his wavy hair, and Lev sucked in a sudden, surprised gulp of air.

Wolves howled and Madeline jumped because the sound was much closer and louder than she'd expected.

"We're trapped. It's a dead end," she said.

Lev loosened his hold, allowing her arms to slide away. But he caught one hand before she'd gone far. He used their clasped hands to pull her around the giant oak. The river was wider than she'd thought. The ravine was so broad that a suspension bridge had been built at one time from their side to the other.

Unfortunately, the bridge was in ruins.

The ropes that had once supported the structure were frayed and weather-beaten. The planks that made up its walkway had fallen to the midway point, and even there, thousands of feet above the rushing water below, the wood looked ramshackle and rotten.

"It won't support our weight," Madeline said. Her stomach felt like it had already fallen onto the rocks below.

"Not for long, but we won't need long to cross," Lev said. His chin jerked up, and he looked back the way they had come. Madeline's horrified gaze was locked on the remains of the bridge, but she could hear the wolves coming. Lev had said the pack had massed together from numerous smaller packs. It had to be their numbers and their witch masters that caused the usually graceful creatures to make such noise chasing them through the woods.

"It will collapse beneath the pack. They'll die even if we don't fight them," Madeline said.

"Not if you cut the ropes when we reach the other side," Lev declared.

He scooped her up again without giving her a chance to protest. There was no more time for argument. To save Trevor, they had to risk their lives, but she'd been prepared to do that all along.

Except Lev didn't head toward the bridge. He turned and ran toward the wolves. Madeline gasped, but it took only a moment to realize that he planned to get a running start for the impossible leap from the edge of the ravine to the first plank on the bridge. The white wolf could easily make that leap...and then eat her when they made it to the other side.

"I will not let you go," Lev promised. Madeline tightened her grip around his neck, but she didn't promise the same. She intended to let him go as soon as she could. Now more than ever, she could see and feel the white wolf close to the surface of his skin. His voice was more gravelly than it had been before. His eyes gleamed. His teeth flashed white against his golden-blond beard when he clenched them.

The wolves are coming, but the white wolf is already here.

She didn't make a sound when Lev jumped. There wasn't time to scream. His legs pumped like the pistons of the mighty train that had brought her to Romania. Only the fuel that propelled him was *Volkhvy*-manipulated Romanov blood. Vasilisa had crafted her wolves out of Ether's energy and bone.

Madeline reached for the hilt of her sword—enchanted blood wasn't enough.

Vasilisa had also forged the ruby sword because Lev Romanov couldn't fight the Dark alone, and Darkness drove the pack that hunted on their heels.

She didn't make a declaration she couldn't keep. This was for now, This was for Trevor. The ruby burst to life and suffused their bodies in its glow just before Lev's feet left the ground. They didn't fly. Madeline could feel the pull of gravity on her body as Lev's momentum propelled them through the air. But they also didn't fall before his toes were able to find purchase on the edge of the first board on the walkway of the bridge. It cracked beneath their weight, but it held long enough for Lev to push forward onto the next and the next. The rotted boards fell away from their progress. Madeline watched the splintered pieces tumble and fall end over end until they splashed in the river.

The wood debris was so much slower than Lev. It fell slowly, illuminated by sparkling ruby light.

And then the man who held her against his chest landed hard on the solid ground of the other side. Madeline drew the Romanov blade as Lev's feet dug two streaks in the earth to stop his momentum. She leaped from his arms as he released her. The rope was already tattered and weak.

Her heart pounded as she raised the sword above her head, because she caught a glimpse of what they'd left behind them. Most of the walkway was gone. Wolves poured from the trees like a black, gray and russet flood. But before the wolves could try to use what remained of the bridge, Madeline lowered the ruby sword and severed first one support and then the other.

By the light of the ruby, the sword's blade was no longer tarnished and dull. It sliced cleanly through the rotted rope. Where there should have been at least some resistance, there was none.

And the suspension bridge fell away from their side of the ravine. Since mostly rope remained, the bridge seemed to float down to the other side of the abyss. The wolves tumbled and rolled over and under and around each other as they came to the edge. Even evil witches spared the pack from the cruelty of sending them onward for nothing. Either that or they had abandoned their horde when they realized it would fail.

A howl shook the earth under Madeline's feet. She stumbled back from the edge and fell to her knees. She knew that howl. It froze her blood and hollowed her bones. The ruby died. Its light went out like someone putting out a fire. Although the blade still gleamed as if it had been polished, the ruby was once more dead and dull.

Madeline used the sword like a cane to push herself up from the ground. She turned to face certain death in the form of the giant monster she'd seen on Krajina months ago. She'd known the white wolf was close to the surface since the moment she first saw Lev Ro-

manov in the tower. It had only been a matter of time
before he would wake.

Except she didn't find the white wolf preparing to
attack her when she turned around. She found only Lev
Romanov. He stood with his shirt and pants shredded
at the seams. Bulging muscles must have been near the
shift when he made that impossible leap. His hands
were fully human, but they were violently curved like
claws, and the tendons on the sides of his neck were
tensed and distended.

He howled again, and the wolves across the ravine responded with submissive yips and yowls. Their sounds
trailed away as the pack disbanded back into the forest they'd come from. Or so she imagined. She didn't
look across the ravine. Her attention was riveted on
the savage man on *this* side. He looked worse than he'd
looked in the tower room at Bronwal. Thunder clouded
his forehead, and fury blazed from his eyes. His teeth
were bared.

This was the beast that had broken and thrown all
the furniture down the stairs. These were the violent
hands that had shredded clothes and books.

Unlike the wolves, she wasn't free to run away.

She had to face the white wolf, because she needed him.

Chapter 10

Madeline didn't sheath her sword, but it was dead in her hand again. Its glow was gone. Lev's howl had snuffed it out. The sword had been created to channel Ether's energy into the warrior who fought beside the white wolf. But the connection between the wolf and the woman and the ruby had to be embraced to be complete.

She wouldn't embrace it. She couldn't. The connection wasn't safe for Trevor. It wasn't safe for her. The fear she'd woken to on Krajina wasn't only a memory. It stared across the ravine and howled in the form of a man.

Lev dropped to his knees, his head bowed down into his hands. He grabbed fistfuls of wild blond mane in his fingers. Was he fighting the shift or begging for it to come and take him away?

Madeline tightened her grip on the sword's hilt and raised the tip in defense. Lev still hadn't looked her way. Her heart still pounded from the death-defying leap they'd made together. Her chest rose and fell as heavily as Lev's, as if she'd also exerted muscle and will to cross the bridge.

Her fear hadn't stopped her from using the connection to aid in the leap across the ravine. In those moments, she discovered the rush of accepting the sword's Call. The ruby was hers. Ether's energy had been channeled through the gem to enhance the white wolf's power. Lev had barely made it to the remaining planks on the bridge midway across the ravine.

But he had made it.

The superhuman feat was more evidence that she couldn't take the connection between them lightly. It was real. It was powerful. And she had to reject it. Lev would shift again. It was inevitable. The white wolf was a part of him. It wouldn't stay dormant for long. She could see the wolf in his eyes, could feel it in his muscles. When he'd leaped from one disintegrating board to the next on the bridge, he'd been more wolf than man. His grace and fury had saved them, but at what cost?

Madeline waited for the ground to shake. She waited for Lev's human form to morph into the creature that stalked her nightmares. If he attacked her, she would have to fight. But even with her remembered skill with the blade, she wasn't sure she'd survive.

Lev's breathing had slowed. He straightened and dropped his hands from his head. And still the shift didn't come. He looked up at the sky and his back expanded, then relaxed as he inhaled deeply. Then he rose to his feet. Slowly, he turned toward her.

His face was a handsome tragedy of scars and resignation.

"We were connected again, you and I. I felt the

ruby's power flow through us. And then it was gone," Lev said. He stepped away from the ravine's edge. Madeline backed away in time with his approach. When he noted her retreat, he stopped. His hands fisted as if he was dealing with some inner frustration he couldn't help displaying. "I join you in rejecting the connection, but experiencing it and then losing it again? I find I would rather have fallen onto the rocks."

She didn't reply. She couldn't. Her lips were numb. Her body was a hollowed-out husk. When the ruby's light had gone out, it had taken a part of her with it into the dark.

Lev closed his eyes. He stood, stiffly, obviously holding himself together while maintaining his distance from her. He seemed to accept the necessity of their separation even as he endured the discomfort of their discord.

Madeline swallowed. She, too, felt less now. Less herself. Less powerful. One third of a whole. But the hollow inside her chest didn't help her to trust the white wolf. If he was part of their triumvirate, then she would walk alone.

Lev's eyes suddenly opened again. His chin lifted, and his body flowed easily and quickly into movement. One second he stood stiffly, and the next he burst into a running leap that took him away from her and into the trees behind them. He disappeared and Madeline let him go without protest, even though her hollowed chest might have echoed his earlier howl.

She slumped as the tension left her body. Her sword arm fell, and the tip of the Romanov blade stabbed the ground. The sun was sinking in the sky. Its crimson glow cruelly lit up the ruby, making it wink in the dying light. She wouldn't go on without him. They hadn't brought any supplies with them as they'd fled, but she would set up a rough camp with whatever she could find.

She would prepare. Either Lev or the white wolf would return, of that she was certain, and she would need to brace herself for one or the other...or both.

He had been fully joined with her again. He'd felt her heartbeat. He'd tasted the mountain air in her gasp, and he'd felt the river's moisture on her skin. Madeline didn't understand. She didn't remember the true nature of the connection's power. She didn't realize all the sensations she was experiencing weren't merely her own.

Sweet torture, dear God, because he did.

It wasn't his desire for her that caused him to run into the forest. It was hers for him. He was left with no doubt that she hungered for his lips and thrilled at his hardness and longed to soothe his pain.

But he'd also experienced her fear and distrust of his shift.

She feared the monstrous white wolf.

She might desire him, but her fear of the wolf overpowered and negated everything else.

Because he and the white wolf were the same.

Chapter 11

Madeline hiked for a half hour before she used young evergreen saplings and several weathered fallen limbs to weave a makeshift shelter. She didn't want to camp in the open air next to the ravine, and a buffer from the cold air coming up off the river seemed wise. There was no way to hide from the *Volkhvy* if they were determined to find her, but she could at least try to make it a challenge for them. She chose a level spot where fresh-cut bows could be spread for bedding. The sharp, pleasant scent of spruce sap filled the air as she worked.

She had no blankets and only the clothes on her back, but she managed to dig a shallow fire pit with a jagged stone and kindle a fire with a piece of flint against the edge of her sword. By the time she achieved a spark, the ember she created with a bundle of dried twigs around dead spruce needles was the only light. It glowed in her hands as she nursed it hotter with gentle puffs from her lips before she placed it on the dried wood she'd already gathered. She lined the pit with more stones to absorb and radiate the tiny fire's heat.

Nearby, a small trickle of water came out of a rocky outcropping. The spring formed a stream flowing delicately but persistently toward the river at the bottom of the ravine. The water was icy cold and refreshing. After she drank her fill, she used it to wash the sap from her hands and face.

Once she had done everything she could with the materials she had at hand, Madeline was forced to sit quietly as her stomach clenched with hunger and the night closed in around her. She couldn't search for food in the dark. That would have to wait until morning. It had been a mistake to leave their packs behind in the sudden rush to escape the wolves.

All alone in the hush of the woods, Madeline missed her charcoal pencils and sketchbook more than granola.

But for the first time, it wasn't the white wolf her fingers itched to draw.

She leaned back against the makeshift evergreen bedding and closed her eyes. She could still see the flames dancing on her lids, but she also saw Lev Romanov leaping over the ravine. She imagined the scene as if she'd been watching rather than being carried in his arms. His clothes had been shredded by the incredible effort of his jump. Not only the first leap, but also every leap after that, across the disintegrating boards. She and the sword had helped him. The power the sword channeled from the Ether had been like fuel, but he'd also come as close as he could to shifting without actually becoming the white wolf.

What had prevented him from shifting all the way?

One day, she would sketch him as he had been at

the edge of the ravine. His near shift was emblazoned behind her eyes every time they closed. But the image she remembered resulted in a very different reaction than the one she'd had to the white wolf.

In that moment, Lev had been glorious, filled with power for heroic purpose.

His arms had stayed tight around her. He'd taken her to solid ground before he released her. And yet, even then he'd remained in his human form. Was he human still, or had he shifted since he left her by the ravine? She hadn't heard any distant thunder or felt the earth quaking. The Romanovs had been enhanced and changed by Queen Vasilisa. It was Ether's energy in their very bones and blood that made the shift possible, and that power, when released, caused the world to shake.

Madeline had seen the white wolf become a man. She could imagine the opposite transition all too well. She waited by the fire, not for the night to end, but for Lev to return to her.

He would be back.

She just wasn't sure which form would appear from the dark forest around her. That she should anticipate one and dread the other was a new and sudden weakness she had to face.

But it was Lev's arms she could still imagine wrapped around her. It was Lev's intense, hungry gaze she could still feel on her lips, and it was his mouth she longed to taste.

Madeline didn't doze. She blamed the mesmerizing fire and exhaustion for her missing the exact moment when she was no longer alone. Only a sudden rush of cold washing over her skin stirred her. Gooseflesh rose on her arms and chest in spite of the fire, and she scrambled to her feet.

A sliver of moon had risen. Enough to join the firelight in illuminating the glistening water and the man who leaned down to drink from the spring as she had done earlier in the evening. He'd already splashed water on his face and chest. His hair was damp, and it glistened with a golden fire-lit sheen. He held the wet, torn remains of his shirt in his hand. He must have used it to wash off with the icy water. What was left of his shredded pants hung low on his lean hips. When he turned at her approach, his eyes were unusually dark in the night shadows. The blue was hidden.

His thoughts should be hidden, too.

But as Madeline stepped toward the bare-chested man who silently watched her, it wasn't only the shock of the cold water she felt. He hungrily soaked up her presence as she did his, and it wasn't merely the track of his gaze from her head to her feet and back again that revealed his hunger for her. His heightened senses absorbed as many details of her as he could—the scent of spruce on her fingers, the nails she had torn when she'd made the fire pit, the pinch of fatigue around her eyes.

But her senses were suddenly heightened as well.

The desire coiling low in her abdomen turned her to fire because it was doubled. She experienced his hunger for her as she hungered for him.

He didn't merely see her. He felt her—the hollow in her stomach, the ache in her heart, the physical need to touch him rising to claim her. Madeline stumbled. She halted in midstep to avoid a fall. His longing was almost too much to experience as his heat combined with hers. His ache and her need collided so powerfully, her body shook from sensory overload.

The ruby didn't glow. She'd left the sword back by the shelter. Firelight flickered over a dull and dead gem.

Yet, unlike the ruby, she and Lev were very much alive.

Lev looked at her, and she felt his desire for her burn in the pit of her belly. It joined her own to burgeon into a truth she couldn't ignore: she wanted him. She didn't want to simply remember the taste of his lips. She wanted to taste them again, here and now. And she couldn't hide it from him any more than he could hide his desire to taste hers. They were connected. Somehow, in spite of the ruby's dormancy and her rejection of its power, they were still connected.

"I would spare you this if I could," Lev said hoarsely. His ruined shirt fell from his fingers to land at the ground at his feet, forgotten. "No one should be tied to a monster for eternity. I feel your fear of the white wolf. It turns my soul to ice. And yet there's fire, too." He took up the movement she had abandoned, stepping toward her as he continued to speak, rough and low. His voice was another revelation of the raw emotions running through them both. "You look at my mouth and I feel the burn of your tongue on my lips. There is pleasure in the wanting. And pain."

Madeline didn't back away. Her heartbeat raced. Her breath came in shallow gasps from lips that tingled with possibilities. The leap must have done this. The sword had come to life, and now they were sensing more than they should of each other's thoughts and desires. The effect would fade as the glow of the ruby had faded. Surely. Eventually.

Tonight was an anomaly.

They were caught in an afterglow of power that

bound them together, even though they were destined
to part.

She should turn away. She should go back to the
fire and keep distance between them until their connection faded.

Lev came to a stop. His body was so close to hers
that the wild scent of mineral-rich spring water and rich
woodsy earth and evergreen enveloped her.

It was her scent, too.

As if synchronized, they both breathed in and out at
the same time in a shared, sensual appreciation of the
natural Carpathian cologne that clung to them both.

Neither of them closed the slight gap between their
bodies. She didn't reach for him. Lev didn't reach for
her. Her fear of the white wolf wasn't a secret. He had
seen it in her sketches, but now he must have *felt* it.
His pause acknowledged her fear and honored it. He
wouldn't touch her. He wouldn't give her the taste he
knew she craved because he also felt her fear. It made
his spine shiver and then it settled, metallic and heavy
as a knot in his throat that could never seem to be swallowed away.

"I'm afraid of the white wolf," Madeline said. It was
an unnecessary confession, but one she was compelled
to make out loud. "He is savage and dangerous and more
furious than any other creature I've ever seen."

Lev still didn't move, but his powerful body trembled
with the will he exerted to hold himself in place. He
didn't avoid her eyes. He met her gaze without blinking.

"*I* am savage and dangerous and more furious than
any other creature you've seen," he whispered. It wasn't
a confession. It was a reminder. He was the wolf she
feared in human form. Scarred, trembling and beautiful, but yes, savage and dangerous. They shared her fear

in their throats and his fury in their chests, but lower, they shared a heat that couldn't be ignored.

"I know," Madeline acknowledged.

Their connection, however long it lasted, ensured that she couldn't fool herself into thinking she desired an ordinary man. A legendary beast faced her. And she ached to taste him again for the first time.

She could no longer remain still. Her hand lifted toward his face almost of its own volition. But he felt her decision and leaned toward her at the same time. His cheek met her tentative palm. Her fingers shook, tickling his skin and causing shivers of response to flow through him *and* through her.

He wanted more. She wanted more. But they both enjoyed the first whisper-soft caress. Her hand wouldn't harden against his face. It was as if she tried to reach out to touch fire, and every instinct warned her to pull away. Of course it wasn't safe to touch him, any more than it would be safe to plunge her hand into flames.

But she was very cold, and the heat called to her with a siren's song she couldn't resist.

She caressed Lev. She explored the different textures between where his cheek was smooth and where scars roughened his skin. His beard crinkled with waves of gold against her tentative touch.

The ruby was dead, but they were enveloped in the firelight's warm glow in place of the ruby's scarlet light, and the connection the sword had caused between them hadn't fully faded away. Not yet. She wanted to play in the flames for a little while before she had to face the morning.

His eyelids had nearly closed when she touched him. Now they lifted and his intense eyes met hers. She would get burned. It wasn't safe to kiss a man with a savage heart. His jaw was hard beneath her fingers as she explored his beard. He was holding himself in check…barely. Just barely. The ferocity of the white wolf was a part of him. She suddenly tried to memorize how Lev looked in this moment, trembling on the second precipice that day. They were going to leap together again. And he was every wolf sketch she'd created—the howls, the hunger, the supernatural power—only as a man.

She would remember and sketch him like this with the wolf in his eyes and her hand on his face.

"I don't even care that this will make it harder. All I've known is hard for too long. I'll have one more kiss to last me forever," Lev said.

His arms came around her and pulled her against his warm, granite chest. Madeline offered no resistance. She allowed him to take her. Her soft, full breasts flattened against him and she gasped at the pleasure that arced from her tight nipples to the throbbing pulse point between her thighs.

"One kiss," she said on a sigh.

She couldn't separate where her heat ended and his began, even before his mouth descended to find hers. He quested to find her in the shadows. His open lips sought hers; his warm breath tickled her skin along her cheek. He breathed her in. Allowed her time to anticipate. There was no rush. His movements were slow and sultry. When his mouth finally settled on hers, he savored her lower lip with a suckling taste. Her knees buckled and she cried out when he teased the lip he'd suckled with his moist tongue.

His powerful arms held her up. He didn't let her fall. They leaped the second precipice together, risking a much more dangerous ravine than they'd risked before. What were rocks and rushing rivers to a long-lost love? One that could never be found? They were merely seeking pleasure to salve the pain.

But, oh, to be tempted and tasted once more. Just once more.

Madeline couldn't breathe. He didn't crush her too tightly. In fact, he held her so gently his hard, muscular body was an enticing contrast to the whisper-soft caress of his hands on her back. His fingers spread heat along her spine, kneading and stroking. He didn't lift her shirt. There was cotton between his hands and her skin. And yet he still stole her breath.

Simply standing. Simply holding her.

He devoured her, but with tender, seeking kisses. It was his tenderness that slayed, that conquered, that made her beg for more.

Their connection might have helped him to interpret her gasps and moans.

But it was her bold, thrusting tongue meeting his and plunging hungrily into the hot depths of his mouth that made him growl and finally, *finally* crush her against him. Now, as she plundered the silken hollow of his mouth, his hands pressed harder and pulled her tighter. She wrapped her arms around his neck, plunging her fingers into his damp hair and taking fistfuls of wet waves to hold him for her sensual exploration of the rough and smooth textures she sought with her tongue.

Now Lev gasped for air. He moaned and fell back against a tree for support. He took her with him, and the tree shook as it caught them both. Madeline gloried in the idea that she had caused him to go weak in the knees. Now she leaned over him as he took her weight against him. Only the tips of her toes brushed the ground. And his chest was no longer the hardest thing about him. The front of his pants bulged with a hot, curving erection. She didn't shy away from the results of her hungry kisses. She pressed against the bulge and cried out her approval when he helped her by lifting her bottom and encouraging her to spread her legs so that she could settle her heated core on him. They were fully clothed.

Madeline's hips matched the hungry movements of her thrusting tongue. No matter how badly she wanted to rip aside their clothing to match the connection they temporarily shared with their bodies, she couldn't. She wouldn't. But the clothing didn't stop Lev from sensing her need. He held her bottom with one hand. He stroked between her legs with the other. He found the spot where she needed his touch the most. She cried out as he rubbed with the perfect rhythm.

"I remember your heat. Your sweet, tight heat," Lev moaned into her mouth between deep, sucking kisses. The heat and friction of his strong fingers pleasured her to a sudden, fierce spasm of release. Only Lev's muscular arm kept her from dissolving to the ground as her body tensed. The arc of her orgasm carried her higher than she'd yet been that day, over and across the abyss that separated them. Then he held her, both arms coming around her as her body shook.

Lev's head fell back against the tree. His broad chest expanded as he finally took a deep breath beneath her. The fire had died down to nothing but embers while they were distracted. It didn't matter. The shadows couldn't hide what they'd shared.

Not the pleasure, or the pain.

Chapter 12

The wolves didn't return that night. The river ran long, and there was no telling how far they'd have to travel to find another bridge or a spot shallow enough for crossing. The *Volkhvy* didn't appear. No doubt they didn't want to risk finding the white wolf instead of their human quarry, especially without the pack to back them up.

Lev had almost shifted when they leaped over the ravine.

She didn't know how far he'd run afterward, but the next morning when Madeline woke, she found her pack by the remains of the fire. Lev had gone back for the possessions they'd abandoned by the trail. Unlike the natural wolves, Lev was tireless even in his human form.

She was happy to see her backpack with its meager supplies. But she didn't express her thanks. The events of the night before were too fresh and raw in her mind.

She now had a vivid memory of his kisses *and* his intimate touch. She hadn't allowed her imagination to go beyond his lips before. Now it ran wild, fueled by the pleasure he'd given her.

It was hard to conceive how even a thousand years of sleep could have clouded previous kisses and caresses from her mind. Her body was more liquid than it had been before. She was more aware of every nerve and every erogenous zone. Her lips were tender, her nipples fully peaked in the early morning mountain air.

Her sensations were all hers, thank goodness. Nothing remained of the unusual connection she'd experienced with Lev the night before. He was completely shut off from her. His absence was a hollowness. Her chest echoed with every heartbeat. Her stomach felt as if she were balanced at the edge of the highest height, waiting to fall.

Instead of pointlessly aching, Madeline rose and washed in the spring. Lev had gone to scout the way. She stretched and went through several rounds of sword positioning while she waited for him to return. Her moves were more graceful than they'd been before. The hilt was hers. It fit perfectly to her hand, even if the ruby didn't glow.

What other lasting effects might exist because they'd embraced the connection?

But even the sword couldn't distract her from the urge to sketch. The image of Lev at the edge of the ravine when he'd been near shifting grew ever more vivid in her mind's eye. She had to commit that moment to the pages of her sketchbook now that it was back in her possession.

She knelt beside her pack and unzipped the compartment that held her drawing materials. Her sketchbook was no worse for wear from its abandonment. She pulled it from the pack and then riffled through the stubs of remaining charcoal until she found one that was still fit for use. Had she drawn back in those days before her long sleep? She couldn't imagine not bringing the vibrant images in her head to life in some way. This time was no exception. In fact, the Lev by the ravine seemed to haunt her even more than the white wolf on the cliffs of Krajina. There'd been something so striking about his tremendous strain as the white wolf had tried to break free.

Madeline lost herself to the sketches, as she always did. One second she pressed the first mark of charcoal into the page. The next she was covered in smudges of coal dust, and a sketch had come to life.

Lev Romanov had come to life, close to shifting and strikingly heroic.

He'd saved her. He'd protected the wolves. And all without shifting completely. The terrible strain in his bulging muscles and his tense features had been poignant for some reason. She captured the beauty of his handsome face and muscular figure, along with some elusive quality of desperation in his eyes she couldn't quite name. Only when the sketch was complete did the compulsion to draw release her. She stared at the drawing for a long time, trying to understand the secret her artistic eye was trying to tell her.

Finally, with a sigh, she gave up and tucked away her sketchbook.

"I've found a game trail that heads in the direction we need to travel," Lev said. He came back into camp at an easy jog. He always made movement look effortless. His muscles responded powerfully to his commands with extraordinary agility that would have looked like work on another man. For Lev, running was like breathing. Automatic. Easy. He had changed out of his shredded clothing into similar pants and a tunic he'd carried in his bag. His vest was the same. She'd held fistfuls of the black leather when she…

Madeline looked up from Lev's broad chest, and her attention landed on the vulnerable pulse point at the base of his throat. She lifted her gaze quickly again. Unfortunately, in doing so, she met his eyes. He had tied his hair back into a queue. Nothing shaded the vivid blue of his irises from view—not night or thick waves of hair.

"We've wasted enough time," Madeline said. "They want to keep me away from Trevor, but I won't let them stop me."

Lev blinked and turned away. He didn't reference the night before. But she could see his lips were pink from her kisses. She wondered if his mouth still tingled like her own. And then she cursed herself for wondering. The wolves and the *Volkhvy* weren't the only challenges she faced. Besides needing to improve her skill with a sword and strengthen her muscles and her mind, she had to steady her nerve against Lev Romanov's allure. The sketches she'd added to her book were a confession she wasn't ready to make.

Most importantly, she couldn't risk waking the ruby again, because in doing so she woke other things that were much harder to resist.

Madeline dug into her backpack for a change of clothes and an energy bar. She hoped the shade provided by the forest canopy over the trail would hide her heated cheeks.

Lev hadn't shifted. Even when he was bathed in the ruby's light, he had kept his human form—but just barely. His clothes had been shredded because his muscles bulged and strained nearly to the point of shifting. He might succumb to the white wolf if she woke the ruby again. And even though she knew he and the white wolf were the same creature in different forms, it was the wolf she feared. As the wolf, Lev had attacked Krajina. He might have hurt her or Trevor if Vasilisa, Anna and his brother hadn't intervened.

Or worse, Madeline might have had to use the sword against him.

She had to wield the sword against the marked *Volkhvy* without calling on its enchantment as she had done over the ravine. Hopefully, they could save Trevor without risking the appearance of a white wolf she didn't fully trust Lev to control.

The morning was sharp, like broken glass. Everywhere he looked, bright rays of sunshine seemed to glint in his eyes, and every step he took seemed to slice into his skin. He'd been hardened against every cut for so long that the pain took him by surprise.

He shouldn't have kissed her. Their combined needs had been too much for the deprivation he'd endured for so long. He couldn't resist her. And she had wanted to taste him so badly, her body had been shaking with the hunger of it. Never mind that his hunger had enhanced and increased hers. Lev hadn't been able to tell where his desire stopped and hers began. Their connection had always been like that. All-consuming. As savage as the beast beneath his skin. As tender as Madeline's sweet, ferocious release.

God. She'd always responded to his touch. They were

match and tinder. Even now. Even now when it tortured him completely. But he had been unprepared for her last night. He'd been shaken from the near shift and their narrow escape. He'd been flayed by the ruby's aura and the way it had knit familiar threads of power between him and Madeline, connecting them together as they'd once been connected long ago.

For brief seconds, he'd felt whole.

But the feeling had been a lie.

Worse was yet to come. The horses were gone, and they were still several days' ride away from Straluci. He could shorten that by a day, but it wasn't going to be easy. The distance was negligible for him even in his human form. Especially now. His years as the white wolf had only strengthened his muscles and his endurance. Madeline was tall, and she was reclaiming the muscles of her athletic build, but physically she would be no burden to him. He watched her as she strapped her sword onto her back. She'd modified the positioning herself to perfectly match up her reach with the sword's hilt. He'd seen her do this a thousand times before. She didn't remember, but her body did. He could see her movements becoming stronger and more graceful.

There was something else she wouldn't remember. They'd counted on his supernatural speed and strength in the past when they needed to. He had carried her into battle many times as the white wolf, movements faster and more tireless than those of any horse.

This would be different. He wouldn't shift into his wolf form. She would never trust him to carry her rather than devour her whole. He would have to carry her as a man. The first challenge would be convincing her to allow it. The second challenge would be enduring the intimacy of her warm body pressed against him.

* * *

Madeline was worried. At top speed, she would be lucky to match half the distance the horses had achieved in a day. Lev couldn't go without her, but she was only going to slow him down. She was stronger than she'd been when she first woke up. But her human strength, unenhanced by the ruby's enchantment, wouldn't be enough.

"I hope your furrowed brow means you've realized we have a problem," Lev said. He approached her as anyone would, with one foot in front of the other, and yet her body reacted as if his walk toward her was a seduction. Her breath caught. Her pulse kicked. Her eyes flicked away from his, only to land on his muscular legs encased in tight leather leggings. Her cheeks heated, because now that she'd actually felt the warm steel of his hips between her thighs, she couldn't help noticing their power and remembering their heat even when he was simply walking her way.

"Losing the horses has sabotaged our journey. The marked *Volkhvy* might have beaten us after all," Madeline said. She forced herself to focus on their enemies rather than her traitorous reaction to Lev as he came to stand near her.

Near was bad. The pull of attraction between her body and his was a powerful force. It was hard enough to resist when they weren't standing close together. It wasn't the sword. It was as dead on her back as it had been before she woke it to help them leap over the ravine. He was a dangerous and damaged man, but she couldn't deny he was attractive. Especially after she'd experienced sheer, wanton pleasure from his touch.

Distance was best.

To show her body who was in control, she stepped several strides back from Lev.

"It will take me too long to reach the portal," Madeline said. She hoped Lev wouldn't notice her skittish reaction to his proximity, but she hoped in vain. He had the white wolf's senses and his predatory nature. His blue eyes narrowed slightly. His jaw tensed. He took a step following her retreat, but then he seemed to catch himself and stop.

"No, Madeline. It won't," he said. It was almost a growl. Each syllable of her name was uttered deep and low. It wasn't fear that made her stomach coil tightly in response. He'd growled her name exactly like that the night before. This wasn't a seduction. This was them planning their next move and their strategy to beat the marked *Volkhvy* stalking them.

And yet his growl made her burn in places she tried to ignore.

She didn't back away when he took another step toward her. Her chin lifted and her spine stiffened. She couldn't will her desire away. She could only try to ignore it. What she couldn't ignore was the reciprocal heat in Lev's eyes when he faced her, toe-to-toe. He looked down at her for several long seconds before he spoke again. The sword didn't glow, but they were suffused in heat just the same. Madeline held her breath because she was afraid her respiration would synchronize with Lev's again. She felt the steady rise and fall of his broad chest. She pretended she could exist without oxygen and Lev's touch.

And then the big, tall man who towered over her dropped to one knee.

She gasped for air as his face ended up only a foot away from her pelvis. He looked from the *V* of her thighs up the length of her torso to her face. Madeline panted as the track of his gaze left a trail of heat in its wake. He didn't reach for her. He didn't touch her. He didn't have to. Kneeling, he seduced her even more than he had by walking and talking. To have such power and pain held in check before her was a heady offering.

One she couldn't accept.

Only she couldn't force herself to turn away.

The sun penetrated the forest canopy and glinted off his golden blond hair. She fisted her hands to keep from reaching to feel its warmth in his waves.

"I'm fast. And strong. There's no man stronger, and only one beast. The white wolf could carry you longer and faster, but I'll offer you this back instead. We need to hurry. For Trevor. There's no other way."

Madeline suddenly understood what the kneeling man offered. Not his heart. But his legs and his arms and his back. His *Volkhvy*-enhanced muscles and a thousand years of built-up endurance. For her. For Trevor.

Her eyes burned. The echo of the howl she'd once released on his behalf tightened her throat. She unclenched her fists, but only to press against the hollow in the pit of her stomach. She willed the moisture in her eyes to dry as he looked up at her, waiting for her response.

He didn't wait patiently. A beast never could. His body was kneeling, but not in subjugation. She could see every muscle he possessed as tense and tight as his jaw. She could see the strain around his eyes and in the firmness of his usually soft lips. If he was stone, he was trembling stone, only seconds away from disintegration.

"For Trevor," Madeline agreed before Lev's wild energy contained for her benefit could tear him apart.

Only then did he reach for her, but he moved so

quickly once her permission released his control that she cried out in surprise. But she fell silent when he merely clasped her hand and pulled her around his kneeling body. She knew then that he wanted her to ride on his back so his movements wouldn't be hindered, as they would if he cradled her in his arms.

She wrapped her arms around his neck and, with no other choice, wrapped her legs around his waist. The intimacy of the position shocked all of her senses, still tender from the night before. He was as hard as she remembered. And as hot. Her body instantly heated against him. She'd felt like liquid when she woke that morning. Now it seemed as if her blood turned to lava.

Lev rose so quickly to his feet that she gasped. She was forced to hold on tighter as he set off. He wasn't fazed by her weight or the burden of her on his back. If his blood was affected by her heat pressed against the small of his back, she couldn't tell as he ran.

Aleksandr didn't pace. His hands were clasped calmly behind his back. He stood with his nose almost touching the cool glass of the wall of windows that over-looked the visible shimmer of the Ether. The cliff house had once been the Dark *Volkhvy's* royal household. The king had lived here, and here the Darkest prince the world had ever seen had been born. He'd grown up influenced by the rift that existed in the canyon. It allowed Ether's energy to seep and flow and shine more closely to earth than it did anywhere else.

Now this cement-and-glass masterpiece of contemporary architecture was his. It had been built as much as a temple to the Ether as a home. Light *Volkhvy* carefully controlled the amount of energy they tapped. Like a black hole, the Ether was a hungry vacuum that would consume you if you were too greedy. The trick was to tap into the energy the vacuum expelled without being devoured.

The witchblood prince had failed to control himself. He'd become addicted to the power. The never-ending vacuum of Darkness had eaten him from the inside out. The prince had been an abject lesson in maintaining control even when you were making the boldest of moves to claim the power, and the people, you desired.

Aleksandr was in control. In this place, control took every ounce of his *Volkhvy* abilities. His effort was supreme, and the rush that flushed his skin and thrilled his pulse was exhilarating. The constantly changing light hovering above the canyon was the only movement he required.

"They failed. The Romanov wolf leaped over a river as if he had wings. No witch or wolf could follow." One of Aleksandr's men had come into the room with the update. He didn't come any closer than the doorway. Not all *Volkhvy* were strong enough to handle the overwhelming presence of the Ether or what the Ether had done to—*for*—their leader.

Aleksandr turned from the shimmering light. His man visibly blanched and stepped back. There were mirrors in the cliff house. Aleksandr had seen his own eyes. Their obsidian sheen was startling.

But he was in control.

He needed as much energy from the Ether as he could absorb in order to finish what he had started. He'd realized it as soon as they'd failed to kill the red Romanov wolf. When Anna, the Light *Volkhvy* princess, marked them all with a sudden flash of emerald power from the enchanted sword she claimed, Aleksandr had known more power would be his only chance to stand against her.

More power and the total disruption of the triumvirate of wolf, sword and warrior woman Queen Vasilisa had created.

He'd failed to stop the red wolf from connecting with his mate. They were united against him now, champions of Vasilisa once more. Just like the black wolf and his powerful Elena, the swan.

He couldn't fail this time. Not with the white wolf. Fortunately, Queen Vasilisa had almost done the job herself. She'd separated Lev and Madeline Romanov for over a thousand years with an enchanted sleep. He only had to keep them apart.

"He shifted?" Aleksandr demanded.

"No. He runs on two legs. He doesn't shift even when attacked. He's only a man." The witch's voice quavered as if he reported to a monster. None of Aleksandr's people were cowards. Rising up against Queen Vasilisa had taken boldness and courage, and none were bolder than Aleksandr himself. He would sit on the throne when they broke her. He would lead the Light *Volkhvy* and the Dark. He would unite them with a common purpose of coming out of the shadows and claiming a world that should be theirs.

He must pay a price for it, of course. His followers looked at him differently now than they once had. Yet loss of their admiration was a small price to pay for a throne. He had their fear. It would be enough.

"Then he can be killed. No man can stand against the *Volkhvy*," Aleksandr said. "And the woman? Is the ruby blade still dead in her hand?" he asked.

"The ravine seemed impassable. And yet they crossed it. The wolf pack couldn't follow. But the woman didn't fight the wolves. She crossed with Romanov and then they both disappeared," his man replied. The witch had edged a little farther away from his master.

"Madeline is no longer an enchanted warrior. Her sword is dead in her hands. Tell our men to continue pursuit. The Romanovs' connection must be disrupted. We failed to capture and kill her on Krajina. We cannot fail again. She must die," Aleksandr ordered. "Before Lev Romanov reclaims his white-wolf form."

"And the baby?" his man asked.

As Aleksandr turned back to the view he opened himself more to the Ether. His body spasmed in painful pleasure as the Darkness rushed in. Mention of the Romanovs' child had only reminded him of Queen Vasilisa. He had to be as powerful as possible before he personally confronted the Light *Volkhvy* queen.

"He will die just as his parents will die. We will feed them to the Ether. The queen tormented her champions with a cycle of disappearances to punish them for their father's betrayal. But I will banish them to the Ether. Never to return. They will die and I will claim the throne," Aleksandr said. "And, perhaps, I will even claim the queen herself."

The man behind him was silent. Whether he had run away or fainted, Aleksandr didn't care. All he cared about was the black energy coursing through his body. No wonder the witchblood prince had been such a formidable *Volkhvy*. Rumor had been that he'd spent as much time in the Ether as possible, risking annihilation for longer and longer periods of time in order to increase his power.

Aleksandr leaned his body against the glass that separated him from the light outside. He could feel its pull. Before long, he was lost in a vision of his upcoming triumph—dead and decimated wolves and warriors and their families. A bound former queen as consort by his side. This cliff house as his royal seat, and the constant pleasure of all the Ether he could take.

He barely noticed his reflection in the glass, or the black tears of happiness that trailed down his face.

Chapter 13

Lev's powerful legs ate miles of mountain one stride at a time. Madeline wasn't a passive passenger. The journey was rough. The path tangled with branches and vines. Her body moved with his along every twist and turn. She dodged and ducked and pressed her face into Lev's neck to avoid sticks and briars.

His kisses had woken something inside her. Not memories, but a longing to remember.

She still saw his savagery, but now she wasn't blinded to other things—he had saved the horses from the wolves by letting them go, he had spared the wolves by not attacking them while they assembled and he had waited for her.

No. She couldn't think about that other waiting. The thousand years of waiting was too overwhelming to contemplate. She could only focus on the days of waiting since they'd first stood face-to-face in the tower room.

He'd waited for her kiss.

And he wasn't a calm and patient man. His wait burned. His wait throbbed. His wait trembled and shook with passion and fury. Yet still, it had been her touch that gave him permission to act on what they both desired.

He had waited for her. He had waited for that touch.

She couldn't reconcile the truths she had learned about Lev Romanov with the truths she knew about the white wolf. Madeline needed the memories she'd lost to help her understand the creature who carried her through the Carpathian woods. Was he a man lost to the beast, or a beast lost within the man? The heat of Lev's exertion caused his shirt to dampen beneath her hands. By midday, she could see moisture trickling down his neck.

And still he ran.

He wasn't an ordinary man, but he was made of muscle and bone, as she was. Her hips screamed, and her thighs trembled from actively riding his every move all morning. Her own hair was damp on her head. Tendrils of moisture-darkened scarlet tumbled into her eyes.

She didn't have memories to help her understand this man who pushed himself so ferociously, but she suddenly knew he would run until he fell down dead if she didn't make him stop. He wouldn't be able to fight the marked *Volkhvy* who had kidnapped their son if he killed himself to get to them.

"I can't hold on much longer, Lev. You have to stop," Madeline said. She didn't shout, but rather murmured into his ear. Her lips brushed his earlobe. She tasted salt. She wasn't sure if it was his perspiration or her own. "I have to rest. I need water and food."

She was certain if she had told him that he needed to stop for himself, he would have ignored her. Maybe as the wolf, he had done this. Run until he collapsed, and then run some more with no one around to remind him to eat and drink and rest. No wonder he'd been lost to the beast for so long. While she'd been sleeping with Trevor, Lev had been alone. Left to the lonesome drive of the wolf in his heart.

"I'll be worthless when we get there if I've died from dehydration," Madeline said.

Lev's speed dropped. He had sprinted all morning. Now his run changed to a lope, which changed to a fast walk. Madeline released his neck and slid to her numb feet when his walk slowed enough to allow it. She took several strides to catch her balance. She was propelled by the momentum, though Lev stopped easily with his muscular legs, still powerful even after they'd been pushed so hard for so long.

Feeling returned to her limbs as she stretched and moved away from the place where Lev had halted. She instinctively put some distance between her aching body and the tall, hard body that had carried her all morning.

But she couldn't help looking.

Sweat plastered Lev's shirt to his broad chest, and his vest didn't hide the muscles the damp cotton revealed. Not his powerful pectorals or his rippled abdomen. His leather leggings were a second skin, stuck to his muscles by perspiration that only served to call attention to his strong legs.

"There's water nearby," Madeline said. The gurgle of a stream teased her ears once Lev's feet were no longer pounding on the forest floor. The fresh scent of water-dampened earth and stone made her lick her lips. They'd eaten their last granola and changed into their fresh clothes that morning. Now Madeline's stomach was almost as empty as her backpack, and her mouth was dry. Modern food left much to be desired. She craved fresh bread and tangy cheese. And a tankard of ale would be nice.

Instead, she settled for the cold water she found not far from where Lev had stopped. She crouched beside the tiny trickle of a mountain brook and scooped up water with her hands. She even savored the mineral bite of the liquid against her tongue as she hydrated.

At least until Lev joined her.

He had taken the leather cord from his hair, and he'd shed his sweat-dampened shirt and vest. Wild waves surrounded his head like a mane. He fell down on the moss beside the brook and stretched out flat on his stomach. He lowered his mouth to the water to drink. The water rushed over his face and hair as he buried his face in its cool flow.

While she had merely hydrated, it was like he completely refreshed himself. His whole body seemed to enjoy the brook and the moss and the cool respite of the shadowed forest glade. When he rose, it was with a powerful, graceful leap to a crouched position. He flipped his wet hair back from his face. An arc of water flew off him as he balanced on the balls of his feet.

And then he lifted his chin and met her eyes.

She should have looked away, but as their gazes connected, she was caught and held by the intensity in his blue eyes. He didn't speak. He stood, silently, and walked toward her. Madeline had taken one last drink and risen to stand beside the brook. She'd meant to turn away, but she'd watched Lev instead, as transfixed as she would have been watching any wild creature bow its head to drink.

"Water will have to be enough for now. We have to

press on," Lev said. "The wolves have found us again. They aren't far behind."

It was hard for Madeline to process his words, because as he spoke he stepped closer to her until his bare chest brushed the tips of her breasts. He lifted one hand to her upturned face. With an outstretched finger, he touched her cheek. She sucked in a gulp of air, but his hand drew back before she could decide to lean into his touch or move away. He had captured a droplet of water. It hung suspended on his finger for several seconds before he gently, shockingly traced the drop of moisture over her lower lip.

When he spoke, his gravelly voice vibrated pleasantly against her. "We do not have to be connected by the sword for me to sense your desire, Madeline Romanov. I have not forgotten the way your eyes reflect heat and your perfect lips part. I will not claim kisses that you have not offered, but know this—your ache is my ache. Your heat is my heat. The ruby might be dormant or even dead, but my desire for you will never die," Lev said. "Nor your desire for me, I think."

It wasn't arrogance. It was perception. Surely, he could feel her heartbeat pound against his hard, hot skin. His eyes darkened as her tongue flicked out to lick the moisture he'd trailed on her lip. But, true to his word, he didn't lean down to kiss her, even though he must see how badly she wanted to taste him.

"I saw the white wolf's horrible snarl. He threatened everyone on Krajina. There was no reason in his terrible red eyes. There was only blind rage. You appeared before I could fight the white wolf, but I would have fought him. I would have killed him to protect Queen Vasilisa and Trevor. To protect your brother and his wife," Madeline said.

"The threat of the white wolf's savagery looms between us," Lev said. "And his savagery is mine. But it will be our savagery that saves you and Trevor from the *Volkhvy*. This, I promise. I also promise you will never have to face the white wolf in battle. I will do whatever I must to prevent it."

"I have looked into the white wolf's eyes and he has no master," Madeline said. She did back away then. She put distance between them before she turned to walk away.

"The white wolf has no master, but he does have a mistress," Lev replied.

Madeline's steps faltered, but only for a second before she continued walking away from the scarred man by the brook. He looked like he could wrestle the white wolf to its knees, but she couldn't be certain enough to trust Trevor's fate to his hands.

No matter how powerful they seemed.

Chapter 14

Madeline Durnova walked the corridors of Bronwal as a lady-in-waiting to Naomi Romanov. What she was waiting for, she wasn't quite certain. She and the other noble ladies Naomi had invited to the castle were companions, not guests. They kept Naomi company when she wasn't on the battlefield. She was a great lady, but she was also the ruby warrior. She wielded an enchanted blade for Queen Vasilisa of the Light Volkhvy.

She was also very sad.

Naomi's husband, Vladimir, was the great gray-wolf champion of the Light Volkhvy. *He was also a terribly frightening man. Madeline wasn't timid. As the privileged younger daughter in a family full of sons, she'd had an upbringing that included climbing trees and fighting her brothers with wooden swords, as well as learning how to sing and sew. She could leave Bronwal at any time she wished if she became unhappy.*

Her problem wasn't unhappiness. It was impatience. Waiting wasn't doing. And even though she waited on a great lady and a ferocious warrior, Madeline couldn't help but feel that her true purpose was missing.

As her time at Bronwal had gone from weeks to months, only one thing kept her from deciding to leave: Lev Romanov.

Naomi's son was the reason many of the ladies in the castle met each morning with a smile. Unlike his serious oldest brother and his stalwart twin, Lev was wild, full of life and laughter. When he walked into a room, everything and everyone became the setting to his gem. He shone. And Madeline wasn't immune to his energy and magnetism.

In fact, she seemed more affected than most.

When Lev was around, her thread knotted, her wine spilled, her breath caught and her feet betrayed her interest with clumsiness. He noticed. He was one of the Romanov wolves. His eyes were the eyes of a predator. They cataloged her every move, every sig and every stuttering phrase.

It wasn't until an early morning walk found her suddenly alone with the youngest Romanov that Madeline realized she wasn't prey.

"I run in the mornings," Lev said. Like her, he'd been on the ramparts of Bronwal for exercise. Unlike her, he had exerted himself to the point that he was panting. His broad chest rose and fell as he took deep breaths. He was dressed in nothing but a thin tunic and light leggings, and his damp hair tumbled around his head from perspiration and morning dew. All in all, Madeline's fingers itched to capture the look of him in the rising sun. Did there exist a golden thread that

would match the color of his beard? Or an azure thread that would simulate the color of his eyes?

"I sometimes walk. To take in the air and think. To see the colors of the sunrise and sunset over the mountains," Madeline said.

"I know. I see you. Often. I've tried not to interrupt. This morning I failed to resist," Lev said.

He looked at her so intensely that Madeline's cheeks heated, but he kept a respectful distance as he slowed his pace to match hers. Yet it seemed that he didn't want to keep his distance. She could feel the weight of his gaze on her lips. His entire body appeared to tremble with a warm energy greater than she'd seen in him before. But he controlled his wildness. She'd seen the white wolf at a distance. She'd never seen the monstrous creature up close.

But suddenly, she knew she didn't want Lev at a distance. He was overwhelming up close, but there was no denying the thrill that pumped through her veins. She liked the overwhelming feeling. The flush. The rush. The sudden irrevocable acknowledgment that she was no longer a lady-in-waiting. She'd found something she hadn't known she'd been waiting for.

Someone.

"Would you like company sometimes? When you walk? I'd like to walk with you," Lev said. He stopped to face her, and Madeline stopped, too. She tilted her chin to look up at the man who made her feel small in spite of her great height. She'd never felt small until she came to Bronwal. The Romanov men were giants compared to other men. She couldn't help assessing his form and figure with her artistic eye. He waited patiently while she looked her fill, surveying him from his booted feet up to his long, wild hair. He was as handsome as a

Romanov was expected to be, but there was something else about Lev that made him stand out from the rest.

He'd been waiting, too.

It wasn't only energy that caused him to dominate a room when he entered it. It was expectation. It was hunger. But not a predator's hunger. She knew the legend of Vladimir Romanov. Everyone did. The Light Volkhvy queen had taken a lesser son of a royal family and made him into an enchanted shape-shifter to stand as her champion.

Then she had forged a sword for his mate.

Madeline's breath caught when Lev reached to gently brush an auburn curl from her forehead. The whole castle was in love with the youngest wolf, but ultimately he would have only one destined mate.

"We can walk together," Madeline agreed.

"And, perhaps, one day we will run. I race over the ground as the white wolf, Maddy. I noticed from the first time I saw you that you longed to run. The longing shines in your brown eyes whenever you look at me. When you're ready, I'll carry you as far and as fast as you want to go," Lev said.

The promise had made her burn with desire for him and for a life she didn't yet understand. She'd started a new tapestry that day. She'd thought it would be of Lev Romanov dampened by dew in the morning light, but as thread after thread met on the cloth in her hoop, as her fingers grew red from the constant pricks and pressings of needlework, the image that came to life was one of herself.

Wielding the ruby sword.

By evening, beneath the orange-red glow of the setting sun and the deepening forest shadows, Madeline was spent. Her hold had weakened and her back was stiff with pain. She'd nodded off numerous times, only to be woken from vivid dreams that filled her with longing. When Lev came to a stop, she couldn't let go. She rested against his back as she tried to will her arms to respond to her mental command. Lev held on to the trunk of a tree with both hands. His head bent down between his arms, and he drew deep gulps of oxygen into his lungs.

Finally, Madeline was able to release Lev's shoulders and slide to the ground. She would have crumpled, but he sensed her distress. In spite of his depletion, he whirled around and caught her as she fell. Because she couldn't catch herself. The muscles of her arms were beyond fatigued. Lev held her, and she had to allow it. She was too exhausted to push him away. Her tiredness gave her an excuse to allow his strong arms to cradle her close.

She couldn't even pretend not to enjoy it. He breathed heavily into her hair, still catching his breath from the forced marathon he'd run. His wild scent of spruce woods and perspiration filled her nose. To her, he smelled heroic. Their heat blended. His brook-washed and wind-tangled hair fell around her face.

"I couldn't outrun them, Maddy. The *Volkhvy* have flooded the pack with Ether energy. They are almost upon us," Lev murmured. He held her away from him then. Just far enough so he could look down into her face. A sudden flood of adrenaline fueled her arms so she was able to lift her hands to his shoulders. She measured their width and breadth with the clasp of her fingers.

Fully rested, she and Lev might have been able to fight off an ordinary pack of wolves. Lev might even have stood a chance against a pack enhanced by the *Volkhvy*. But only the white wolf and the ruby Romanov warrior could face the threat he described.

Lev suddenly leaned to scoop her into his arms. He took a moment to brace his legs against the new burden, and then he carried her to the base of a large tree. He settled her into a nook created by the giant oak's exposed roots and an earthen bank that was collapsing beneath its weight.

"I won't hide while you fight," Madeline protested. Lev silenced her with a hard kiss against her lips. The kiss felt like a goodbye. He was going to try to shift again. She felt the fury of the white wolf in his flexed muscles before her hands fell away.

"They will regret challenging a Romanov wolf," Lev said. "And terrorizing his family."

She believed him in spite of his extreme fatigue. Because in spite of hers, she was going to rise and fight by his side.

She struggled to her feet, but there was no thunder from the shift. The earth didn't quake beneath her as she used the gnarled tree roots to pull herself out of the nook. Lev still wasn't able to shift. His human form remained. His back was to her. She stood beside the tree and forced her hand up to her shoulder, where the hilt of the ruby sword waited for her grip. Only hers. It had been made for her, after all.

Lev Romanov was her husband. She was his warrior mate. Even if they couldn't be together, she would wield the blade against their common foe. For Trevor.

"You are beaten," a voice proclaimed on a rise above them, just as the Ether-manipulated wolves poured around the bank to flank them on either side.

Madeline looked up. On the rise, a marked *Volkhvy*

stood in a long gray coat. The witch was male, with a perfect pale face and cruelly joyous eyes. His sharp cheekbones matched an even sharper smile. His figure looked as though it could have been cut from glass, all gleaming angles in the setting sunlight. And his hands were outstretched toward the wolves. His fingers glowed with a citrine hue, but the yellow was tinged all around the edges with obsidian.

"If Vasilisa couldn't beat us, do you honestly think you have a chance?" Lev asked.

Madeline drew her sword. The rasp sounded as confident as Lev's growl. But the ruby didn't respond to her desperate internal call. They were going to die. There was no way they could win. She'd rejected the ruby's power. Now it rejected her.

Lev was only a man. She was only a woman. Their bodies had already been pushed to their limits by the long day of grueling travel. The wolves around them had bottomless black pits for eyes. They were filled with Darkness. So filled that it leaked from their eyes like oil to mat their fur and coat their fangs with filth. The witch on the rise suddenly swept his hands together as if he was a conductor commanding a symphony of rabid teeth and fur.

The wolves erupted. They ran toward Madeline and Lev with a cacophony of unnatural shrieks. They were a terrible horde, more than a pack. The marked *Volkhvy* had made a horrible desecration of the poor animals.

Madeline raised the ruby sword, but her hands shook on its hilt. The wolves had been made into hellhounds. They rose from the Ether rather than hell.

But Lev's howl suddenly ripped from his body. His back was still to her. He stood between her and the attacking wolves with his arms outstretched and his hands curved into claws. His shirt split at the seams. The muscles of his thighs bulged the leather leggings until she knew they were seconds from splitting, too. His supernatural howl drowned out the pack's cries.

Once again, he didn't shift into the white wolf, but he was more than a man.

The witch on the rise yelled a warning to his horde of demon wolves. Madeline's attention flew from the witch to the wolves as they swirled around to close in on Lev's position. They ignored her. After all, her sword didn't glow. She was barely able to stand on her feet.

A hard smile curved Madeline's lips. A certainty rose in her heart. She'd dreamed about sewing a tapestry that revealed the Call of the sword. She was suddenly certain that the dream had been a memory that had been woken because of her connection with the enchanted ruby when Lev had leaped over the ravine. She remembered Lev on the ramparts of Bronwal. She remembered his wildness, controlled, and his offer to help her run. She remembered the first touch of his big hand, gentle on her face. She couldn't remember riding on the white wolf's back, but she was suddenly sure that she had done so. She was stronger and braver than the marked witch knew.

Like the tainted wolves, the marked witch on the rise was ignoring her, too. His attention was fully on Lev Romanov as the first wolf leaped on Lev's back to bite and rip the already shredded material of his shirt. Wolf after wolf after wolf followed. Their attack left smears of black Ether taint on Lev's skin.

But he met every foe with ferocious energy that had been given to him by the Light *Volkhvy* queen. His muscles were as hard as steel, and his scars gave testimony to his fierce survival experience. He flung the wolves off him again and again. He fought them with nothing but his fists.

Ether flowed from the wolves' eyes and black foam coated their mouths.

Lev was undaunted. Madeline looked from the wolves to the witch on the rise. The glow from the marked *Volkhvy*'s hands was now more black than citrine. And his eyes had gone as obsidian as the wolves'. His fingers were stretched in the wolves' direction. He followed their movements, or their movements followed his. She couldn't be sure which. But a dawning certainty did claim her as she watched.

The witch wasn't only influencing the behavior of the wolves. He was channeling Ether's energy into the pack.

Madeline closed her eyes. She envisioned Trevor's sleeping face. She couldn't remember his laughter. She couldn't recall his tears. One day—one day soon—she would see her baby smile.

She was undaunted, too.

One foot responded. And then the other. She moved, and no one noticed. The horde of wolves tried to devour a man who was more beast than they were. He beat them back. He would not fall. At least not before she climbed the small rise that seemed like a giant mountain to her exhausted legs. She climbed anyway. One step after another. The marked *Volkhvy* only had eyes for his horde. Black liquid foamed from his lips now. He screamed at his wolves, every bit as rabid as they seemed.

She remembered the revelation of the tapestry she'd sewn. Thread by thread, the ruby sword she now held had Called her to Lev Romanov's side. She couldn't accept its enchantment now. Lev was far removed from the young, controlled man he'd been. He was haunted and hounded and nearly out of control these days because of all he'd been through during the curse.

Her steps were punctuated by Lev's howls. He didn't have to summon four paws and a horrifying snarl. He was the white wolf. The white wolf was Lev. She finally knew it. There was no separation. Her husband was the Romanov wolf.

But she was a warrior, enchanted connection or not. She didn't need the ruby's glow. She could accept its long-ago judgment that she was worthy of wielding its power without accepting the power itself.

Madeline plunged her sword into the marked *Volkhvy*'s chest and out his back. She aimed for his heart and met her mark. Black blood gushed around the blade. But it was the witch's shock that was her true reward. He hadn't seen her as a threat. He'd hardly seen her at all. His mistake had enabled her to slowly climb the rise and fell him, even as she faced him.

The marked witch collapsed to his knees. As he fell, Madeline pulled her blade free from his dying body. His last move was to reach for the gaping wound. His hands no longer glowed.

"You're only a woman," the witch said, coughing. More black blood bubbled up from his lungs to join the foam on his lips. "You can't…"

"You obviously have no idea what I can and will do," Madeline said. She only allowed her sword to fall to her side once the witch's eyes glazed over in death. She used it as a prop against the ground to keep herself on her feet. And only then did she look down to where Lev stood.

The whole horde of wolves was strewn around him. They weren't dead. She saw them breathing, and some of them were already trying to rise. There was steam all around. The black taint of Ether was evaporating from the wolves. Steam rose from Lev's skin as well. The taint had smeared on him during the attack.

But there was also blood.

As hard as Lev seemed, he was still human. Not marble. His scars proved it. More scars would join them now. He had beaten off a savage attack with nothing but his fists.

Madeline gasped when Lev turned away from the wolves toward where she stood on the rise. The fight wasn't over yet. Not for him. His eyes blazed and his teeth were bared. He tilted his head toward the rising moon, and the tendons on either side of his neck were taut. His eyes closed and he raised his fists to the sky before a howl erupted from his chest. He expressed his fury with every cell of his human body, and it wasn't enough. He was denied the shift as she was denied the ruby's light.

She felt the echo of Lev's howl in her own chest.

He was the wolf as she was the warrior, but she didn't utter a sound. The dead witch who had collapsed at her feet began to disappear. First his spilled blood evaporated as black steam, and then the cells of his body disintegrated into the air to follow the tainted blood into the Dark nothingness of the Ether that inexorably pulled them to rejoin its constant cold hunger.

Madeline shivered. Was that what Lev had endured while she was sleeping? In moments, the dead witch and his blood were gone, as if they'd never existed in the first place.

She looked from the empty spot on the ground to where Lev stood. He'd fallen silent. The wolves all around him were dragging themselves to their feet and creeping away into the forest shadows. Lev followed her attention to the wolves and allowed them to retreat. One turned to look at him briefly before it melted into the trees. He'd described the alpha wolf to Madeline, and she recognized the poor creature now. After a pause, the alpha disappeared in the shadows. Even though Lev's body was still stiff with fury and tension, he showed the fallen creatures mercy. Their eyes no longer gleamed an oily obsidian. The Ether had begun to evaporate from them as soon as the witch was no longer actively channeling it into their bodies, and now the fog had disappeared, returning to where it came from.

The wolves were freed, and other than the bruises they'd suffered from Lev's defense of their attack, they appeared as if they'd survived the marked *Volkhvy's* manipulations. Madeline looked down at the sword in her hand. The witch's blood had also evaporated from her blade. It was clean enough to sheathe now, and she did so slowly with a grimace of pain.

Suddenly, her body was spent once more. The adrenaline of necessity had flowed away and she was left more exhausted than she'd been before. As the blade slid home with a comforting swoosh, her knees crumpled beneath her. One second she was standing. The next found her on the mossy earth.

She wished she could draw the moss around her like a soft green blanket. But before she could try, Lev was there. He'd leaped for the rise when she fell. In spite of all he'd been through, he was there to stop her head from hitting the ground. He caught her as her body leaned to the side.

It was a considerate gesture, even though his chest was probably much harder than the ground.

"You fought back at least fifty wolves," Madeline said. She had every intention of pulling away and standing up. In a minute. After the next breath or two. But apparently, every cell in her body needed to rest. She couldn't make herself rise.

"You killed the witch," Lev said. He spoke into her hair, and she could have sworn he nuzzled his cheek into her tangled locks. "The ruby doesn't shine, but it doesn't matter. You shine without any need of enchantment."

She could barely reconcile the ferocious creature she'd witnessed fighting off the wolf attack with the gentle giant who cradled her now. Lev was every bit as tall and muscular as he'd always been, but he growled soft words of encouragement instead of howling.

"The marked *Volkhvy* disappeared. Was that what it was like for you? For Soren and Ivan and all the people of Bronwal?" Madeline asked. If she'd been less fatigued, she would have kept her curiosity to herself. Lev Romanov was damaged beyond repair by the years he'd spent trapped as the white wolf. She'd witnessed firsthand his destruction of the tower room and the way the whole castle avoided him. His pain and anger were evidence of wounds that had penetrated deeper than the ones that had scarred his skin.

He stiffened against her and his hold tightened. His tension had returned. He drew his face back from her hair as she waited for him to reply. Long, silent seconds passed.

But he didn't stand up and walk away. That was a good sign.

"The curse came down on us like the black fog of Ether-tainted blood from the wolves in the clearing below. We were consumed. Devoured. There was no chance of escape. I searched for you. I called until I had no voice left. Until I had no mouth left to yell. Even in the cold nothingness of the Ether, I think I tried to scream. Once every hundred years, Vasilisa allowed Bronwal and its people to materialize for one month, but we always returned to the Ether again and again," Lev said.

"She thought your father had killed her daughter," Madeline whispered. She couldn't imagine what it had been like for a father and husband to lose his family. Especially one used to being an unstoppable champion of the Light. She remembered him as he'd leapt the ravine. She remembered him as he'd fought the wolves. Lev didn't give up. No wonder he had railed against the Darkness for hundreds of years.

"Anna was caught up in the curse and tortured for centuries—by her own mother," Lev growled.

"She and Soren fought the Ether together. He was her constant red-wolf companion. They survived," Madeline said.

"Anna is a witch. Just like her mother. *Volkhvy* can't be trusted. Light, Dark, marked—they're all the same," Lev said.

"Vasilisa protected me and Trevor as we were sleeping. She kept watch until we recovered," Madeline said.

"She's used your memory loss to tell you a tale that absolves her of guilt. Your 'illness' was of her making, Madeline. Queen Vasilisa caused your enchanted sleep. It was part of the curse. She took you from your home and family. She stole everything from Trevor. She stole your past from you," Lev said. His body shook. He pushed her away as if he didn't trust himself not to crush her in his fury. She had rested long enough that she was able to keep her balance as he withdrew his support to stand. "She stole you from me. She severed our connection. You and Trevor were imprisoned in crystal, and I was left alone."

Madeline closed her eyes and swallowed. Her throat was numb. Behind her eyelids, she saw the shattered glass of the coffin-like bed she'd first woken up in on Vasilisa's island. The queen had told her that the white wolf had woken her too soon, and that was why she'd lost her memories.

But the white wolf hadn't shattered the glass.

Vasilisa had broken the glass and taken Trevor from her arms. Had the queen done that in response to Madeline beginning to wake up, or had she done it in order to wake her? Judging from Lev's anger, if the white wolf had finally found the island after centuries of searching, Vasilisa would have needed something to stop him.

Something. Someone. Her. The ruby warrior who rose to do her queen's bidding as naturally as her heart beat.

Had the Light *Volkhvy* queen put her to sleep and then woken her up too soon, all to punish the white wolf, once her champion, but now her greatest enemy?

Madeline forced herself to breathe. She gathered her strength and brought her legs up beneath her. She rose because she couldn't remain on her knees when Lev was trembling with rage nearby. Not because she was afraid. Trevor wasn't with them. She wasn't afraid of any threat against herself. Her only fear was not reaching Trevor in time to save him from the marked *Volkhvy*.

Her concern for Vasilisa hadn't completely faded. Lev had been a wild beast for so long. He believed the tale he told. But she wasn't sure what to believe. Just as it was hard to reconcile beast from man, it was hard to imagine the kind, motherly woman on Krajina as an evil queen.

The last Madeline had seen of Trevor, he was swaddled in a blanket and cuddled securely in Vasilisa's arms. She had to believe that Vasilisa would protect her baby until she could get to him, or she'd go insane.

"You aren't alone now. Our connection is severed. It has to be. Neither of us has any idea when or if the white wolf will return, or if he'll be rational or a savage beast when he does," Madeline said. "But we're together now, and we'll beat the marked *Volkhvy*. We'll save our son."

"With my bare hands if I have to," Lev vowed. His anger fled before his determination. Or maybe fueled it. His fingers were fisted, but he no longer shook. His tension was a calm one, filled with intent. "There's something you need to know."

Madeline braced herself for more emotional revelations. She was already reeling, unsure of what to believe, but haunted by the story Lev had told her. His tale seemed to continue even after he was finished, as if the lover and father he described were deep within her mind, moving rock after rock of the avalanche that had smothered her memories.

"The alpha was leading that pack," Lev said. "I think you freed him from their control, but there are others." He watched her face. She didn't falter or fall even though she understood immediately what he meant. "It was only a small portion of the pack I discovered before."

"They won't give up," Madeline said.

"The *Volkhvy* won't allow them to give up," Lev said. His hatred of witches was evident in every forceful syllable, with no distinction allowed between Dark and Light.

"We won't give up, either," Madeline replied.

Lev stepped toward her. He was bleeding. His clothing was not only torn, but was also stained with his blood. Suddenly, he looked all too human. The white wolf seemed like nothing but a savage dream, one that they couldn't count on to materialize and save them. For once, Madeline wasn't as certain as she had been that the white wolf's continued elusiveness was a good thing.

If Lev shifted, the white wolf might not distinguish between witch and warrior. There was always the danger that he would shift into a savage beast that would tear them all apart. But with his human body injured and exhausted, if Lev didn't shift, he might fall beneath the next wolf attack.

Madeline fisted her hands. Trevor wasn't with them. As for herself, she would gladly risk the white wolf in order to save the man.

Lev had to be hurting, but his injuries didn't stop him from scooping her into his arms. This time he held her tight against his chest. She wrapped her arms around his neck, but he supported her weight with no help from her at all. He didn't look down at her face.

"It's too dark to travel," Madeline warned, although the moonlight seemed brighter than usual, as if the night hovered in perpetual gloaming around them. "And you're hurt," she continued.

"I can see," Lev said. "And I'm used to the pain."

He was closer to the shift than he'd been since he became human on the cliffs of Krajina. The night was no impediment. He could see a crystal-clear black-and-white world. The edges of the trees and their needles and budding leaves were sharp against the sky, as if they'd been cut from paper. The shadows receded and the path was clear. Every pebble beneath his feet was defined in spite of the absence of light.

Madeline's features were also starkly revealed to his near-wolf eyes.

He had to look away.

He couldn't bear the sympathy and concern that furrowed her porcelain brow. Or the confusion she confessed to by the way she bit her lip and narrowed her eyes. She couldn't remember. So why would she listen to a man she'd seen fight Ether-mad wolves with his bare hands? To her, he must seem nearly as mad himself, driven wild by his time as the white wolf.

Only he knew it had been the wolf that had kept him sane.

One way or another, the Ether was going to claim him, whether he sought its oblivion as the white wolf or as a man.

He had found her. He would find Trevor. Then he would free them.

From the *Volkhvy* threat and from himself.

His booted feet pounded against the ground, but he didn't feel the impact. His body responded to the demands placed upon it as it always had. His blood dried. His wounds knit. And the pain of the wolf bites was nothing compared to the pain he had lived with for years.

He had failed to save his family when they needed him most. He could only save them now. Save them as a last act of defiance against the Dark before he gave himself to the hungry vacuum that had taken so much of him. He already felt as if he had a black hole of Ether where his heart should be. What did it matter if his body followed?

Lev concentrated on the warmth of the woman in his arms. He liked that the sword pressed between her back and the crook of his arm was a reminder of her strength. He had watched her kill the witch. Like him, she'd used only muscle, blood and bone—no enchantment.

He would go into the Dark to spare his family from

the beast he'd become. Not the white wolf, but the perpetually tortured man. When he disappeared, he'd know that he was leaving a warrior behind to love and protect Trevor forever.

Madeline didn't need him or the enchanted gem. When she plunged the blade into the evil witch, her red hair had been highlighted by the moon's rise. He'd almost allowed an attacking wolf to reach his throat because he'd been so startled by the vision of Madeline with an entirely natural scarlet aura.

He held her close now, but in that moment he'd remembered hundreds of times when he'd seen his beautiful, powerful wife defeat a Dark foe. She was the ruby warrior. He could never again be the champion who deserved her love. He could only—finally—let her go.

Chapter 15

She'd thought Lev had run fast before. She'd been wrong; he'd given her a chance to hold on. This time, he had only himself to consider. She was safe in his arms, and his feet flew. Her body responded to the pace with a swooping stomach, and it seemed as if the breeze his speed caused got inside her head. Late-night terrain sped by in a gray blur. She had to focus on his bearded chin to keep the motion sickness away, but better his chin than the pounding pulse at the base of his throat.

When she looked at that vulnerable spot, her fingers itched to press against it. The move would be far too intimate. Especially because it was driven by visions of the wolves he'd managed to knock away. She wanted to feel his pulse. Needed to confirm that he was alive and well. What if any of the wolves' fangs had met that mark? There were deep grooves on either side of his neck. His shoulders were dark with dried blood. She tried to be careful with her hands so she wouldn't disturb his wounds, even though she was fairly certain he would ignore the pain if she did.

She didn't need her memories to know she didn't want Lev to die. She'd seen enough to know they could never be together. But she'd also felt enough to know she'd always regret the necessity of saying goodbye.

He'd fought the wolves off with his bare hands. He'd promised to do the same if he had to with the marked *Volkhvy*. He'd been glorious in the moonlight. But he had also been completely wild. There were times when he was so driven by his rage that there was nothing civil left in the man.

If his tale was true, the fault was all Queen Vasilisa's. Madeline's hands tightened on the hard muscles she held, but Lev didn't flinch. He only sped on. Vasilisa had manipulated the Romanovs' blood. She had enchanted their muscles and bones. She had created the Romanov shifters. Even Trevor would one day be both human and wolf. *Volkhvy* channeled the power of the Ether. The Light *Volkhvy* were careful and controlled… usually. Vasilisa had created her champions, and then she'd punished them unmercifully when she thought Vladimir Romanov had killed her only child. There had been no control in her curse. It had been a mother's vengeance. Pure and terrible, but even more terrible because it had been based on a mistake.

Madeline held on to Lev as he carried her closer and closer to the portal that would take them to Queen Vasilisa, and she remembered his words.

Your "illness" was of her making, Madeline. Queen Vasilisa caused your enchanted sleep. It was part of the curse. She took you from your home and family. She stole everything from Trevor. She stole your past from you.

If what Lev said was true, Madeline's vengeance would be pure and terrible, too. She could feel a hot, hard knot of heavy anger in her chest. It was made of iron, but the iron glowed red, as if it had been heated over a forge.

She had woken ready for battle but had found a confusing world she didn't fully understand. Without memories to guide her, she was left with only instinct and desire. She'd automatically trusted her queen, but how much of that had been inspired by Vasilisa's *Volkhvy* abilities to manipulate her? Hadn't she felt the queen's cool touch in her mind, soothing and calming? What if Lev was right, and the Light *Volkhvy* queen wasn't so Light after all?

Since she'd found Lev in the tower, instinct and desire had drawn her closer and closer to him. How could she trust a story that claimed her heart and imagination with its poignancy? She couldn't even trust her deepest drives now, because they all led her straight into Lev's arms.

She could only hold on and try to remember. She could only prepare herself to fight, and hope when it was time for battle, she would know which was her enemy—the witch or the wolf.

Aleksandr was finally ready to face Queen Vasilisa. He could feel the black power of the Ether pulsing inside him. His veins bulged with it. They gleamed darkly in a visible network of lines that branched infinitely to cover his entire body, barely contained beneath his skin. He was covered like a tattooed man, except his art was on the inside, drawn by the Ether when he'd welcomed it into his soul.

Walking was difficult, he had to admit. Every step

seemed just shy of falling into a hole he could feel but not see. The vacuum was painful, but the feedback of energy was orgasmic. The pleasure helped him endure the fear of falling. The euphoric pulse of Ether in his blood turned the fear into exhilaration.

What was a witchblood prince by birth when compared to one who had claimed his place with strategy and daring?

Gregori and his family had been complacent fools. Spoiled royals who hadn't deserved the place of honor the Darkness had allowed them. A true king must win his throne. Aleksandr would never suffer the fate of Gregori. He wasn't spoiled and complacent. He'd worked hard to rise in the ranks of the Light *Volkhvy*. And now he'd worked hard to lead his followers in an uprising against Vasilisa that would succeed.

Ether was a tool.

Only a tool.

Once he had defeated the white wolf and prevented him from reclaiming his mate, he would also destroy the other Romanov wolves and their mates. He would decimate the entire Romanov clan. Then he would release the Ether energy he'd absorbed.

He would be the only king and champion the world needed.

But he might allow Vasilisa and her former warriors to live, if they agreed to serve him well.

When he laughed, he could feel the Ether energy bubble up like a thick liquid in his throat. The marked witch beside him startled at the gurgling sounds and shied away. It did take some getting used to—his appearance, his power and the Dark sounds his body made.

Not everyone could handle the transformation the

way a witch meant to be king could. Aleksandr had always had to suffer fools and weaklings. The witch beside him was making silly noises of continuous distress as they continued down the hall. Aleksandr ignored the whimpers of his follower. He was intent on his prize—the throne—and Vasilisa's warriors on their knees. He added to those visions the picture of an entire family of wolves' heads on display. Vasilisa had doomed the Romanovs when she favored them.

But surely the Romanovs had known that truth for a very long time.

Chapter 16

She and Lev had met every morning and every evening for weeks. Only on rare occasions did he touch her again, but always with fingers that shook as if he strained to remain distant and gentle. If the attraction he felt for her throbbed inside him the same way hers for him did, then his control was legendary.

Madeline ached.

And she worked all her frustrations out onto the tapestry with needle and thread.

On those rare occasions when Lev brushed her hair back from her face, or reached for her hand to steady her on a stair, she sewed into the wee hours of the morning as she burned on the inside.

The tapestry was almost finished, and he had yet to kiss her. She'd had to remain dissatisfied with merely the heat of his gaze on her mouth. She could only imagine what it would be like to suckle the full swell of his sensual lower lip between hers.

The worst times were when he was summoned to the battlefield and she was left to walk alone. Once, he'd come to her as the white wolf before leaving. She hadn't been afraid. Not really. She'd trembled because of the extreme display of his power. It was the first time she'd reached for him. Madeline had looked up at the giant wolf looming over her, and she'd raised her hand to his snout. The white wolf had allowed her to cup his ferocious jaw. He'd held himself still while she smoothed her hand down his neck to his barrel chest. She'd pressed her palm into his fur until she found his mighty heartbeat.

Only then had she truly understood the forces at work in their lives.

"Come back to me," she'd said. But her voice had startled the massive creature and he'd whirled away from her touch. She'd watched him run from Bronwal toward a fight with the Dark Volkhvy.

Her time with Lev Romanov was precious. Her longing for his kiss grew supreme.

The next time she saw him, Madeline didn't wait for his touch. It was only the second time he'd come to her inside the castle. He'd returned from battle to find her in a drawing room sewing by the fire. Her tapestry was almost complete. It was held stretched by a large wooden hoop she could move from section to section on the large work of art. She was currently working on the hilt of the sword in her fingers. She'd never held anything but toy blades, clumsy wooden practice swords made for young boys. Yet she knew how each finger made of thread should be placed.

Lev came into the room. He'd seen the tapestry once before. They hadn't spoken of what it meant. Or how it revealed the Call of the sword that throbbed in her breast. But this time, when he approached the fireplace near where she sat, Madeline stood, allowing the hoop to slide off her lap to the floor.

"I want to run with you," Madeline said. "Into battle. Into our future together."

"I know," Lev replied. He stopped only when her body prevented him from pressing closer, but his hands were at his sides. He pulsed with energy and hunger and desire, but he waited as the white wolf had waited— for her touch. His fists were clenched. His jaw was hardened. Only the fact that he had come looking for her and his slightly parted lips revealed his desire.

Madeline reached up to grasp the back of Lev's head. He gasped at the first brush of her fingers beneath his hair. She burrowed them intimately against his warm skin and held his strong neck beneath her palms. Their eyes met, and she saw the white wolf in his, contained. She appreciated his control. He'd allowed her innocence the time to give way beneath her longing to be free. Free with him. Free to taste and touch.

Madeline pulled his face down to hers, and he followed her urging like a drowning man diving into a refreshing pool. When their lips met and merged, Madeline cried his name into his mouth. Only with that obvious sign of her arousal did he hungrily take what she offered. And he did it so ferociously that Madeline's knees gave out and Lev's strong arms coming around her were the only thing that kept her on her feet.

Lev's tongue plunged against hers. Rough, moist velvet twisted and twined in a dance that caused her heart to race as fast as the white wolf could run.

Their first kiss caused the ruby's glow to shine from their eyes, and the sitting room was lit more brightly than the fire by enchanted light.

* * *

Madeline had slept for so long encased in a crystal coffin on the island of Krajina. This wasn't like that. Birdsong echoed in her ears. Warm sun caressed her cheek. And the sharp, sweet scent of flowers filled her nose. Not the cloyingly sweet scent of roses from Vasilisa's garden. But a scent both fresher and more familiar.

Yet what could be more familiar than the scent of a garden in which you'd spent over a thousand years?

Madeline opened her eyes and then closed them right away when a bright blue sky dazzled above her and caused moisture to well up. She sat and blinked the tears away as she opened her eyes again. This time, instead of a prismatic fantasy world glimpsed through salty water, Madeline saw the sloped curve of a mountainside. The slope was awash in a deep violet color that appeared almost crimson by the light of the setting sun.

Spring blossoms painted an entire field of wildflower bushes. The woody stems of the bushes clung hardily to the uneven craggy terrain, and their dark green leaves trembled in the breeze.

"We're almost there. I wasn't sure if you'd passed out or if you were only sleeping. I thought I'd better stop for water to make sure it was the latter," Lev said.

"You don't like when I sleep," Madeline said. She didn't know how she knew it. Maybe it was in the tightness of his face. Maybe even several feet away, she could still see the pulse in his throat.

"Every time you open your eyes it's miraculous," Lev said. "Like *I'm* waking from a nightmare."

Madeline took the water he offered. She didn't ask where he'd found the dented container he held out to her. It was a strange cylinder of metal she'd seen before, on Krajina and the train, but instead of being filled with a sweet, sparkling beverage called a "soda," the empty can had been rinsed out and filled with fresh, cold liquid from a nearby stream.

"Even Vasilisa's enchantments couldn't keep humans and their trash completely away," Lev said.

She drained every drop, ignoring that much of the liquid spilled from holes in the container to dribble onto her cheeks as she drank.

But once her thirst was quenched, she noticed the scent of the flowers again. And then she knew.

She'd been on this mountainside surrounded by these wildflowers before.

The empty container fell from her fingers as Madeline reached for the nearest bush. She plucked a blossom from it and brought the petals to her nose, then stood as a rush of recognition flowed over her. This place was a memory. She whirled around to share her discovery with her companion, but he already knew.

Because he'd been here with her.

They'd been here together.

It wasn't only the wildflowers she remembered.

He must have washed in the stream. He was wet. His hair dripped into his eyes and his bloody, shredded shirt was gone. Cleansed, his injuries didn't look as bad as they had the night before. He healed quicker than an ordinary man. She didn't just intuit that knowledge; she remembered it. Her mind flooded with images of times when Lev had been hurt and she'd seen him heal. The memories were indistinct and foggy. But they were there.

Other memories were clearer. Probably because they were inspired and rooted in the place where they stood.

His taste. His touch. Their bodies entwined. She'd inhaled the scent of the flowers deep into her lungs, making their sweetness a part of her, as she'd found an orgasmic release beneath him.

She remembered.

Lev's eyes darkened in the sunset's glow. He remembered, too. Had he laid her here in the hope that the memory might come back to her?

"We had to leave Straluci to be alone. It was always full in the spring. It seemed as if the Dark *Volkhvy* thawed with the ice and snow. There were so many more of them then. Ivan followed Vladimir's practice of housing a large contingent here to guard the pass. A first line of defense. As for you and me, we lost our winter retreat," Lev said. "You can almost see the towers from here. If you know where to look."

She knew where to look. She didn't even have to follow his gaze. She saw the tips of three towers and wondered if the fourth tower had crumbled away. The copper spires that had once glared in the sun and given the castle its name now had a greenish patina, but even that camouflage didn't fool her.

Madeline looked from the copper-tipped towers to Lev. He brought his attention back to her more slowly, as if uncertain of what he would find. His nearly bare chest angled back toward her as his face came around. His lean hips turned.

Lev's hard physique startled her every time he moved. He caused her breath to catch—his strength, his grace in spite of his injuries and his obvious tension. The sudden return of her memory about their former intimacy in this place only heightened her already heated response to the physical attraction she'd felt to Lev Romanov from the start. She didn't remember everything. But she remembered enough to be mesmerized by the man who was a dangerous stranger on one hand and the closest person on earth to her on the other.

He moved so slowly that the wait seemed torturous. It was only moments, but those moments caused her heart to pound and adrenaline to rush beneath her skin. She was afraid the rush was fueled by anticipation.

Madeline knew the look in Lev's eyes even before their gazes met. When he lifted his eyelids, she wasn't disappointed. She also had to admit she was anticipating other things. Dangerous things. Like the promise of heat in his gaze as his attention fell to her lips. She moistened her mouth, suddenly aware that she was breathing more heavily than she should, like after holding her breath for too long. His attention followed the dart of her tongue. Then he lifted his gaze to hers once more.

"Tell me to walk away," Lev said. "Far away. Now. Or I'm going to kiss you again. And more. Much more."

He stepped toward her. Only one stride. And Madeline couldn't breathe again. Her throat closed. Her chest constricted. She had to struggle to speak, but she forced herself to respond because she didn't want him to mistake her silence for a protest.

"Don't...go," she rasped, and her voice was nearly as gravelly as Lev's.

He reacted as if he'd been shot. He swayed on his feet. He lifted both hands up to push his fingers into his wild, wet hair. He held the thick blond waves off his face as if he needed to see her more clearly to be sure of what she'd said. Then he closed his eyes. Swallowed.

"I think I heard you wrong, Madeline. You're going to have to repeat yourself," Lev said. His pained growl caused her stomach to tighten and heat to coil and curl low in her abdomen. They shouldn't do this. It was a terrible decision. One that would torture her when they were forced to part. He was giving her every opportunity to reject him the same way she'd rejected the sword. He might be savage after his years as the white wolf, but not here. Not in this moment.

Not with her.

It was a bad decision, but it was hers to make. She stepped toward Lev as if she stepped off a cliff to spread her wings and fly. His chin came down. His hands dropped from his hair, and his eyes opened. He sensed her movement toward him. And then he watched her take another step. He didn't rush forward to catch her. He allowed her to spread her wings.

"Don't go," Madeline said. This time her voice was strong. "Come to me, Lev. Come to me."

"Always," Lev responded. His voice wasn't strong like hers. There was a howl in his tone and a waver to his usual growl.

Vasilisa had told her about Lev's brother, Soren. How he had hunted for the white wolf for hundreds of years. How he had remained in his shifted form of the red wolf for centuries, even though that meant he could only be a loyal wolf companion to the woman he loved. Anna and the red wolf had been inseparable. Neither had known she was *Volkhvy*, the Light *Volkhvy* princess. When the truth was discovered, Soren's hatred of witches had almost torn them apart, even though Anna heard the emerald Romanov blade Calling her to become Soren's warrior mate.

Lev had run from everyone for so long. Anna said it was because he was searching for her and Trevor. He'd been driven. Tireless. Near madness by the time he'd found Krajina.

Now the blossom she'd picked fell from her outstretched hand as he came to her.

Madeline raised trembling fingers to his face, and Lev leaned into her palm. She traded the flower petals for his beard of burnished silk. His skin was hard, but vulnerable above the golden hair. He was so tall that he had to lean down, even though she was tall herself.

And in this field, he was hers, as he had been ages ago.

He suddenly fell to his knees and reached to pull her hard against his face. He nuzzled her lower abdomen, seeming to find the heat that had coiled there a few moments before. Madeline buried her fingers into his damp hair. She gloried in the heat inside herself and from his open mouth as he kissed and nipped her through her clothes. The heat in her abdomen was nothing compared to the heat that flared and flowed between her legs.

She had been afraid he would devour her as the white wolf. Now she was afraid he wouldn't devour her soon enough with his lips and teeth and tongue. Her memories were hazy. She needed to be reminded by Lev, here and now.

Madeline relaxed her knees, and he felt her intention. He loosened his hold to allow her to sink down to the ground. They kneeled, face-to-face. She tilted her chin to meet his eyes, and it was Lev's turn to lift his palm to her cheek. He held her more firmly than she'd expected. His thumb curved beneath her chin, and his fingers spread to cup her jaw. He urged her head back and she was caught—both by his strong hand and by the flush of desire on his pale face. When he leaned to press his lips to hers, she gasped. The sudden relief of his full, sensual mouth sucking her lower lip became a torment seconds later as a flood of response pulsed between her legs.

She remembered his tongue pleasuring her to heights

she had never imagined. She remembered the tickle of his beard on her thighs, and his long wavy hair between her knees.

Lev's tongue mimicked the same plunging, darting, licking movements he'd used to plumb her feminine depths all those years ago. In this field, surrounded by a riot of colorful flowers, she'd cried out to the heavens. Now she gasped and met his wicked tongue with hers. He growled his appreciation as they explored each other's mouths. And all the while, she ached to have his tongue on her and in her more intimately than this.

"Will you lie back for me, then?" Lev murmured into her mouth. "Let me help you remember."

She was too hot to wonder how he knew what she was thinking. She fell back on the soft grass, but before she settled, Lev masterfully cupped his hands beneath her knees to spread her legs and pull her closer. Her shirt rode up as her body slid on the grass, and Lev immediately zeroed in on the bared stomach her sliding shirt revealed. He swooped down to nuzzle her naked skin, and she gasped his name as the heat of his mouth scorched her.

Lev froze. His fingers tightened on her legs. He raised his head just enough from her stomach to look up at her face. Their eyes met. The tip of his beard hovered against her skin, causing gooseflesh to rise and a tickling sensation to zing to the pulsing flesh still covered beneath her leggings.

"Say my name again," he urged. His beard brushed her stomach as he spoke, and Madeline sucked in air. She bit her lip as he noticed her reaction. His eyelids grew heavier, and he teasingly leaned down to trail his beard along her quivering, exposed flesh. He watched as her reaction intensified the closer he came to the juncture of her thighs. "Say my name again," he repeated.

"Lev," Madeline breathed. She couldn't help it. His name was infused with all the longing she'd been fighting for days. "Lev. Please," she added.

"Always," he repeated. She recognized it as a declaration. She stiffened, about to protest his promise of forever, when his hot lips pressed against the skin just above the waist of her pants. His hands had moved from her legs. She hadn't noticed. Until his fingers hooked in the stretchy material of her pants and eased them down an inch. Followed by a slow tasting kiss with hints of moist tongue. Then another inch, followed by the swirling delight of more tongue.

She couldn't help it. Her hips had started to respond to his nearness and the moist heat of his mouth. She wiggled her bottom against the grass as he slid her pants farther and farther down. His mouth followed, until he paused to appreciate the mound of scarlet hair the lowered leggings had finally revealed.

"My ruby warrior," he said, and his breath tickled across her.

She didn't argue. For now, she could be the woman he remembered, and he could be the man who had loved her in this field a thousand years ago.

His tongue. Oh, God, his tongue.

Lev looked up to see her pleasure as he used one final pull to take the leggings halfway down her thighs. He fully exposed her womanhood, and then he dipped his head to delve into her with his tongue. He found her most tender flesh, and she cried out. Her hands spasmed in his hair and pulled him closer as her hips rose off the ground. He hummed his approval as his tongue met her thrust.

She called his name louder than she'd said it before. Her head fell back and her legs were suddenly bare. He'd moved to pull off her pants, but as always, his moves were so quick and graceful that his mouth was back against her before she noticed the loss of his heat.

She came against his mouth as he nuzzled into her most intimate folds. In their field, she cried his name to the sky as her body shivered and shook.

When he pulled away without speaking, Madeline struggled to open her eyes. She rose on her elbows to see where he had gone, and quickly realized he hadn't moved far. He kneeled between her legs.

He reached for her knees when she looked for him.

"I'm here, but you can still send me away. I'll go. It will kill me, but I'll go," Lev vowed.

"We'll have to part soon enough. Stay. For now," Madeline said.

Lev was still fully clothed. She could see his erection bulging against the tight leather of his pants. But he didn't release himself, and she was too overwhelmed to reach for him herself. Instead, when he lay down beside her on the grass, she rolled to press against him and bury her face in his chest.

Her hazy memories were still distant, but they'd claimed the field once more. They couldn't claim each other or the sword. She couldn't risk an enchanted connection that might bring the ferocious white wolf in contact with Trevor. But as the moon rose above them to darkly illuminate the flowers, Madeline was glad they'd always have the rhododendron mountainside.

She would never forget tonight. The ruby sword sat silent and still several feet away, where Lev must have moved it when he laid her down to search for water. It was dull. The dead gem didn't gleam. Beside the sword

was her nearly empty pack. It held only her sketchbook
and used pencils. They were out of supplies. Far in the
distance, many miles away, she thought she heard a
sound that might be the echo of a howl. Lev didn't stir,
so she knew there was no danger.

Yet.

The portal wasn't far away. Soon, they would see
Trevor again.

Lev had fallen asleep. The incredible journey had
tapped every ounce of his strength, limitless though
he seemed. She almost reached to touch his face, but
stayed her hand. This field was theirs, but Lev Romanov
wasn't hers. Not anymore. And he never would be again.

Always.

They didn't have much time. And they certainly
didn't have forever. At one time, she must have thought
he was her future. They had married. She had accepted
the Call of the ruby sword. She couldn't remember what
that had been like. She knew they'd lived a war-filled
life. The battle against the Dark *Volkhvy* was constant
in those days. Yet they'd decided to have a baby in spite
of the Darkness.

And she had failed to protect him.

Even now, Trevor was in jeopardy because she had
failed. She hadn't been much of a ruby warrior. She
could only vow to be a better mother and warrior from
here on out. That would be her always. It would be a
lonely vigil, but she would undertake it because she
had to.

She watched Lev Romanov sleep. His broad chest
rose and fell. His hair had dried, and it waved around
his face. His hard features were softer, his scars sur-
prisingly visible in the night. It must be the star-filled

Carpathian sky that made midnight seem more like dusk than the pitch-black of night here in the mountains.

Carefully, she traced one scar on his cheek with a gentle finger.

He would never be hers again, and no one else would ever take his place. How could any other man follow a legend?

Briefly, before Madeline fell asleep, she wondered why Lev had pleasured her without seeking release for himself.

Chapter 17

Lev was hurt, and he couldn't shift to speed his healing. The wolves had ravaged his body. He was beaten and bruised everywhere he wasn't bleeding, and the grueling run to escape the wolves had taxed his abilities after the attack. As the white wolf, he could have carried Madeline farther and faster. But even the wildest of the Romanov wolves had his limits.

Straluci was close. The *Volkhvy* and the wolves they controlled were also drawing closer. He'd outrun them for now. Even injured, he could beat natural wolves. But he thought he could detect the ozone scent of Ether's energy on the early morning breeze. The wolves weren't natural wolves. Not anymore. If the wolves that tracked them now were also being flooded with Ether channeled into them by their *Volkhvy* masters, it wouldn't take them long to catch up.

Lev waited for Madeline to wash up in the stream

he'd found. He'd done the same, but the tainted mouths of the wolves that had attacked him had done more than rip his skin. He could feel his Romanov blood fighting the black stain of infection the wolves had shared with him. The shift would clear it in an instant, but in his human form, his body had to wage a slower fight. He would still heal, but it would take too long.

They needed to reach the portal and use it to find Vasilisa and Trevor before the wolves and the marked *Volkhvy* caught up with them. But the portal would take them through the Ether itself, and he wasn't strong enough to fight the vacuum, not when tendrils of Ether's energy had invaded his blood like a disease.

Madeline couldn't go alone. Not with nothing but a dead sword by her side.

He mentioned nothing to Maddy when she came back from the stream. The skin around her eyes was already pinched with worry and fatigue. They would press on to Straluci and be there by nightfall. Once there, he would reevaluate his condition.

He would gladly risk his life for Trevor and Madeline. But if he disappeared into the Ether before he could rid them of the *Volkhvy* threat, he would fail greater than he'd failed before.

He wouldn't allow that to happen. They were awake now. They needed him. Ether-tainted blood or not, he needed to succeed.

He would make certain that Madeline and Trevor were safe from Vasilisa. And then he would disappear to keep them save from the white wolf as well.

Something was wrong.

Madeline put her sword in its sheath and tightened the straps around her chest. Then she shrugged into her

nearly empty backpack. But the entire time she prepared for travel, she could sense increased urgency in
Lev. He'd been up with the sun, and to the stream and
back before she rose. His hair had already dried in a
wild blond mane around his face. The streak of white
in front startled against his golden beard when the wind
blew. But it was his hard, unsmiling face that drew her
attention again and again.

Perhaps he regretted the night before.

It certainly hadn't been wise for them to get carried
away with memories and physical attraction. Even now,
she had to fight the urge to go to him, brush his hair back
from his face and kiss the frown from his lips. Long
ago, she would have done exactly that. She knew that
now. Just enough of her memories had been unlocked
for her to know that she'd loved Lev Romanov once.
He had been the wildest of the Romanov brothers—the
most likely to shift and stay shifted for long periods of
time. He'd also been a ferocious fighter. She'd loved all
of those qualities about him. She'd remembered their
combustible desire last night, but she'd also remembered
the face of a softer, younger version of the man who was
currently made of steel flesh. The Lev Romanov she'd
loved as a young woman had been wild, but he'd also
been much easier to tame.

Waking to this older and more ferocious version of
Lev had been overwhelming.

But she suspected it was more than their past and the
present stolen moments of intimacy coloring his mood.

Lev was hurt.

She'd become so accustomed to his powerful grace
over the last few days. This morning he moved slowly
and carefully. His shoulders were as stiff as his face, and
he grimaced several times when a particular reach or

stoop strained at the wolf bites on his skin. Lev healed more quickly than an ordinary man, but the wolves he'd fought had been more savage than ordinary wolves.

"Straluci is half a day's hike up the mountain. We should get started," Lev said. If he noticed her appraising his condition, he didn't acknowledge her concern. He merely started out, one long stride after another, and she was forced to hurry to keep up. Her stride wasn't exactly short, but Lev was over six feet tall. "We need to keep up a brisk pace. Let me know if you need help," Lev said.

The fact that he didn't carry her spoke volumes about his condition. Or maybe it spoke volumes as to how he felt about last night. Madeline vowed to keep up or die trying rather than be a burden. Not only did she want to spare him the extra effort, but she also didn't want to spend hours in his arms, pressed to his chest, the two of them so close together.

Last night had been a mistake. She was certain they both knew it. She was also certain it would be only too easy to make the same mistake again. He wasn't the same man. She wasn't the same woman. But their bodies were still drawn together even after all this time.

"Our stalkers are out there. I can pick up a hint of their scent on the morning breeze. But we have time to reach Straluci. If we hurry," Lev said. "I think."

Madeline hastened her pace to match Lev's as his increased. They were practically jogging up the mountain toward the place where she thought she'd seen a hint of tarnished copper towers in the distance last night. The terrain was rough and rocky. They left the scent of flowers behind and walked once more into air tinged with spruce and pine.

But Madeline's nose twitched occasionally. It was

impossible, but she thought she detected a whiff of Ether's stormy ozone scent every now and then as they hiked. It had to be her imagination, though. She didn't have Lev's nose. She only had visions of the attack from yesterday—the wolves leaping on Lev as the Ether forced into them by the *Volkhvy* drove them mad.

She was being hunted by a pack of tainted wolves and their *Volkhvy* masters, but it was her thudding heart that spurred her onward. It beat for her baby. Not for the man who led the way toward Straluci. He was once again a stranger to her this morning. His thoughts and feelings were shielded behind his stony face. Perhaps he had loved her and Trevor at one time, but the white wolf had long since taken over his heart. He helped her now because he sought vengeance against the *Volkhvy*.

His reasons shouldn't matter. She should just be glad for the aid. This way she could accept his help and easily say goodbye once Trevor was saved.

If only there wasn't a pang between every heartbeat that seemed to whisper Lev's name.

Chapter 18

Straluci was a ruin, but everywhere Madeline looked, she seemed to be able to see the past superimposed over the present. The stained-glass windows that gave the castle its name, along with the copper towers because of the way they used to shine, had been mostly shattered. Here and there a gemlike glimmer of remaining glass hinted at the spectacle that might once have been. Was it her imagination that gave the structure four intact towers where it now had only three? Or did she actually remember the fourth stretching high into the Carpathian sky? Was it her imagination that gave each tower a long furling banner that held the striking image of a different wolf—black, red, white and gray?

"There were banners. One for each of you," Madeline murmured.

Lev didn't reply. He stood beneath the looming structure, and he seemed as out of place and time as the castle itself. He was too big, too hard and muscular, and far too experienced to be a mere hiker who appeared out of the woods to gawk at a rediscovered piece of history.

Maybe she looked the same, with the sword on her back and centuries of sleep in her eyes.

"The fountain was in the center courtyard in the middle of the keep. When the tower crumbled, it looks like it fell inward. We might find the fountain crushed by rubble," Lev said.

"No," Madeline replied. She couldn't follow Lev as he headed into the arched doorway that had been left uncovered by a wooden door long since rotted away. Straluci wasn't like Bronwal. It had stood here forgotten for hundreds of years without being unnaturally preserved by Vasilisa's curse. There was nothing left but metal and stone. The skeletal nature of the small castle haunted her.

She was suddenly frozen. She should be dust. The life she was beginning to remember was long gone. Her memories were as skeletal as the ruin in front of her. She might never fill in all the details she'd lost.

The world opened its gaping maw all around her, full of unfamiliar and alien things, full of people and places she might never understand. She was a skeleton with a dead sword on her back, surrounded by a strange landscape she didn't know how to navigate.

Madeline closed her eyes and swallowed, forcing the world to narrow once more. She breathed in and out, and listened to the sound of her heart in her ears.

Her heart beat for Trevor and whispered for Lev, so she forced herself to step forward into the future, whatever that future might be. One foot after the other. She approached the doorway and paused once more while she tried to make out which way Lev had headed in the shadows. The ruby sword was in her hand. She hadn't intentionally meant to draw it from its sheath. The move was comforting because it was instinctive. She wasn't only a skeleton, after all.

Lev gave away his position by disturbing a flock of doves. They startled and flew up and out a hole in the deteriorated roof in a flurry of distressed cries and fluttering wings. The roof was nothing more than oak beams that had almost petrified before being eaten by beetles and riddled by weather and the passing of years. Sun streamed in through the roof and illuminated the way she needed to go.

Madeline squared her shoulders and stepped into Straluci. If the portal was destroyed, they would find another way.

The swirl of dust motes the birds had left in their wake sparkled in the sunlight, and Madeline was once again caught by a sudden memory: sunlight through the stained-glass windows of Straluci had given the entire castle a multicolor glow on bright days. The castle had shone on the inside as well as the outside. It had been a small fortress used to guard this side of the mountain, but it had also been a spring retreat. Her and Lev's spring retreat. In between winter and summer, they had spent time here away from the heavy demands of a warrior's life.

This was where Trevor had been conceived.

One of the windows on the east side of the castle had been protected from breakage. The wall was an interior one that faced the inner courtyard. Madeline stepped into the warmth of sunlight that formed a prism through the windowpanes. Multiple shades of pink, violet and red washed over her just as the memories of making love to Lev blossomed in her mind.

* * *

The first time had been impulsive. He'd returned safely from a terrible battle and found her alone. She'd kissed him, and the kiss had led them passionately into other things. They'd both already known at that point that the sword was Calling her to be Lev's mate. Neither of them wanted to resist. Her continued work on the tapestry was a declaration. When she'd also been brave enough to touch the white wolf and bold enough to claim their first kiss from Lev's lips, it was natural for all else to follow.

He took her down to the floor in front of the fire. And then he pulled up her skirts to discover the delicate whispers of silk stockings on her legs. She laid back and watched him as he'd reached higher to find the ribbons that held her stockings in place. But she gasped his name when he inched her skirts even higher so he could lean down and loosen the scarlet ribbons with the grasp of his white teeth. He drew back from her upper thighs, but only to stretch the ribbon free from the top of her stockings. First one. And then the other. Madeline reached for his hair. She fisted a handful of his wild mane in her fingers, just as his mouth had found tender skin instead of ribbons.

"Ask me to stay. Tell me you want my hot tongue, Maddy. Tell me to taste you," Lev ordered.

Her body had been hot for him when they merely walked together. The whisper of his lips against her thighs as he uttered the erotic instructions caused her to wiggle her bottom against the floor as the heat between her legs turned wet with excitement.

"Stay, Lev. Lick me. Love me," Madeline said. She'd never made love with a man before. She'd only dared to

touch herself once or twice when thoughts of Lev drove her to ease her frustrations alone.

But the budding connection with the ruby blade, and Lev's encouragement, made her bold. She loved the way the big, muscular man's hands trembled on her legs when he reached to do her bidding. He pulled her silk drawers loose. They easily drooped down her hips beneath his insistent fingers. She heard the fabric rip, and she blushed with the idea that she might have to explain the tear to a maid.

His hot mouth descending on her made all thoughts of modesty evaporate. He thrust his tongue on the same spot she'd used to ease herself when thinking of him. Only this time, a hot, wet tongue was a million times more pleasurable than her own fingers. She cried out his name as the sensation took her, and he murmured hers in return against her throbbing flesh.

There was no modesty. He pulled off his britches and showed her how to give him the same pleasure he'd given her. She rose and took him in her hands. He blazed against her fingers. His flesh seemed hotter than the crackling fire. He kneeled between her legs, and she leaned over to lick him the way he'd licked her.

Lev jerked and cried out her name. He fisted his hands into her tousled hair, and she was spurred on by his reaction. She held him and closed her mouth gently over the hard, swollen tip of his erection. He trembled beneath her mouth as she tasted him for the first time.

And then he rocked his hips. Just enough to work the very head of his shaft between her suckling lips. Her body quickened again. She clamped her thighs against the tingling as she grew more bold, taking him deeper and deeper still into the hot, moist depths of her mouth.

"Maddy. I'm going to do this between your sweet

thighs. Do you want me there? I tasted your excitement. I want to feel it, too. I want to thrust into you. Like this. But harder. Deeper. Tell me you want to feel me. Welcome me inside you." Lev gasped as he gently indulged in careful thrusts between her eager lips.

Madeline moaned against the hot, hard, salty skin she pleasured. She did want to welcome him inside her.

"I've never been with a man, but I want to be with you," she murmured as she came up for air.

"Maddy, you're with a man now. A man and a wolf. To be with me means more than marriage or mating. You'll wield the ruby sword against the Darkness. You'll stand by my side and fight for the Light Volkhvy. It won't be safe or settled. The sword is Calling you. I'm on my knees for you," Lev said. "But you can say no." He stilled her head with his hands in her hair. He gently tilted her face up so he could meet her gaze. "I came to you as the white wolf so you would know me. All of me. I'm no ordinary man. And marriage to me will not be easy."

"I've always known you're not ordinary. Deep down, I've always known I was meant for more. I thought the tapestry was going to be you. I've never seen anyone like you. You take my breath away," Madeline confessed. She released him and he lowered himself to press her back against the floor. She wrapped her legs around his hips and cradled his erection between her thighs. But he didn't penetrate her. He simply allowed his heat to rest against her.

"But when I saw the image I was creating, I realized there's never been anyone like me, either. I alone can stand with the wildest Romanov. I am unique."

There was only the slightest pain when he thrust inside her. She welcomed him with her body and her *words. She begged him to complete their physical union, even as her connection to the sword became complete.*

The memories were as hazy and soft as the light, but that didn't make them any less powerful. Madeline trembled. She closed her eyes again and swallowed against the sensations she suddenly recalled—Lev's taste and touch and his powerful, perfect rhythm matching hers as they claimed each other.

Her eyelids flew open when Lev released a triumphant shout outside in the courtyard. She was forced back to the cold, harsh reality of the here and now. There were no monsters in Straluci, at least none she could slay with her sword. She sheathed the ruby blade and continued on to find the man who had once been her lover.

Lev stood beside the fountain portal they hoped would take them to Vasilisa. Madeline walked toward him. The triumph in his shout had been short-lived. He looked disappointed now. As she approached, she could see why. The marble fountain was a breathtaking work of art. It had been elaborately carved. Its basin curved outward like rolling waves preparing to crash into the courtyard. In its center rose the figures of four wolves, poised as if they were seconds away from leaping onto the crest of the waves. They faced north, east, south and west. Their tails touched as if they had been frozen for eternity in the act of watching each other's backs.

But the fountain was dry and filled with leaves and debris.

It seemed as dead as her sword.

The courtyard was ringed with overgrown rowan trees. Currently, their branches twined toward the sky and from one tree into the next as if they were joined together. Fresh green buds were beginning to burst open in the sunshine. It was their dead leaves from previous years in the fountain. There hadn't been anyone here to tend the grounds for a very long time. The rowan trees had reached out to each other as if to hold hands against the neglect and desolation.

"We'll clean it out," Lev said. "The bottom of the basin is brass. We'll polish it and fill it with water once more. Hopefully, it's still connected to the queen."

Madeline's hopes had fallen, but as they got to work removing the leaves from the basin, she watched Lev's strong back, arms and legs in the act of doing whatever was necessary. She joined him in the task. They weren't skeletons. They weren't dust. Not yet. There were still battles to be fought…and won.

It was the hardest here. Lev's entire body strained against the need to shift. The Ether taint tried to blacken his blood. It tried to expand within him, reaching icy tendrils closer and closer to his heart. He held out against its cold hunger with as much determination as he used to fight against the white wolf as it tried to claim him.

It didn't matter that the shift would save him. It would also hurt him because it would hurt Madeline. He'd seen her sketchbook. He'd seen what she thought of the white wolf. But there was more…

He'd known the truth ever since he leaped the ravine, and he'd been fighting the shift with everything he had since he ran away from Madeline once they'd safely reached the other side.

They were still connected. And he'd felt her fear of the white wolf and of the man he'd become.

As he jumped the ravine, he'd rejected the full shift.

He'd somehow held on to his human form. For Madeline. The ruby's penetrating glow had been like fire in his veins. Because he'd rejected it, the power had scorched him from the inside out, shredding his clothes and sizzling his nerve endings.

Even though she rejected the ruby and he rejected the shift as soon as he'd realized he had a choice, they had always been connected. He'd slowly ascertained that she could see and hear and smell things an ordinary woman couldn't—from the noise of a faraway river to the wolves to the ozone whiff of Ether on the breeze. Her senses were augmented by their connection.

Madeline was still the enchanted mate of the white wolf.

Lev's mate. Found, but still lost. Lost forever, because now he knew she would never be able to accept the creature he'd become. He knew it because he'd sensed those feelings in her. He'd won. He hadn't shifted. But Madeline had seen the shift in his eyes.

As they cleaned out the fountain, he ached with the torture of working by her side. They were nothing but a parody of the team they'd once been, because he had become a monster while she was sleeping. He couldn't blame her for rejecting the ruby, or for rejecting him.

He could have shifted in the blink of an eye. He could have plundered the earth with his rage and pain, as he often had before.

But he didn't.

He helped Madeline clean out the fountain, though they didn't know if it would still act as a portal to take them to Vasilisa. He helped, and his body quaked with the need to shift, which he denied.

And the Ether continued to darken his blood.

* * *

They cleared the fountain of debris by evening, and then they took turns polishing the brass they'd uncovered. It was tarnished, but Madeline emptied her canvas backpack and Lev tore it in half, and they used the pieces of rough fabric as abrasive cloths, supplemented by some handfuls of sandy grit Lev scooped from the nearby flowerbeds.

Finally, as the sunset began to paint the sky with orange and gold and brilliant pink, the brass had reclaimed some of its former gleam. They'd also uncovered and unclogged the natural spring conduit that filled the fountain, the seepage already forming in the basin.

"At this rate, the fountain won't flow until morning," Madeline said. She was grimy but satisfied as she looked over the job they had accomplished together. The fountain no longer looked abandoned. It looked like it was only a matter of time before it became a portal again. The water in the basin hadn't covered the brass yet, but it was rising incrementally as she watched. Once the height of the water reached the base of the wolf sculpture, it would flow up the channels created in the marble when the wolves were carved. When the water reached maximum height, the gentle pressure would allow the trickle of water from the wolves' snarling mouths.

The effect was of four champion wolves riding the waves they created from within themselves.

"They're coming, but there's still time. We'll rest tonight. And use the portal in the morning when the sun reaches its zenith," Lev said.

Madeline turned her attention from the slowly filling fountain to the man at her side. He hadn't said she should rest. He'd said, "We'll rest." All afternoon, he'd worked tirelessly without complaint, but now she noticed Lev's injuries still seeped black beneath his shirt.

"Your wounds need tending," she said.

"Inside," Lev replied. His agreement startled and worried her. For the first time since she'd found him in the tower room, she doubted his hard invulnerability. She took a step in his direction and raised her hands toward him before she realized what she'd done. When she caught herself, she lowered her hands and fisted her fingers, hoping he hadn't noticed her concern. "But first we'll need wood for a fire," Lev continued. "And a container for heating water. I think I know where to find an ax." He looked away from her, but for some reason Madeline thought he hadn't missed her reaction.

"I'll find the kitchen. Maybe there'll be some pots that haven't been looted," Madeline said.

Lev was already walking away in search of the ax. The idea of cutting down one of the rowan trees didn't seem like a desecration. It seemed as if the trees had waited for them to return to this place that had been so special to them before. Now one of the trees would provide a few branches to keep them warm for the night as they tried to prepare for the battle ahead.

But instead of battles and tending Lev's injuries, it was memories of making love with Lev that filled Madeline's mind as she went back inside to search Straluci for supplies. Was it a coincidence that the longer she spent with Lev Romanov, the more she remembered about her former life?

Chapter 19

She found the half-collapsed kitchen and was able to dig an iron kettle from the rubble. Its handle had rusted through on one side, but it seemed intact enough to hold water—but even better, she found a larger copper tub that had been used for bathing. It had been battered and dented by a fallen ceiling beam, but the beam had long since rotted so that Madeline could shift the tub free of the stone and bug-eaten splinters that remained.

Cleaning the fountain had left her and Lev sweaty and coated with grime. She ignored the flutter in her stomach that tried to coil into desire when she imagined getting clean…or helping Lev get clean. The tub would be too small for him, but that, too, sparked visions of the large man overfilling the copper bath. She pushed away visions of washing his muscular chest. It was pure practicality. Or if not pure, it was at least pragmatic to wash his injuries before she tended them.

Of course, she had no medicine or bandages, so cleaning his wounds might be the only treatment she could offer.

The tub wasn't nearly as heavy as the iron kettle. She placed the kettle in the copper tub and hauled them both back toward the only other source of noise in the castle. She could hear the distant sound of wood being placed for a fire. The sound echoed with surprising loudness in the empty hallways and passages she traversed.

Lev had chosen one of the smaller rooms to build and start his fire. It was a smart choice. The front hall was too expansive, and even with its larger fireplace, the heat would have dispersed too quickly in the vaulted ceiling and the missing portions of the roof. He'd chosen a room sheltered by a stone wall that had collapsed on one side. The collapse had created a three-sided nook near the fireplace.

There was a spot by the fireplace for the copper tub she carried. She placed it there without comment, but she felt Lev's eyes follow her movements. Was he, like her, imagining things he shouldn't? The rebellious flutter was another reaction to the sensual imagery that arose in her mind.

"We'll have to carry water from the courtyard," Lev said.

Madeline lifted the iron kettle from the tub with a bold flourish, even though she was feeling shyer by the moment. Needing to wash Lev's injuries was reason enough to haul water from the fountain. This wasn't seduction. It was necessity.

But Lev's fire-lit eyes seemed to see all the way to her quaking middle.

He rose from the fire he'd been stoking. It had combusted into a small furnace of heat and light that illuminated the nook with a reddish orange glow. Her sword was dead. The ruby didn't shine. But the quality of the light reminded her of the connection that was possible between her and Lev, and how hard it was to deny.

She held the kettle toward him, but he ignored it as he approached. His attention was riveted on her face. Could he see the flush on her cheeks? Did he recall the perfect rhythm they'd found together in this place long ago?

"You've remembered more. It's slowly coming back to you," Lev said.

"My memories don't matter," Madeline said. His chest bumped into the iron kettle. The one-sided handle rattled in her hand. Only then did he reach up to take it from her, but only to move it out of the way so he could step closer still.

He held the kettle down to his left side, then raised his right hand to brush her frazzled hair out of her face. She tilted her chin to meet his eyes. There was no reason to pretend his touch didn't affect her. It did. What she needed him to know was that the effect he had on her wouldn't sway her intentions.

She would save Trevor. She would walk away.

"I know," Lev said. "And I agree. I know what my years as the white wolf have made of me and why we'll never be together as a family again. Above all else, I intend to protect you and Trevor from what I've become."

Hearing her own fears spoken aloud made her uncomfortable. As if they were less logical when they came from Lev's lips. Of course, she had reason to fear the white wolf. He had been a complete savage for centuries. He had been poised to attack on Krajina until she stood against him. She couldn't risk Trevor's safety to the whims of a wild animal.

And yet she couldn't forget Lev's arms around her and the way he'd carried her to safety, even putting his own health at risk. He'd pushed himself to get ahead of the pack. He'd ignored his injuries to get her to Straluci. He'd ignored them further as he helped her prepare the portal.

"I'm not afraid," Madeline said.

"You're brave. You don't bow to fear. You refuse to let fear stop you," Lev corrected. "But that doesn't mean you aren't afraid."

"I'm not afraid for myself," Madeline conceded. "I would face the white wolf. Anytime. I've seen him in you. He shines from your eyes. And for myself, I'm not afraid. But Trevor has been through enough. When he wakes up, he needs a chance to laugh and play."

Lev's hand was gentle as he placed his warm, calloused palm against her cheek. Madeline didn't pull away. She didn't lean into his touch, but she didn't pull away.

"I'll give him that chance. I promise," Lev said.

Before she could second-guess the move, Madeline turned and placed a light kiss on Lev's hand. He drew in a great gulp of air in surprise, but then he held himself very still, as if he was afraid any reaction would drive her away.

"I believe you," Madeline whispered, then backed away.

Lev concentrated on the chore of filling the copper tub. It was a mindless exercise of repetitious motions, much like running. He wasn't free to shift and run away, so he filled the tub that Madeline had found. His wounds pained him. His long-sleeved T-shirt had fused to several of the bites as the blood dried. His every move caused the shirt to threaten to pull away from those injuries and make them bleed again. But worse still was the murmur of Ether in his veins. It sounded like the nightmare times he'd been lost to the Ether as part of the curse. In that black vacuum, the nothingness wasn't silent. It was sibilant with the constant hiss of voices even his wolf ears couldn't distinguish.

Not everyone had returned from the Ether during the continuous cycle of materializations. Many disappeared over the years. Between one Cycle and the next, they would simply be gone. Some never returned, even once Vasilisa's curse had been lifted. His father, Vladimir, had been one of the first to disappear. He and some others had never reappeared, even after the curse had been broken. When he returned to Bronwal as a man, he'd found the people rebuilding, but there were far fewer than there had been before.

Now it was as if his very blood echoed with the cries of those who had been lost to the nothingness. The murmur was a reminder of the nightmare he'd endured.

Lev could remember one of his last rational thoughts before he'd given himself fully to the white wolf. He'd wondered if Madeline's voice and Trevor's cries were a part of the Ether's murmur. He had tried so hard to find them, only to discover that Vasilisa had had them all along.

Finally, the tub was nearly filled.

He heated the last few pots over the fire in order to make the bathwater hot. Stream rose from the copper tub as a result. He had to admit it was a welcoming sight after so many frigid rinses in mountain streams.

Madeline returned, and her arms were full of items she had salvaged while he was busy filling the tub.

"Nothing is left from our time, but I found several

things that must have been abandoned by curious visitors through the years," she said. She held up a dried and cracked sliver of soap and a rag that looked like it had once been a white T-shirt.

And then she opened her other hand to reveal a straight razor.

"I polished the blade on a stone," she explained.

"I filled the tub for you," Lev protested. He raised his damp hand to his face and tugged on his beard. He had barely trimmed it since he reassumed his human form.

"We'll take turns," Madeline replied. "But you'll go first."

She'd already washed her face and her hands while he was busy. Now she turned to place the T-shirt in the last pot of water that bubbled on the fire. The boiling water would disinfect the old material so she could use it as a washcloth without depositing more germs than she cleansed away.

"This will end badly," Lev warned.

Madeline faced him. He stood in the firelight with his arms akimbo, as if he didn't know what to do with his hands now that his chore was finished.

"Yes. We've already agreed to that. Tonight is a reprieve from unhappy endings. You took care of me when you saved me from the wolves. Now it's my turn to take care of you," Madeline said. "Your injuries aren't healing the way they should. Let me help you, Lev."

He nodded. Just a simple up-and-down motion of his chin, but his agreement opened the door to possibilities that set the flutter in her stomach to somersaults.

Madeline dipped the sharpened straight razor's blade into the boiling water for a few minutes. Then she used a stick that Lev had brought inside for the purpose of lifting the pot by its broken handle away from the flames.

She set the pot on the hearth so the water and the T-shirt in it could cool.

While she was busy with those preparations, Lev had bent over to take off his boots. First one and then the other. Madeline heard every rustle and every sigh. She could almost feel his relief as his tired feet hit the cool stone floor.

"Do you need help with your clothes?" Madeline asked. She was trying to force nurse feelings to the fore, almost impossible when her "patient" had driven her wild with his lips and tongue the night before. Definitely impossible when she remembered what it was like to feel him thrusting deep inside her while her body pulsed around him with its release.

"I couldn't answer that honestly if I tried," Lev said. "And I don't want to try. I want you to strip me. Forget these injuries. I can only think about being naked with you."

When she turned to face him, she caught sight of her sketchbook. She'd dumped it out of her backpack because they'd needed to utilize the canvas to polish the brass in the bottom of the fountain.

Lev had brought it inside. On top of its cover were several charcoal stubs.

She looked from her salvaged possessions to the man in front of the steaming tub. His courtesy warmed her, and the warmth joined the flutter in her middle. He knew the sketchbook was precious to her, and even though it portrayed him as a savage beast, he'd saved it for her.

The sketches weren't a lie. She'd seen his savagery for herself. Both as the white wolf and as the man. He'd fought the Ether-tainted wolves with his bare hands.

For her. For Trevor, the warmth inspired by his courtesy said.

Also not a lie. But it would be dangerous to place too much confidence in his ability to control the wild wolf that had managed to take over for hundreds of years. She couldn't trust him, but for now, they were alone and he was hurting. She could help him. She could also admit her feelings weren't merely altruistic. She was no nurse. The heat from his consideration met with the heat that already rose in her whenever he was around.

She stepped toward him and raised her hands to the torn hem of his shirt. His eyes widened, but he didn't flinch away. He held still as she raised the shirt from his waistband, and he stared intently at her face. Was he trying to gauge her intentions? If so, she wondered if her expression showed concern mixed with mounting desire as she pulled the ruined shirt up to reveal his rippled abdomen and muscular chest.

He didn't look away when it was time for him to lift his arms to help her remove the shirt. He stared down at her, and only the shirt passing over his head interrupted their locked gazes. The color in his cheeks above his beard was high. She could feel the heat of a flush rising in her cheeks as well.

The shirt pulled away from several of his wounds, but he didn't cry out. Madeline flinched for him, and her attention fell from his eyes to his torn skin. The blood that seeped from the wolf bites was tinged with black. Her instinct was to try to wash it away, but the miracle of his epic run following the attack struck her all over again. Even burdened with her weight and his injuries, he had practically flown across the earth.

Madeline dropped his shirt to the side, and without thinking of the consequences, she allowed her fingers to trace the uninjured skin she had exposed. He sucked in air and held it as her touch feathered over his neck and shoulders and down the hard plane of his chest, where she paused over the steady, powerful thump of his heart before continuing down the impossibly toned muscles of his abdomen. Her memories were of a different, softer man. Still fierce. Still strong. But not honed by centuries as a mad wolf.

By the time she reached the laced waistband of his leather leggings, the heartbeat in her chest was pounding in the same rhythm as his heartbeat. The beat seemed to make her fingers vibrate and echo throughout her body, even though she was no longer pressing her hand above his heart.

She had rejected the sword's connection. They were no longer bound together by Vasilisa's enchantment. But their bodies seemed to fight the severing force of her will and his acceptance of her decision.

Her heartbeat synced with his. Her breathing adjusted to the rise and fall of his chest. And the bulge and heat of the erection that showed beneath the leather, as she gently worked the leather cords of his lacings free, echoed the heat throbbing between her own legs.

"Madeline," Lev said hoarsely. She'd heard the howl that had caused the rough quality of his voice, but that didn't stop his growling tones from tightening her stomach until the flutter she hadn't been able to ignore was caught and held in a fist of increasing need.

Reclaiming her memories of how they'd been together wasn't enough. She needed this Lev. Here and now. She needed more than what they'd shared in the wildflowers last night. She needed to physically join with him, even though no greater connection could be allowed. Come what may tomorrow.

He had been infinitely patient with her undressing. His stillness was heady in and of itself. Such a powerful, hard man waiting on her pace and allowing her to lead the way. But he sighed when she finally parted his lacings to allow his erection to spring free into her eager hands. The velvety skin of Lev's penis burned her fingers as she teased her touch around his shaft. Then he groaned and grew tense once more when her fist finally, boldly closed around the hot, curved length of him.

She had held him like this before. He had thrust into her hand and cried out her name.

His leggings slid midway down his thighs as his legs trembled in reaction to her strokes. Her body also reacted, but the trembles deep inside her intimate folds were hidden. She suddenly wanted him to know. She wanted Lev to feel her reaction to his erection.

"Step into the tub and let me wash you," Madeline ordered. She reluctantly released him, and he moved back from her touch long enough to push his leggings off his powerful legs. He kicked them aside and stepped into the steaming water of the bath.

Nude, Lev Romanov was a striking sight. She paused in the process of taking the boiled T-shirt from the cooling kettle. The water trickled back into the pot as she forgot the cloth she'd been wringing out. She could only stare. He was fully erect. The tight fist in her stomach released as her insides turned to molten liquid. She wanted nothing more in that moment than to rip off her clothes and beg him to join with her.

But his injuries still needed cleaning.

Madeline shook herself and flicked out the warm, wet cloth. She carried it over to the tub, trying not to focus on the evidence that he was as heated by desire as she. Lev watched her approach. He didn't reach for her. But he did fist his hands at his sides, as if not reaching required effort.

She dipped the sliver of dried soap into the water that lapped around his lower legs, but to do so meant she had to lean over. She appreciated the view as she rose. Every inch of his muscular legs. Every inch of… other things.

Madeline looked up at Lev as she worked the soap into the cloth in her hands. He had closed his eyes. The pace of his breathing had increased. So had hers, and now they matched. The color in his cheeks was high. She watched his face as she began gently lathering his neck and shoulders. His eyelids flew open and their gazes connected with an electric snap that made her gasp.

"You pleasure me and torture me all at the same time," Lev growled.

"I want you. And I want to take care of you. Just for tonight, let me savor this time," Madeline said. As she spoke, her soapy hands slid over his hard skin. She covered him with lather, inch by inch, appreciating his lean form, soothing his pain and increasing his need until his entire body trembled beneath her hands. She dropped the cloth into the water and took extra time with only her soapy fingers on his erect shaft. He moaned and groaned and sighed her name as she pleasured him in the guise of washing him until suddenly his hands came up and he held her shoulders. She met his eyes and paused. Her hands fell away from a steely cock that had been seconds away from orgasm.

"Rinse. Now," Lev ordered. And Madeline didn't argue. She went to the hearth and picked up the kettle. She filled it with water and then poured, washing away the lather. Lev watched her work with glittering eyes that were no longer as patient as they'd been before. The difference caused a thrill to take over where the flutter had been. Her nipples peaked, and goose bumps rose as she waited for him to act again, order her to do something.

Lev's body glistened in the firelight as the lather ran down his hardened flesh. His scars and the marks the wolves' teeth had caused on his skin didn't detract from his sculptural beauty. His rock-hard penis jutted out from golden curls, proving that however carved he seemed, he was hot and real and, at least for tonight, hers to enjoy.

She bent to scoop another kettle full of water, but Lev bent down to stop her. She allowed the kettle to sink to the bottom of the tub as he gripped her shoulders and encouraged her to stand. His hands were strong, though gentle on her arms, but they were also insistent.

She'd been right. His patience was gone.

Suddenly, he crushed her to his wet chest and lowered his lips to hers. She only had time to gasp before his hot, questing tongue speared into her mouth to twine with her own hungry tongue. He delved deeply, tasting and exploring and taking her last breath. Her head grew light. Her knees buckled. But he held her so she didn't fall. He eased up, but only seconds before she thought she would faint.

And she didn't mind at all.

Because his ferocity was hers. His passion was hers. She gasped for air and mourned the loss of his mouth at the same time. He allowed her to reach up and throw her arms around his neck. He lowered his hands from her arms to her hips. Somehow her feet were off the floor, her legs were wrapped around his waist and his engorged cock was pressed against her hot core.

Her face was above his now. She tried to kiss him again, but he spoke against her lips instead.

"I'm going to empty this tub and fill it with fresh water for you. But I'm going to undress you first. I want you to sit naked by the fire so that I can see every inch of you while I prepare you a bath. I want to see your hard nipples and the lush globes of your breasts. I want to see the auburn bush between your legs. I want to make those red curls glisten with anticipation," Lev murmured. The movement of his mouth on hers teased, and his words enticed. Heat rushed to the juncture of her thighs as she thought about him enjoying her nudity as she'd enjoyed his. She moved her hips as her ache increased, and he laughed in response.

Madeline was stunned into motionlessness. Then she reached to cup the sides of his face as if she could capture the smile on his mouth and the sound of his laughter in the palms of her hands.

"We'll get there, Maddy. We'll get there," he teased, and he held her bottom in two powerful hands so she couldn't resume her wiggling. He stepped from the tub and crossed the room to stand by the fire. She didn't protest when he untwined her legs from his waist and placed her feet on the floor. She was facing him in the firelight. His thrusting cock measured the distance between them.

She waited, trembling, for him to strip her as she'd stripped him. She didn't have to wait long. He raised one hand to her chest and undid the buttons of her shirt, one by one. She breathed lightly but quickly as he exposed her flushed skin.

"You're even more beautiful than I remembered," Lev said. His hands hastened to move her shirt aside when he undid the final button. The fabric swept off her shoulders and down her arms in a cottony whisper that tickled the same way desire was tickling the insides of her thighs with need. "You're also sweeter than I remembered. I discovered your sweetness last night. And since then, I've been dying to taste you again."

He leaned down to illustrate his hunger with his lips on the curve of her neck. Madeline's head swooned backward as she gave him greater access, and he took her offer with a sucking kiss against the vulnerable pulse point at the apex of her neck.

Her push-up bra cupped and displayed her breasts at a delicious angle. He stood back to look at her, and she could see his appreciation in his eyes. She looked down and saw her dusky areolas and pink nubs of her nipples showing through the pale peach lace. As she watched, he cupped her left breast, then caressed her swollen nipple through the thin material of the bra with his calloused thumb.

"Lev," Madeline breathed. It was half protest, half plea. He laughed again in response.

"Now you know how hard it is to be patient when you're being pleasured by someone you desperately need to take" Lev said.

With a sudden jerk of his hand, he twisted her bra free. The lace sprang loose and fell to the floor, forgotten. The fire's warmth fell on her breasts. The dancing flames illuminated her hard nipples and the flush of desire on her pale skin. She was left in nothing but leggings and boots, but not for long. Lev's hands were already on her waist. He jerked the stretchy material of her modern buff leggings down…and he went with them. She placed her hands on his broad shoulders as he worked her body almost roughly to pull at the leggings, and to wrestle the boots off her feet at the same time.

She welcomed the hurry. She wanted to be bare. She needed to be naked. For him. Only peach lace remained when he tossed her pants and boots aside. And her auburn mound showed through, level with his kneeling face. She didn't resist when his hands came around her hips to pull her toward him. But she did emit a surprised yelp when his hot mouth opened and he gently closed his teeth over her throbbing mound. The heat and pressure teased her even through the lace.

And then he stood.

"When I come back, I want those off. I want you on the hearth by the fire, and I want to see how ready you are for me," Lev said.

He turned away so suddenly that Madeline swayed. Cool air rushed back at her in his wake, in spite of the fire. She watched as he easily picked up the copper tub, even though its weight had been increased due to the water it held. His muscles bulged, and she admired his broad back as he walked out of the room.

I want to see how ready you are for me.

She was ready. And she wasn't too shy to let him see.

Madeline hooked her fingers in the waistband of her underwear and pulled them down. She stepped out of them and tossed them to the side. She wanted a bath; she wanted Lev to give her a bath. But most of all, she wanted the large erection she'd held in her hands deep inside her. He would fill her to the limit. She remembered perfectly the stretch, the fullness. That absolute perfect friction of their sliding together.

And even though it was probably wrong to desire him more, here and now, she was sure it would be even better. His hips would be harder and more frenzied between her thighs. His body would be a hot sculpture come to life only for her hands and her heat. He was a beast. Definitely. There was no doubt about it. But he would be her beast tonight. And she was warrior enough to take him.

Madeline settled on the heated stones of the hearth. They were almost hot against her bottom, and the heat radiated elsewhere. She wiggled against it and felt the pleasurable flush rise to tease her.

Lev would dump the tepid, used water from the tub. Then he would come back, any minute now, and find her just where he'd told her to wait by the fire. Madeline raised her hands to her aching breasts, so she could cup and caress them, and remind herself of his teasing hands. Her nipples were responsive and tender. Sensation zinged from the brush of her fingers straight to the pulse between her legs.

She clamped her thighs against the feeling, but then she remembered his orders. She thought she could hear his step in the hall. Madeline leaned against the hot stone at her back. The fire had died down, but it was still crackling enough to cause beads of sweat to spring up on her forehead and upper lip.

She was naked, but she wasn't cold at all. In fact, she'd never been hotter. Lev stepped into the room carrying the empty tub just as Madeline spread her legs. Across the room, his eyes were dark from the firelight, but she saw and felt him take in her display from her head to her feet…with a long pause in between. His pause was like a physical caress. Madeline could almost feel his fingers teasing the flesh between her thighs.

"You're going to kill me, but I'm determined to fill this tub," Lev said. He placed it on the floor with a clang and rose. The tub had shielded his erection from her sight. Now she appreciated how hard and ready he appeared. So much so that she pressed her hands against her hot stomach to quiet the ache there.

"Look at you. It's going to take more than that to ease your need. When I come back, I want to see your fingers wet, Maddy," Lev said. He picked up the kettle and turned to head back to the fountain to fill it. She'd gone motionless at his latest order, but as he headed back outside, she gladly obeyed. It wouldn't take him long to fill the kettle. Madeline moved the hand she'd pressed against her stomach down to her damp curls. She threaded her fingers into the nest to find the moisture he wanted to see. She gasped, her excitement heightened because he'd told her to touch herself and share her physical response with him.

Lev came back in the room as she raised her damp fingers back to her stomach. He crossed the room and placed the kettle on the fire beside her. And then he stepped to her. He reached for her hand and raised her wet fingers to his lips. He suckled first one and then the other. The hot suction and the sultry act caused her to gasp, but she didn't close her eyes. His erect penis was so close to her face. She went even wetter as she saw how much he wanted to replace her fingers with his cock.

She leaned forward, and he didn't stop her. She took the head of his penis in her lips. But he stopped her by grabbing a fistful of her hair before she could take him deeply into her mouth.

"You're hard to resist. Did you know that? I can hardly pull away. I have to feel your hot lips. Just for a second," Lev groaned. Madeline sucked as much as he would allow her to suck—only a teasing inch between her lips. She was so hungry for more. She moaned in frustration and then, because he wouldn't allow her to have more of his cock, she bathed the head with her tongue. Again and again, until his legs shook and the hand in her hair grew almost painfully tight.

"Oh, yes, Maddy. I'm going to take you tonight. I'm going to make you scream," he promised.

Madeline wiggled on the hot hearth, and he let go of her hand and her hair, but he also stepped back. She licked the salty taste of him from her lips. They were full and swollen from the suction she'd used on the head of his cock. He reached to take the water from the hearth with the tree limb. He carried the kettle over to the tub and tilted it so the steaming water would pour out.

Madeline felt as if her body was steaming as obviously as the bathwater. Lev looked back at her. He paused in the doorway with the empty kettle in his hand.

"I'll be back," he said.

This time her instructions were left to her own imagination. She tingled with the anticipation of his return. The taste of him on her lips made her crazy for more. It was easy enough to rise to her knees on the hearth and give herself what she needed. But it wasn't enough. Only he would be enough.

She was rocking her hips against her own fingers when he stepped back in. Lev slowly crossed the room to the hearth. Through narrowed lids, Madeline watched him approach. She didn't stop. She continued to rock. She'd felt this way almost since she first found him in the tower room. He heated her blood. He drew out every ounce of ache and need her body could feel. He should see what he did to her. Just as she could see what she did to him.

He placed the kettle on the flames, but he only had eyes for her. He stood for several moments, watching and appreciating before he leaned down to take her salty lips with his. He kissed her gently this time, licking all the perspiration from her upper lip, suckling her lower lip as her hips still moved against her own hand.

"Oh, Maddy, love. You are mine, aren't you?" She startled at his words and her hand fell away, but he continued. "No. I know. We are bound to be apart. But you're mine. And I'm yours. There's no denying it, no matter our circumstances," Lev said against her lips.

Madeline gasped when he replaced her hand with the nudge of his hot penis. Yet he didn't penetrate her. He only teased. He slowly eased his large cock high between her damp thighs, so he nudged her most tender flesh. She cried out his name and grabbed his shoulders.

"Say it, Maddy. Admit it for me. Just for tonight. Admit that you're mine," Lev said. "Forever."

Her "yes" was forced through teeth that chattered because her need for him was so great. When he stepped away to pour another boiling kettle of water in the tub, she thought she would cry.

"Only a few more trips," Lev promised.

The kettle was large, and the tub wasn't made for soaking. Madeline cuddled herself in the heat of the fire while Lev continued his chore with no more teasing. None was necessary. She already burned hotter than the fire itself. And his hands fumbled with his tasks, as if he was impatient to be through.

Finally, after several unheated kettles, the tub was filled enough for their purpose.

Madeline uncurled her legs, but this time Lev picked her up and carried her to the tub instead of the kettle. He set her down in the steaming liquid and rose before her. Madeline looked up at him as he soaped his hands. He didn't use a cloth to wash her, but rather, used his large palms. He lathered her from head to foot, even scrubbing her long hair with gentle, kneading fingers. It was a different kind of sensuality than the one they'd shared moments before—it was passion paired with consideration.

But when he kissed her between rinsings, she knew he was going to fulfill his earlier vow. His tongue mimicked a rhythm she recognized. He thrust deep into her mouth. He claimed her, and she welcomed it.

Yes. She sketched, but she also wielded a sword. It would take a furious desire to make a warrior scream. Only Lev Romanov, out of the entire world, could match the fury of the need in her own belly. Before the last of the soapy bubbles were rinsed away, Madeline wound her arms around Lev's neck and refused to let him bend to dip the kettle one last time.

"I was wondering when you'd grow tired of my teasing," Lev said.

"That I managed to survive with your soapy fingers between my thighs speaks volumes about my control," Madeline replied.

"I don't doubt your control. It's mine I've been testing," Lev said.

"No more control. I can't bear it anymore. I want to run with you this time. Let's ride this together while we can," Madeline said.

"There are no beds. No blankets," Lev warned.

"I only need you," she insisted.

He lifted her away from the water with her grip around his neck. She held on long enough for him to wrap his arms beneath her bottom. This time, when she hooked her legs around his waist, they were both naked. Her core settled against his hot stomach, and his erection bumped her bottom.

Lev took her weight with him to the floor. He shielded her from the rough flagstones with his warm, hard body. And then he moved his hands from her bottom to the aching need between her thighs. He opened her and centered his erection, but he didn't thrust his hips upward. He merely raised his gaze to hers. She saw the howl—she also felt the howl rise in her own breast. She felt the desperation of the search he'd undertaken to attain this incredible moment of reconnection.

And still he didn't take her.

It was Madeline who claimed the beast. She lowered herself on the erection he offered, and she accepted the incredible pleasure and pain of the tight fit and luxurious friction between them. She cried out his name. It sounded very much like the white wolf's howl. And with that, he went wild beneath her.

Her whole body was rocked by the power of his movements, but she clenched her thighs and held his shoulders and responded with the eager, fierce thrusts of her hips. She took him. He took her. And they both found their shuddering release that seemed to be echoed by the earth beneath them.

He didn't shift. The wolf was in his eyes, and the white wolf's song burst from his lips as he came, but he didn't shift. Thunder rolled and the earth rumbled, but it was Lev beneath her when she collapsed, replete, in his arms.

Chapter 20

The water had cooled, but Madeline added another log to the fire and reheated a kettle for the task she intended to undertake. She'd donned nothing but her tunic against the chill. Lev was still nude. He sat against the crumbled stone of the hearth and watched her work.

His muscular physique was distracting in the firelight. Especially now that she'd ridden him like a wild woman. She felt his hard, lean hips between her thighs. She knew how he could fill her. More than that, she knew how she craved to make him howl for her, with her. Even with a look of relaxed satisfaction in his eyes, he still looked ready to pounce, and his readiness matched the tender thrill between her legs. But he watched and waited as she prepared some sudsy warm water for his shave. They had no towels, and the razor she'd found was far from ideal, but she was determined to see his face tonight.

Please, God, there would be time for other things as well. But this she had to do before they made love again.

She placed the steaming kettle beside him on the hearth as his glittering eyes followed her movements. He was no longer as relaxed as he'd been. She knew the firelight must silhouette her otherwise naked body beneath the thin white cotton of her shirt. The direction of his gaze hardened her nipples and caused her well-pleasured femininity to tingle. He held himself still as she forced herself to take her time. She dipped her trembling hands into the hot water to moisten what was left of the sliver of soap she'd found, then worked it into a sudsy lather in her palms.

"You're killing me, second by second, as I wait for your touch," Lev said. His rough voice had become like foreplay to her. The fabric of her shirt touched her peaked nipples as she moved, but his howl-ravaged voice seemed to brush against her ears and skin. The timbre and texture of his tones were naturally sensual, but the intent in his eyes and the hardening of the flesh that lay heavy on his left thigh increased this sensuality.

"I'm going to touch you, Madeline. I'm going to kiss you and take you again and again," Lev growled. Her body responded with a tightening that made her gasp, and hot moisture flooded her insides. She wanted his explicit promises. She needed his lust. It mirrored hers, after all. "Tonight. We have tonight. The wolves are coming and the fountain is filling. By the morning, we'll have to travel through the portal and face what we find on the other side. But tonight, I'm going to ease centuries of longing. I'm going to fill you and taste you. I'm going to lick your sweet pink folds and suckle the nub that will release your pleasurable screams. I'm going to claim every impossibly tight, hot inch of you.

Hard, Madeline. So hard. Because you'll love it. You're no timid maiden. You want me to take you as you took me earlier.

"Remove my beard. Reveal my hidden face. But know this—I will still be savage with need no matter how you civilize my appearance. And I will prove it with the way I claim you when you're through."

Madeline shook with desire by the time he'd finished his sultry speech. He hadn't moved. He merely waited for her to shave him as he'd promised. But he was fully erect now. His penis jutted up from the nest of golden curls at the apex of his thighs. It reached all the way to his lean abdomen just beneath his navel… and it was thick and flushed with color. He was obviously as excited as she was.

"I'd better get started, then," Madeline spluttered. Desire made her lips seem hungry and swollen against her tongue as she moistened them. His eyes followed the dart of her tongue and then the movement of her throat as she swallowed.

"You should kiss me once more. Like this. So you can compare the difference when you're finished," Lev teased. It was a challenge. Suddenly, Madeline knew they had always been like this—playful but urgent. Testing themselves against each other as they teased their desire higher and hotter. What they'd done earlier, when he'd refilled the tub as she displayed herself according to his wishes by the firelight—that was a game they'd played before. Both bold and submissive. Taking turns on top and beneath each other.

It would be so easy to toss down the razor and straddle him right now. She could ride him again the way she had before. He wouldn't resist. They both wanted it. But it would also be a loss on her part. Because it was his turn to take her, and it was her turn to tease him unmercifully until he did.

Hot memories came soaring in as more moisture flooded her. She was slick and breathing heavily when she reached for his face with soapy hands. She did straddle him then, but even as she lowered herself to her knees, she kept her moist heat off his lap. She hovered above the tip of his erection. Her body barely brushed against his chest and stomach as she worked the soapy lather into his beard.

He groaned then. His head dropped back, and he closed his eyes. His arms reached out on either side of him to brace against the hearth and also to grip its hot stones with his hands.

She knew the game now. And she remembered how to play. As his knuckles whitened, she began to brush her heat against his naked stomach. Her shirt was long, and it was in the way. But the thin cotton barrier could easily be removed.

He must have felt her moist heat as she felt his hot, lean abs. His beard was crinkly and thick beneath her fingers. She soaped it thoroughly, but her attention was fixed on his full, parted lips. She almost kissed him when he licked them. She wanted to—wanted to devour his mouth. Instead, she leaned against him to press her barely covered breasts against his chest. She rubbed her body more boldly against him, and his eyes opened. His head was still thrown back, but he looked at her with intense eyes that glittered through his lowered lashes.

"Maddy, I'm going to spread your legs and bury myself so deep. Are you going to howl for me? Are you going to howl my name?" Lev asked.

Madeline leaned toward his mouth. She didn't kiss

him. But she moved her soapy hands out of the way so she could speak against his parted lips.

"Yes," she answered. She met his eyes and made her mouth into an almost-kiss that teased her as much as she intended to tease him. "I'm going to howl. I'm going to beg. I'm going to come so hard you will hardly be able to thrust against my tightening. But I'm so wet, Lev. I'm so ready for you. You'll slide even as I clench."

She felt him lose control then. Just a little bit. Just enough to thrust his tongue into her parted lips and catch her unaware. The sudden penetration made her gasp, and she lost control, too. She sank into his mouth for a deep, exploratory taste. Her tongue danced against his. And then his tongue thrust again. And again. He mimicked the rhythm of his promised claiming. Her body tightened, almost as if their words had already come true. She felt the sudden soar of pleasure she only expected from much more intimate play.

Only from the thrusting penetration of his tongue.

She moaned, and her soapy hands tried to find purchase on his broad shoulders. They slipped and slid, but he maintained his hold on the hearth. He was only kissing her. He kept control of all else.

Then Madeline brushed against his erection. She lowered herself just enough to tease her heat against his hot shaft. Once. Twice. Then she caught herself. She reached for his beard again and gripped both sides of his face. She pulled herself away from his lips and held him still while she caught her breath.

Lev was breathing heavily as well. His chest rose and fell against her sensitive nipples.

"You're killing me," he growled.

"Then you will be a clean-shaven corpse," Madeline responded. But she couldn't hide what his hungry kiss had done to her. Her lips were swollen. She could feel the heat of a flush suffuse her skin. The sensitive flesh between her legs throbbed with need.

She released her grip on his beard with one hand and reached for the razor beside the kettle. She'd sharpened it on a stone. It was no longer rusty; its edge was sharp enough for the task at hand. She dipped it in the water and brought it, dripping, to his face.

She wanted to kiss him again. She wanted to end this sweet torture and make love to him until he was senseless beneath her. Instead, she applied the blade to his left cheek and swept down in several rasping movements that plowed golden hair before them.

"Your hands are shaking," Lev noted.

He was right. She was so excited, her fingers weren't steady. He'd almost caused her release with his kiss. She wanted more of him. Now. Right away. He'd said she was killing him. She was almost dying herself.

"I want you. I need you inside me. I want to come around you," Madeline said softly. Nevertheless, she focused on the shave. First, she took off the excess hair in half a dozen swaths. She had to hold the beard with one hand and gently saw with the razor in her other. It couldn't have been a comfortable process for Lev, but without scissors, she had no other way.

He didn't flinch. He didn't pull away. He leaned against the hearth and let her remove his beard without complaint. Perhaps his focus was on the sway of her breasts or the heat radiating off her body. She tried to ignore those things for now. And the slow but sure revelation of Lev Romanov's lean, handsome face helped her to succeed.

Little by little, scrape by scrape, Madeline followed the perfect angular contours of Lev's cheeks and jaw.

The golden curls fell away beneath the rough blade. And every revealed inch of his skin was a beautiful disaster. He was marked by fine white scars. But not marred. Never that. He had been born so perfect that the faded scars only influenced his appearance by giving him a depth and history he wouldn't have had before. She remembered. His perfectly smooth skin. His younger, untouched face.

Tears sprang up in her eyes, but she blinked them away. She didn't want him to think she was sorry over the face she revealed. Not when she was only sorry that she hadn't been there to help him fend off whatever blows had caused the marks on his skin.

In the firelight, the scars were only visible because she leaned close to shave him. Most people wouldn't notice them at all. But most people weren't his wife. She'd kissed his unmarked chin.

Her gaze lifted and their eyes locked. He seemed to see the emotion swimming in hers.

"Don't cry, Maddy. I survived," Lev said.

Madeline paused in her work. The razor had found bare skin. There was only a little bit left to do.

"The scars I see are nothing compared to the scars I can't see. You carry scars beneath your skin, Lev. And I fear they aren't old and mostly faded away," Madeline said.

"Those I might not survive, but we'll face that battle tomorrow," Lev said.

He reached for the razor in Madeline's hand. He was no longer holding the hearth. He dropped the razor into the kettle of now tepid water. But his eyes didn't leave Madeline's face.

"I have lost you even as I've found you, but I refuse to let that spoil our time together. I meant everything

I said earlier, Maddy. There are promises I intend to keep," Lev said.

He rose beneath her effortlessly, as if she weighed nothing at all. His arms came around her and he lifted her with him, and suddenly they were both standing before the fire. But he didn't pause there. His hands dropped to the hem of her tunic and he pulled it up. She didn't resist. In fact, she raised her arms and allowed him to pull her shirt up and over her head.

Her bared breasts came up against the hard plane of his chest, and she thrilled at his strength and solidity. He was a rock. Immovable and hers. Not forever. Witches came between them. And the white wolf that wouldn't rest within his heart.

But nothing would come between them tonight.

"Tell me you want me to keep my promises, Maddy," Lev said. He leaned over her. His large palms were hot on her lower back as he spread his hands to lightly hold her in place.

Madeline answered by twining her arms around his neck. He was tall even next to her. And so strong. So hard and lean. His big Romanov build had been honed to nothing but muscle and bone by his centuries of running wild. But such muscle. Such bone. Her heart pounded in her chest. Surely he could feel it against him.

"I want you to keep your promises. I want you to take me. Hard. Completely. No holding back," Madeline breathed. Her confession was a sigh, but she tilted her chin up so he could see the intensity in her eyes. "I'm not afraid of the savage, Lev. I only shaved you so I could see you as clearly as you deserve to be seen. Every moment you ran. Every second you searched. Every battle you fought. For ages. For me."

He lowered his head and groaned her name against her mouth as he crushed his lips to hers. She welcomed his hunger. Her swollen lips had already been tingling in anticipation of another kiss. His mouth was hot. The stubble the ancient straight razor had left on his skin was slightly rough against her, but she didn't protest. She clutched him close, holding on to the back of his head, where much softer hair tangled in her fingers.

There was no soft bed waiting for them. There was no softness at all. But when Lev backed her up against the cool stone wall, Madeline cried out urgent encouragement. There was no place she'd rather be than pinned between the wall and Lev's big, hard body, with nowhere to run and hide from the desire to join with him.

He lifted one of her legs high, and she hooked it around his hips. He held her there as he found the wet, throbbing core she'd been teasing him with all night long. He buried his other hand in her hair and held her with a fistful of scarlet waves as he entered her with a single impaling thrust. They both cried out into each other's mouths.

"Maddy… Maddy," Lev gasped again and again as he slammed into her.

"Yes…yes," she said with each thrust, and then she screamed his name. She had come hard and fast. The shave had been almost more foreplay than either of them could handle.

The name she screamed was one that had been beloved to her long ago. A name that she'd discovered was beloved to her still.

It was savage, but it was their savagery, not just his. They were savage for each other. Madeline knew they always had been. She remembered. Their passion was forever, even if their coupling couldn't be.

Lev stiffened and shuddered violently as his release followed hers into her orgasm-tightened folds. His body jerked and his head fell back, and Madeline opened her eyes to watch him become gentle and vulnerable for her. Only for her. It had always been so. She couldn't remember every moment. She didn't remember everything. But she remembered this. Their carnal connection was deeper and more meaningful than the enchanted connection they had to reject.

They had lived terrible lives of hardship and battle. There had been blood and terror. Triumph and loss.

But there had also been this. They had found each other during times of intimacy. They had played while the world burned around them. They had created life with their love, and they had both treasured Trevor. Their family life had been a bubble of harmony amid the chaos of the war between Dark and Light.

Until an unexpected enemy had torn them apart.

Vasilisa. Queen Vasilisa. Suddenly, Madeline knew that Lev would never let her treachery against them go unpunished. He wasn't only with her to help save Trevor. He had agreed to help her because he intended to make the Queen of the Light *Volkhvy* pay for what she had done.

Vasilisa had helped her and Trevor since Madeline had awoken on Krajina. Or so she'd thought. She'd been certain that the queen was her best counselor and companion. She had allowed the Light *Volkhvy* unrestricted access to her child, and she had considered Vasilisa a nurse as well as her leader.

Lev had said it was all a lie. That the queen had misled Madeline to cover up her shame.

She was no longer certain that Lev was wrong. He

might not be the same man he'd been before the white wolf claimed him for centuries, but he wasn't merely a beast. He had exercised extreme control with her every time they'd been intimate. Even against the wall, he'd required her permission to continue. He had respected her needs and desires, sometimes shaking with the will it took to keep himself in check.

Those were not the actions of a wild man. His passion was savage. Lev was not. At least not when he was human.

Madeline quietly helped Lev freshen the water in the tub as she sifted through all these thoughts in her head. When he helped her wash up, she didn't resist. His gentle ministrations after the ferocious eruption of sex was only more proof that he might be thinking rationally when it came to what Vasilisa had done.

He'd been awake. She hadn't. If Queen Vasilisa had forced her into an enchanted sleep to "protect" her and Trevor from the curse she'd leveled on everyone else at Bronwal, then the queen was responsible for the sudden waking that had left her impaired by her memory loss. But that meant she was also responsible for waking Trevor more slowly to give him time to adjust.

If it was true, the whole scenario meant Queen Vasilisa lived in a world of gray, not black and white. Suddenly accepting that the Light *Volkhvy* queen might not be so light made Madeline's heart thud in her chest.

"I scraped your back against the wall," Lev said. She could feel the bumps and bruises he rinsed with water from the tub. She could also feel the pleasant tenderness in all the right places.

"I was rough, too," Madeline replied. She traced the marks her nails had left on his shoulders as she rinsed the sweat from his skin. They were nothing compared

to the wolf bites or the past injuries that had left him
scarred. But she was tall and strong, and she'd given
as good as she'd got.

"The fountain is filling. We used very little water
compared to what's welling up from the spring we unclogged. We should get some rest while we can," Lev
said. He didn't wait for her to protest. He pulled her near
the fire and urged her down to the floor with him, par-
tially cushioning her against his big body to buffer her
scraped back from the stones. He stretched one muscular arm beneath her head like a pillow. Every move
caused the thudding of her heart to increase.

Not from desire. Her body was completely satiated
from their earlier lovemaking. The intensity they'd
shared had left her satisfied. Her heart raced because
she'd remembered enough about Lev and their relation-
ship to know that if Vasilisa had done what he'd accused
her of doing, the queen was in terrible danger.

Madeline cared most about Trevor's safety. She
couldn't allow Lev to harm Vasilisa as long as she
thought the queen was helping her child.

Even as he cradled her gently, she knew he would tear
apart a witch who had placed his family in jeopardy.

Chapter 21

His witches and the wolves they controlled had failed to destroy the white wolf or his former mate. Fortunately, Aleksandr's plan was still in motion. The world he saw through the windows of his private jet was a black haze, but it was still his world to claim. As he flew toward the Carpathian Mountains, the sword, Lev Romanov and the former warrior, Madeline, were all together, but their enchanted connection had not been reforged. They were separate, and therefore, they were weak.

And the credit for that was his.

His attempt to kidnap their child had created chaos and confusion. Setting a giant pack of wolves on their trail had hounded and harried them even further. By all reports, Romanov had been injured.

Aleksandr could hear the cries of the souls lost in Ether as a distant hum beneath his skin. The Ether he'd absorbed was filled with those cries. Perhaps even filled with the souls themselves. He had wondered for a while if the lives it ate increased the Ether's energy output. Perhaps Vasilisa had fed and strengthened the Ether with her curse. After the wolves attacked Lev Romanov, Alek had begun to hear the echo of those cries from far, far away. His witches had channeled the Ether into their pack of wolves. Now the wolves had infected Romanov with Darkness. Alek could hear the same cries of the lost that flowed through his veins from Romanov's blood.

The white wolf could have expelled the Ether with one good, long run. Romanov wouldn't be able to shake it off as easily. Alek's witches also reported that the white wolf hadn't appeared. Romanov had seemed close to the shift during the attack. He had fought off the Ether-charged pack with his bare hands.

But he *had* used hands, not teeth or claws.

Alek had failed to stop the red wolf and his mate, Anna, from claiming their connection to the emerald sword. They'd managed to claim it even when Alek had possession of the sword. Anna had taken it from him. It had practically leaped into her hand. But the powerful triumvirate of Romanov wolves would be diminished if even one was lost. He still had the chance to tear them apart by killing the white wolf and his family.

But first, he had to find the child.

Their plan to kidnap Trevor Romanov had encountered an unexpected glitch when Queen Vasilisa herself took the baby and disappeared. Aleksandr's people had been searching tirelessly since. To no avail. Even with the Ether's help, Alek could not find her. He'd discovered her island, but from there, her trail had vanished into thin air.

Thankfully, the former wolf and warrior had led his people to a portal that would take them straight to the queen herself, wherever she was. Anywhere in the world. Alek was flying there now. He used Dark energy to power his plane because he was afraid to travel through the Ether itself. He could already feel its vacuum tugging on every cell in his body from the inside out. He would risk only a step through one of Vasilisa's portals. He couldn't chance a long journey.

Alek raised a stained handkerchief to wipe at his weeping eyes. He was so filled with power that it constantly overflowed. It never occurred to him that his former self might be crying at what he'd become. He simply wiped away his oily tears and flew on toward his destiny.

He would be king.

Once Vasilisa and her wildest wolf were destroyed.

Lev woke with Madeline snuggled so close to him that it seemed she had tried to crawl into him while they slept. Her cheek was pressed to his neck, and it was damp. The tears she was too strong to shed during the day often claimed her as she slept—this was something only a lover would know. He had guarded that secret vulnerability in their former life together. He would guard it still.

Unfortunately, she had also wrapped one leg around his hip and snugged her most intimate heat against his loins. He had to rise and leave her in order to protect *his* vulnerability.

His desire for her was his greatest weakness. Especially if he must let her go to save her.

He washed off with the cold water from the fountain. The chill had a dual purpose. It washed away the salty residue of her tears, and it cooled his rampant erection. She had begged. She had screamed. She had clawed his skin. In spite of the cold water, he couldn't get her pleasure in his wildness out of his mind. She had woken from her enchanted sleep weakened by her loss of memory and her fear of the white wolf. Now, her memory was slowly returning. She'd moved past her hesitation with him.

But there was still the white wolf to contend with.

His blood was poisoned by the Ether taint, and it wasn't going away. His human form couldn't heal. The chill of the fountain water was nothing compared to the chill that had infected his blood. He could feel the Ether's nothingness inside him, as if its vacuum would devour him from the inside out.

He'd seen a witchblood prince devoured by the overwhelming flood of Ether he'd welcomed into his body in order to become more powerful. That same process had begun in him without his permission. The tainted wolves had broken his skin with their teeth, and the Ether channeled into them by the marked *Volkhvy* had spilled over into him.

If it claimed him, he would be leaving Madeline and Trevor to Vasilisa's cruel, unpredictable mercy. But he'd come to realize that the only way he could cleanse his blood of the taint was to shift.

He would have to terrorize Madeline in order to save her. She might have accepted and even reveled in the wildness that stayed with him even in his human form, but she would not welcome the white wolf near their child. And he couldn't blame her. He had respected her caution through every attack. He had held the instinctual drive to shift at bay. He had stayed in his human form—or mostly human—for Madeline.

In part, because he shared her concern. He had always been the brother most claimed by the wildness during the shift. She thought he would be as feral as he'd been for centuries if he shifted again. She wasn't wrong. He could feel the fury for Vasilisa burning in his chest even as the chill of Ether poisoned him. He'd felt it for too long not to recognize it as the white wolf's rage.

Trevor was colicky. Madeline had been up most of the night with her fretful baby and she was groggy from lack of sleep, but once she found a lullaby that seemed to soothe him, she rocked the cradle gently and hummed without stopping in spite of her exhaustion.

His little flushed face had finally gone back to the usual rosy hue that predicted the strawberry blonde fuzz on top of his head would eventually lean more to red. He'd fallen into a peaceful sleep while she hummed and rocked tirelessly.

If only Dark Volkhvy *were as easy to vanquish as colic.*

Lev had been called away to battle. He'd made her promise to stay, but she'd only agreed when the baby seemed to grow ill. Lev had been too solicitous over her during the pregnancy, and even now. Not that she wasn't drained from caring for a newborn. But she was a Romanov warrior. She was the wielder of the ruby Romanov blade. It was time her husband remembered that.

As the baby slept, she continued to rock the cradle beneath a large tapestry. She had begun to sew the likeness of herself when the ruby sword Called her. At first, she hadn't known who the female warrior was, but stitch by stitch, prick by prick, her identity had been revealed. By then, she was already hopelessly in love with the ferocious Romanov who became the ter-

rifying white wolf in the blink of an eye. He shook the world when he shifted.

But he had shaken her world the first time he met her.

Madeline began to think of several ways she could remind Lev Romanov that she was the fierce warrior he'd married, a mate who could meet his ferocity on the field and on the bed, no coddling necessary.

But a step sounded in the hall outside and interrupted her thoughts.

Queen Vasilisa swept into the room. As always, her elaborate white gown and long white hair formed a startling sight against the stone castle walls of Bronwal. Madeline continued to nudge the baby's cradle, but she curtsied deep before her liege just as she would have done if Vasilisa had been sitting on a throne.

It wasn't until she rose from her deep curtsy that Madeline realized something was wrong. Queen Vasilisa, normally so perfect and pale, was flushed. Her cheekbones were as bright red as Trevor's had been when he was crying. In fact, Vasilisa's eyes were rimmed with red and shadowed with circles that looked like two large bruises on her beautiful face.

"You must bring the baby and come with me," Vasilisa ordered.

Madeline picked up Trevor from his cradle. She didn't hesitate. A toy Trevor had been sleeping with fell to the floor. It was a white wolf she had fashioned out of spare cloth. She had given the wolf vivid blue eyes with her embroidery thread. Trevor had laughed and loved the toy wolf right away.

The toy's legs sprawled out loosely on the floor, and for some reason the way it had fallen bothered Madeline. Its legs were twisted, its little face pointed at the sky as if it would howl in pain.

"What's wrong? What has happened?" Madeline asked. She reached for her ever-present ruby blade. It was in a scabbard she'd hooked on one of the bedposts. Vasilisa didn't reply. She simply turned and walked away. Madeline followed Vasilisa out the door, glancing back only once. She saw the tapestry in the firelight standing watch over the empty cradle. Madeline carried Trevor in one arm and her sword in the other. She followed the queen down the hall.

The queen walked with purpose toward the old chapel that held the mirror portal. There was no one around. The corridors were deserted. Trevor began to fuss against Madeline's breast. She began to hum the same lullaby that had worked on his colic before.

"That's right. Sing him to sleep. I wager you're getting sleepy as well," Vasilisa said with an odd, tight voice Madeline had never heard her use before.

"If something's wrong, we should go to Lev. He can help us," Madeline said.

"He's no use to us now. No use at all," Vasilisa replied.

Madeline would have stopped them. She would have refused to go on. But they had reached the chapel, and Vasilisa had reached to take the sword from her hand. She only released it because she needed both hands to cradle Trevor to her breast. Her arms seemed weaker than they should be, and she could hardly keep her eyes open.

"What has happened?" Madeline asked again.

Vasilisa reached for Madeline. The ruby in the sword flared bright, and by its light, Madeline saw the queen take her arm and pull her toward the mirror portal.

She didn't want to take Trevor through the portal. He was too young. The Ether was too cold. Even one step in its chill would be too much of a risk for a newborn. But Vasilisa tugged, and Madeline stumbled after her.

Queen Vasilisa began to hum the same song Madeline had been humming. For some reason, the lullaby sounded eerie coming from the pale queen with her bruised and red-rimmed eyes. Madeline managed to balk then. Her heels attempted to dig into the stone floor. She was not a small woman. She towered over the queen. But it didn't matter. The queen had all of Ether's energy to increase her strength.

The mirror swallowed the queen, Madeline and Trevor. And Madeline's screams.

Madeline woke up with a start. Lev was gone. He'd left his leather vest rolled beneath her cheek in place of his arm. The memory she'd dreamed was fresh in her mind. Why hadn't she realized that Queen Vasilisa had been crying? Her red-rimmed eyes and the bruise-like shadows underneath them had been in response to Vladimir's betrayal. She'd decided to curse Bronwal, but she'd still thought of protecting Trevor. She'd come for them and taken them to Krajina as the curse had fallen. Madeline could remember those empty, echoing corridors. How had she ever forgotten those halls or the eerie lullaby that had put her into a sleep that would last over a thousand years?

She couldn't allow Lev to hurt Vasilisa, even though the Light *Volkhvy* queen had torn their family apart. She had been protecting Trevor from her rage and grief, and she had kept him safe all the same. It had been her singing, after Madeline woke abruptly when the white wolf found the island, that kept the baby from waking too quickly.

Wherever they'd been taken, Madeline hoped Vasilisa sang for Trevor still. She prayed he would be guided gently into this new, modern world. And it was entirely up to her to make sure the white wolf didn't finish what he'd started before Vasilisa could help Trevor wake, slowly and carefully, from his long enchanted sleep.

Lev wanted to punish the queen for what she'd done. Madeline understood. The memory her dreams had unlocked was still too vivid in her mind. She remembered the leaden weight of her limbs as the sleep had claimed them while she was still trying to hold the baby to her breast. She remembered the desire to cry out for her husband, knowing without a shadow of a doubt that he would save them if she could only muster the strength to fight the enchantment long enough to call him.

She'd failed.

She'd trusted her queen, and even now she had to wonder if that mistake had actually been a blessing in disguise for the baby. If she'd resisted more effectively, they might have been lost to the Ether rather than sheltered on Krajina for all that time. For herself, she would have preferred to fight the Darkness by her husband's side. She might have helped him hold on to his humanity. She might have protected him from some of the scars, both inside and outside. But when it came to Trevor, she had to be thankful he had slept, blissfully unaware of the passage of time and tides and how they had eaten away at his legendary father.

Madeline had woken to a nightmare choice between her lover and her child. She didn't want to raise the ruby blade against Lev. Not even if he shifted into his white wolf form. She might reject their enchanted connection, but they shared a different connection that needed no *Volkhvy* interference to enhance it.

If she stood against him to defend Vasilisa, even that connection might be severed. She would lose him. Truly lose him, for the first time.

Her determination to protect Trevor propelled her up and out of the crumbling castle in search of Lev. They would have to use the portal together. She had to be certain he didn't go ahead of her and attack Vasilisa before she could stop him. She buckled the modified straps of her scabbard over her chest and arranged it as she headed to the courtyard. The ruby was still dead and dull. It didn't matter. She'd been awake for weeks. Every day she became stronger. She'd remembered how to wield the blade. Each day she remembered more. Her body moved more gracefully, each muscle remembering its purpose as she pushed herself to be ready.

The confidence of a warrior had been rekindled in her veins and burned brightly in her heart. For Trevor.

She was wide-awake now. She didn't need the light of the ruby to guide her.

Lev stood by the fountain. The water from the spring had filled it to the brim, and a forceful flow poured from the statues, creating small, gurgling waterfalls from the open mouths. The streams of water fell away from the main body of the fountain into a channel that carried the water away and back into the ground. In contrast to the rushing water, the middle of the fountain at the base of the wolves' feet was still and serene. Like glass, it reflected the sky as the sunrise painted the horizon with an orange-and-yellow glow.

"They've found us. I can smell the wolves on the breeze. I can hear their paws scrabbling on the ground. They roil toward us as one entity made of many. There will be no posturing. No chance for me to challenge the alpha and take over the pack. It is completely under the control of the *Volkhvy*, who drive it ahead of them," Lev said.

Madeline strained her hearing. She thought even she could detect a rustling. As she listened, the noise increased, coming closer and closer, like an approaching storm. Only it would be a downpour of tainted fangs that caught them, instead of rain.

"Hurry," Madeline said. Her hand had automatically gone to the hilt of the sword over her shoulder. "We should use the portal before the wolves reach us."

Lev turned toward her. His hair was wild around his shaven face. Her heartbeat stuttered, and her breath caught. The morning sun created a halo of his blond waves, but if he had been an angel, he would be a vengeful one. She could see the anger tightening his jaw, better than she'd been able to see it before. Shaving him hadn't made him civilized. It had only revealed more sharply the man he'd become.

Her heart skipped because he didn't repel her. Just as her sketches had revealed, she was fascinated by his passion and fury.

She had reclaimed her warrior spirit, and she was no longer afraid of the wolf that showed in his eyes.

"We can't escape them. They will follow us through the portal. We will face whatever is on the other side, as well as the pack and the witches who control it," Lev said. He stepped toward her, and Madeline's hand fell away from her sword without her giving it permission to stand down. This was how it would be. She didn't want to fight him. Her instinct was to fight alongside him.

"And there's something you should know," Lev continued. "The wolf attack infected my blood with Ether taint. I'm fighting the Darkness with every breath. If I use the portal, the vacuum might take me before I step through on the other side."

"No," Madeline said. This time, instinct drove her to reach for him instead of her sword. She grasped his arms as he faced her. His muscular biceps were so warm and strong beneath her fingers. He couldn't disappear. He was forever and always. As much as she'd feared the white wolf, she'd expected to see him again one day the same way she expected the sun the next day when night fell. She had been wary of his feral nature, but deep down, she'd believed that he could be reached. Not tamed. Never that. But brought back from the savage edge of madness, where he'd been driven by the curse.

"You'll shift," she told him. "You'll heal. The white wolf will shed the taint as you shed your human form."

A howl sounded in the distance. It was a howl made up of a hundred wolves' howls, but all strangely together in one deafening cry. The synchronicity was unnatural. It jarred every expectation because it was impossible. How could wild creatures be so joined and manipulated? The pack was one weapon aimed against them, and it had reached the rhododendron field.

"You don't want me to shift, Madeline. The white wolf woke you too soon. The first sight you had of me, I was at my most feral. I had finally sensed you after centuries of searching. I was mad from grief and pain and exhaustion. And fury. I wanted to tear Vasilisa limb from limb. You and Trevor were there the entire time. I thought you were gone. And worse, she *still* had you. That was what drove me wild. You were still in her clutches. A witch. The worst of the *Volkhvy*. She used and abused us all," Lev said. "And I couldn't stop her. I had failed to help you for centuries. I wanted to tear myself limb from limb." He stood with his arms at his sides as she held him. His face was hard and tight. Moisture swam in the blue of his eyes. He fisted his hands, trembling with emotion.

Madeline was suddenly claimed by the same emotion. Her body trembled, too. Her heart pumped pure fury through her veins. Her teeth clenched, and a growl rose in her tightened throat.

They thought they had rejected the connection.

But it had been the connection that woke her from her long enchanted sleep.

She had risen to face the white wolf in battle, but it had been the wolf's emotion she'd been feeling. Lev had come back from the wild when they connected once more, and he had come face-to-face with his failure. His fury had been directed as much at himself as the queen. She'd been a nearly empty vessel, woken too soon to bring her memories back to life within her. She'd only had Lev's thoughts and feelings to guide her actions, and his main thought had been one of self-loathing.

"Vasilisa shielded us from the curse and from you. You couldn't have found us, Lev. No matter how you tried. I was sleeping. I couldn't hear you. Or call you," Madeline said. "I tried. As the sleep claimed me, I tried to call you. But I realized what was happening too late. I failed, too."

"You raised the sword against me. I was going to take the blade. Through my heart," Lev said. "But you didn't plunge the sword."

"Of course I didn't," Madeline said. "I was feeling your rage. But my love prevented me from killing you in either form."

She'd been so focused on Lev's emotion coursing

through her that she hadn't noticed the morning sunlight was no longer orange and yellow. It was red.

Lev broke his gaze from her. He looked over her shoulder. And Madeline could see the glowing ruby in her sword's hilt reflected in Lev's eyes.

"We have to save Trevor. In the end, even if we can't save ourselves, we have to save Trevor. You have to shift. We need your help to defeat the marked *Volkhvy*," Madeline whispered. She heard with Lev's ears. She detected the scent of the pack with his nose. They didn't have much time.

"If I shift, I might be as feral as I was before. Filled with fury. Driven by pain," Lev warned. "I've been holding off the shift ever since we leapt the ravine. I realized then it was your fear that had stopped me from shifting before. And I wasn't going to ignore it to shift even once I knew that I could."

Madeline raised her hands from his arms to his face. She cupped his hard jaw in her warm palms and stared deeply into the ruby light in his eyes.

"You are filled with fury and driven by pain in either form. And I love you. Because your pain and fury is for us. It's fueled by love. And your desire to protect us," Madeline said. "Shift. Shift and we will both survive the leap through the Ether to save our son. Both or neither this time, my love. I won't survive without you or the wolf in your heart."

Madeline suddenly knew the truth that her artistic eye had seen at the edge of the ravine. She'd captured that moment in her sketchbook. Lev hadn't been trying to shift. He'd been holding the shift at bay. For her. Out of respect for her fear. His love had held back a supernatural compulsion, and she had somehow seen the extreme sacrifice and beauty. She'd had to draw him in that moment.

And that had been the moment she remembered her love for Lev.

Wolves began to pour into the courtyard through the wall surrounding it, crumbled by time. Like black water through the cracks of a broken dam, they came. Madeline drew her sword and whirled in one smooth, clean motion. Ruby light flared. But it wasn't her sword's light that caused the wolves to swirl in a confused mass before they could attack.

It was the sudden earthquake that shook the castle ruin and the entire mountaintop on which they stood. Stones fell, crushing some wolves in the avalanche of debris. The aura of Madeline's ruby protected her.

And then it protected a massive white wolf as well.

He was hers, and she was his. Her heart expanded as if it beat in a huge barrel chest of a monster. Her lungs expanded as if they filled with oxygen for the first time in centuries. The white wolf turned to look at her, and his red eyes no longer filled her with dread. It was her ruby's light that caused his eyes to glow.

She was by his side. With all four paws on the ground and his powerful bite and his leap and his run, no adversary could stand against them. He was strong. He was tireless. For her. The lost time was over. They were found now. He had found her. He had found himself.

He wasn't feral.

He was Lev, the white Romanov wolf.

And he was the wild.

The Carpathian forest called to him. The sharp scent of spruce. The ancient creak of rowan. The mineral bite of water that flowed over rocks in never-ending rivulets of refreshment. It was all for him, and in him—the ground beneath his paws and the prey that fueled his run.

It was all for him because, in him, it was a gift for her. His bite. His leap. The muscle and bones beneath his fur. The hunger in his belly and the rage in his heart was all for her. He would strengthen her by standing by her side. Protect her by destroying her enemies.

There was a greater enemy than these puny wolves that prepared to attack. There was someone else to find. But for now, he had found Madeline, and he had found his purpose again. To stand. To protect. To fight beside his warrior mate and her ruby blade. All his centuries of constant vigilance and preparation had led to this moment.

He hadn't been feral or mad. He'd been obsessively training. He'd been hardening himself and strengthening his abilities. For her. For Trevor. For his family. It hadn't been madness. It had been a wild love only the wildest of Romanovs could understand.

The white wolf had always known he would find his warrior, even when his human soul had lost hope.

"We need to prevent them from using the portal. We can't allow them through," Madeline said. Her words gave him a direction in which to point his ferocity. He had always been the wildest of the Romanov wolves. The fastest. The most agile. Because he had learned to give himself completely to the shift. Madeline had always been his lifeline back to his human form.

Until she hadn't been. He'd remained a wolf for centuries because the wolf was needed. If he hadn't been needed, Madeline would have called him home. Others tried to call, but he didn't listen. He listened tirelessly for Madeline's call instead.

And now he was needed once more.

He'd always known she would find her way back to him. He'd been tireless all this time so he would be ready for this moment, when he was called once more to fight by her side.

Chapter 22

The wolves temporarily broke the control of their *Volkhvy* masters because their instinctive fear of the white wolf was so strong. But their masters weren't far behind. Once the witches caught up with their pack, they retained control by tightening their grip on the Ether in the wolves' blood.

Madeline could see the marked *Volkhvy*. They had appeared on the sections of the wall that still stood. One. Two. Three. Then a dozen more. Anna had marked them all. She could see the shadowy bands of bellflowers shining darkly against the pale skin of one forehead after another. An ozone-scented breeze came with the witches. Their manipulation of the Ether had kicked up an unnatural storm. Instead of rain, drops of Ether appeared above their heads and fell in an oily drizzle. The ruby aura of her sword protected her. Since the wolves weren't fortunate enough to have a shield, their fur became matted with oily residue.

But they ignored it.

The witches had halted their temporary milling about They massed into a cohesive force once the marked witches appeared. And with violent, synchronized gestures, the *Volkhvy* set their tainted pack on their prey.

Madeline and the white wolf stood between the pack and the fountain. They couldn't afford to die and leave Trevor unprotected. But they could at least reduce the number of wolves that would follow them through the portal.

As soon as the first tainted wolf leaped and the white wolf tore him in half, Madeline knew they could do more than reduce the numbers. The white wolf wouldn't let any of the tainted wolves pass. With him defending the portal, she was free to go after the witches. They would divide and conquer as they'd done before, only on a much larger scale. Then again, as large as Lev Romanov was as a man, he was a giant as a wolf. She would have to live up to his size and strength.

She had taken down one witch with a dead ruby sword. The confidence of the white wolf pulsed through her. They were connected. They'd always been connected; she just hadn't known it. Now she didn't just know, she embraced it. Her confusion and fear no longer stood between them. She and Lev were a perfect team. Her sword glowed, and all the strength and agility she'd rebuilt over the last few weeks was enhanced.

Thirteen witches were nothing to a Romanov warrior and her wolf.

She took the marked *Volkhvy* down one by one. Even though she wielded an enchanted blade, it was her determination that propelled her on each climb up the deteriorated wall. The witches had given themselves over completely to controlling the pack. Their focus was on the battle with the white wolf. Madeline took advantage of their distraction and killed them. One after another. By the fourth witch, she was drenched with sweat and shaking. By the tenth, she was barely able to make the climb. The white wolf was no longer white. His coat was marred by the black oil of Ether taint and by the wolves' blood. The witches had already killed the wolves. They had become zombie vessels poisoned to death by the Ether that controlled them.

The white wolf laid their desecrated bodies to rest one by one just as she sent the evil *Volkhvy* into the Ether. She stabbed all of them through their black hearts with her ruby blade to ensure that they would never be able to hurt another wolf or another child.

The last three witches finally realized what was happening and disappeared, risking the Ether that already filled them to travel away from her blade.

Madeline collapsed to her knees. The ruby light faded, but not entirely. The gem was alive with the power of her connection with Lev. It had taken the white wolf's ferocious devotion to her to feel it. Lev had fought the connection. For her. He'd wanted to give her the chance to turn away.

He hadn't realized the white wolf would never turn away, no matter how much it hurt to stay by her side.

The white wolf was Lev's heart. He confessed it without saying a word. Madeline struggled to her feet and went to the monstrous beast who had helped her defend the portal. He shied away from her hand, either because he was covered in grime or because he would never be tamed—she couldn't be sure.

Madeline let him slip away. He stopped several paces from the fountain and turned around to face her. The ruby's light was still in his eyes, even though she had cleaned and sheathed her blade. It wasn't a reflection. Her eyes would look the same. The ruby's power was in them as long as they accepted it.

For now, they couldn't afford to push it away.

They still had a baby to save.

Madeline approached the fountain, giving the white wolf his space. He watched her suspiciously, as if she might try to put a collar around his neck if she came too close.

"Were you always this ridiculous, you silly beast? I'm only going to wash my face," Madeline said. She scooped up water from the fountain and did just that. The white wolf sidled closer. "You could use with a face-washing yourself."

And then Madeline splashed the huge white wolf that dwarfed her and the statues of all the Romanov wolves.

"It wasn't you I feared. It was Vasilisa all along. I felt your fear of her. It woke me. It colored all my perceptions of you. And your anger at yourself. You shared that with me as well," Madeline said.

It was time to step through the portal. But she had one more thing to say to Lev. She'd already told the man. Now she told the wolf.

"It wasn't your fault. You weren't to blame. But you know that in your wolf form better than you know it in your human form, don't you? You didn't focus on fault. You focused on being ready when the time came," Madeline said.

The white wolf blinked at her. She saw Lev in his eyes.

"Come back to me when it's time," Madeline said. "Just as I came back to you."

The white wolf whined. He lifted a giant paw and placed it in the icy water that flowed up from somewhere deep inside the mountain beneath them.

"I understand. It's time to go," Madeline said. "And I'm not sure how much you can understand, but I have to try." She reached and grabbed the white wolf's fur before he could slip away. She tightened her hold, and he turned his massive head toward her. She wasn't afraid. He wouldn't hurt her. The certainty of that filled her as surely as she could sense the powerful beating of his heart beneath her hand. "Vasilisa is helping Trevor. She's preventing him from waking too soon. I know Lev hates all witches. He distrusts them. For good reason. But to protect Trevor, we can't harm Vasilisa."

The white wolf blinked at her. His muscles trembled beneath her grip. She didn't let him go.

"I don't know what we'll find on the other side of the Ether when the portal takes us to Vasilisa. I only know I won't allow you to harm her. We must save Trevor. We must protect him," Madeline said. "He needs Vasilisa's help."

The white wolf whined again, and she allowed him to pull away from her hand. He didn't jerk. He didn't leap. Instead, he pulled gently.

"As big as you are, I suppose I should be grateful of the consideration, but seriously, haven't you learned by now I'm not going to break?" Madeline asked.

Her body did protest when she leaped into the fountain to stand beside Lev. This time she didn't try to hold him. He wasn't tame. He wasn't a companion or a pet. He was her wild wolf. And in this form, he barely knew his name.

He might not have understood her words about

the queen. It might be dangerous to allow him to step through the portal as the white wolf, but somehow, she thought the wolf was more malleable than the man. Lev might not be capable of standing down. When he saw Vasilisa again for the first time since he'd found his family, he might react more ferociously as a human father. It was a risk she had to take. To trust the wolf. Because there was no way of knowing what they would find on the other side.

There was no place close to Vasilisa's portal for the plane to land. Aleksandr had to risk the Ether in order to reach his quarry before it was too late. His body was already filled to overflowing with the black rush of the Ether itself. He could feel it travel inside him, along with his blood. Its chill coated his heart, slowing its beat. All of his visible veins gleamed darkly beneath his skin in a spidery network. And now, as he rose from his seat on the plane, he looked down to see that the viscous liquid was seeping from his pores to flow in thick tendrils on top of his skin.

He no longer knew how he escaped the constant vacuum. Every step took effort. Every inhale and exhale was bubbly and wet. But he couldn't abandon his chase. If the white wolf and his warrior reached their baby and triumphantly reclaimed their connection, he would lose everything. He'd sacrificed his autonomy to win. He had all but given himself to the Ether. All he had left was his goal: to defeat Vasilisa and rule the *Volkhvy* in her stead.

Aleksandr stood in the center of the plane, which was rocketing over the Carpathian Mountains. Far below, Lev and Madeline Romanov had all but defeated his witches and their wolves. Only a few had escaped through the Ether as a last-ditch effort to retreat. He'd felt the ripples of their travel in the Ether that flowed in his body. He'd heard their warning screams in his head.

The white wolf had appeared. Lev Romanov had shifted. Perhaps Aleksandr should have retreated as well, but the Ether rode him too insidiously to consider escape. There was no going back. There was only the battle ahead.

It required no effort to channel more Ether to surround him. All of his effort was spent trying not to be devoured as the black sphere formed. He couldn't risk traveling through the Ether. He would travel with it instead.

Within moments, the sphere was thick enough to protect him. Never mind that he trembled within the black hole it created inside the plane. He fought its hunger, continued to fight it as the bubble sank through the floor of the plane and out into the Carpathian sky.

The sphere of Ether fell with him inside it. It carried him to the ground. At impact, the sphere burst, expelling him as if it had given birth. The ground was drenched in oily fluid, but in moments it had become thicker. Its cold embrace was drawn back to his body, and he was suddenly covered with flowing Ether as he'd been before.

Only this time, the Ether rooted itself into his pores, settling more firmly against him like a living, lurching second skin. Aleksandr was hundreds of pounds heavier than he'd been before. It took all his remaining strength to pick up his feet and put them down again in a shambling march as he set out to find the portal that would take him safely through the Ether to Vasilisa's side.

Safely.

Oily laughter erupted from Aleksandr's black lips at the thought. He tamped down the panic that rose with the eerie outburst of humor.

He was no longer sure the laughter was his own.

Chapter 23

The cold of the water was more than mountain chill. As they allowed themselves to sink down, the water rose. Like living mercury, it climbed their legs and engulfed their bodies with a shimmering flood. Vasilisa's portal sucked them into the Ether. Madeline floundered. It felt almost as if the sleep was claiming her again. She panicked. Her sword nearly slipped from her hand. But on her other side, the white wolf sensed her sudden terror as the portal reminded her of her long, inexorable sleep. He pressed his massive body against her instead of shying away. He was wild, but he was hers. He supported her body for the one step necessary to take them through the Ether and out the other side.

Madeline fell forward, soaking wet and coughing up spring water.

There was no fountain on this side. There was only an unwelcoming rocky terrain. The air was hot and dry.

Using her sword unceremoniously as a prop, Madeline pushed herself up from the ground.

She had expected an army of marked *Volkhvy*. Or a dank prison, where the queen and Trevor were held in a cell. What she saw confused her. Reddish soil dotted green with scrubby vegetation held no signs of life or habitation. The sky was a vivid blue, like Lev's eyes, and it stretched as far as she could see across desolate plains disrupted only here and there by flat plateaus. Nearby, boulders as big as the white wolf and smoothed by constant wind were very different from the craggy gray rocks of home.

"The portal didn't work. It didn't bring us to the queen," Madeline said. But she was interrupted by a rumble and a harsh rasp of stone on stone. Her knees bent and she whirled, expecting to see the white wolf shifting, but he was nowhere to be seen. He hadn't materialized by her side. She was alone with the rasping. She brought the ruby blade up before her with both hands on its hilt. The ruby's glow was dim. She could barely discern its light in the sun. She would face whatever she'd found, but her heart was hollow. Had the Ether eaten Lev? Had there been taint left in his blood as the wolf after all?

"You have found me. Just as I knew you would. We've been waiting for you," Vasilisa said. She stepped from the maw of a cave that had been revealed by a giant boulder rolling away from its opening. "You know how I like to use natural inaccessibility to aid my power. Welcome to the Arizona desert. It's far removed from the places where Ether bleeds through into this world," Vasilisa explained.

"You took Trevor through the Ether before the

marked *Volkhvy* could take him from you," Madeline said. "You weren't kidnapped. You escaped."

"There was no time to come for you. They were on us too soon. Aleksandr was more powerful than I had planned for. I never imagined, after the witchblood prince, that any witch would be foolish enough to absorb the Ether itself," Vasilisa said. "Much less one of my Light *Volkhvy.* I should have known better than most that the Darkness calls to everyone in desperate times. And Aleksandr was desperate for power. He sensed an opening as we struggled to recover from all the discord my curse had caused."

But Madeline could only look at the squirming bundle in the queen's arms. They were separated by half a dozen yards of rocky earth, but she could see the bundle was a baby—a wiggling baby. Little fists waved in the air, and pudgy feet kicked. Fists and feet that she remembered in spite of all she'd forgotten.

"Trevor's awake," she whispered.

Her sword slipped from her hands and fell onto the dusty earth.

"You sought a hideaway where you could continue to wake him slowly," Madeline said.

"When I allowed Lev to find you, I allowed you to wake too soon. I'm to blame for your memory loss. I didn't know what else to do to save my daughter from the white wolf. You interrupted his hunt for her," Vasilisa said. The baby in her arms had captured a lock of her long silver-white hair. She allowed the following tugs without batting an eye. "I'm sorry. Even though I would do it again, I'm sorry."

"Anna is precious to you," Madeline replied. "Just as Trevor is precious to me." She wanted to rush forward, but she had no idea if Trevor was well enough to leave Vasilisa's arms.

A howl interrupted them. It rose long and loud from a supernatural throat that was raw from centuries of howling. The white wolf had come through the portal. As he entered, his cry shook rocks from the cliffs around them. He landed between Madeline and the queen, blocking Madeline's view of the baby.

"Lev, she saved him. She's been protecting him the whole time!" Madeline shouted. The white wolf didn't look her way. Once his feet settled, he stalked toward the queen.

She had no choice. Madeline bent to scoop up her sword. It was glowing brightly now. As bright as she remembered from those glorious days of unity long ago. The gem's gleam made no sense as she prepared to stand against her partner in defense of her queen. Vasilisa wasn't their enemy. She was an ancient complicated being who had made mistakes. But she didn't deserve to die. Especially not when she held their baby's life in her hands.

"Trevor needs her, Lev. And so do we. Aleksandr and the marked *Volkhvy* are still our common enemy," Madeline said, more calmly. How do you reason with a wild wolf? Or a wild man, for that matter? She could sense his heightened emotion, but not clearly. Like her, he was feeling anger, fear and relief. His heart pounded slowly and powerfully in his massive chest.

It beat for her and Trevor. The white wolf couldn't speak, but she could sense his savage devotion.

"No, Madeline. Trevor doesn't need me anymore. He's ready to come back to you," Vasilisa said. She faced the white wolf without quaking. He was on her now—his giant snout only inches from her head. The queen looked up without fear at the looming wolf that had formerly been one of her champions. Her beautiful features were soft and serene, even as she revealed a truth that could possibly seal her fate. Why would Lev let her live if she was no longer needed to keep his baby alive?

"She loves her baby, Lev. Just as we love ours," Madeline said. Terrible teeth were inches away from Trevor's waving hands. He'd released the lock of Vasilisa's hair.

And now he grabbed the white wolf's snout.

Madeline gasped. It hadn't been that long since she was certain the white wolf would hurt them. Knowing better now didn't make it easier to see her baby touch the monstrous face.

She stumbled forward, but she was too slow. She hadn't even raised her sword when the white wolf's mouth opened and closed on the baby's swaddling clothes. Vasilisa didn't flinch. She allowed the white wolf to lift Trevor from her arms. The baby squealed with delight, and giggled as Lev turned around. Madeline lowered her sword. The white wolf carried the precious bundle toward her. He stepped gracefully and gently over rocks to avoid jouncing the baby. Trevor's smile indicated he was experiencing no fear or pain. He kicked his feet and laughed.

Madeline dropped her sword once more to take the baby when Lev reached her. He lowered the happy baby into her outstretched hands and opened his mouth to release his hold.

Tears streamed down Madeline's cheeks. She looked from Trevor up into the white wolf's eyes. Lev's eyes, not the wolf's, met hers in return. They were all together again.

"Do what you will. I hurt you. I hurt you all. I deserve the harshest judgment. Anna is well now. And all my wolves have claimed their mates," Vasilisa said. She hadn't moved. Lev jerked away from them. He whirled and leaped back toward the witch that had separated him from his family. He landed in front of her, a giant wolf in front of a delicate, lithe woman—yet Vasilisa was capable of summoning immense power to defend herself if she needed to. But she didn't. She simply bowed her head and waited for whatever fate might befall her.

"Lev, she hurt us, but she also protected us. She came for us as the curse was falling. She sang us to sleep and sheltered us on Krajina. You tried to tear the world apart as you searched for us. That same savage love lives in her breast. For Anna. For family. For us. Forgive her. Forgive yourself," Madeline said.

Thunder split the sky, and the earth shook. Madeline braced her feet against the quake and held Trevor closer. The thunder didn't scare the baby. He laughed as his father made the world tremble.

Suddenly, Lev stood before Vasilisa in his human form. His nudity didn't make him appear vulnerable. He was a mighty creation of blood and bone and enchanted blood. But he'd also created himself anew in the years of the curse. He was hardened and honed, tireless and scarred and relentless.

Madeline's heart soared even as her stomach fell. She'd been right to fear that Lev in his human form might be more dangerous to Vasilisa than the white wolf.

He was hers. He was Trevor's. But he was no longer merely a champion and a Romanov. He was a father and a husband. One who had never given up on his wife and child.

Even in his human form, Lev towered over the queen. Vasilisa raised her head to meet his eyes. Her face was still calm. She didn't cower or cry, didn't summon the violet gleam of her power. Her hands stayed at her sides.

And suddenly, Lev went down on one knee before the Light *Volkhvy* queen. She had saved his baby from the Darkness that had tried to devour Trevor's innocence— the darkness she had caused and the Darkness of the marked *Volkhvy*. Trevor had been the line she wouldn't cross. The line that defined her right to be the Light *Volkhvy* queen.

Vasilisa did start then. Her face crumbled, and as it filled with sorrow and joy, she looked older than she'd looked before. Time touched her as Lev Romanov proclaimed his loyalty to her once more. Soft wrinkles appeared at the corner of her moist violet-blue eyes and around her pale lips.

"A touching display. I'm almost sorry to interrupt," Aleksandr said. He stepped from the portal on an oily black carpet of Ether that poured along under his feet from where he'd come. Several of his marked followers appeared with him. And following at their heels were half a dozen zombie wolves that cavorted around their masters in spite of looking the worse for wear. Black tongues lolled and wounds seeped, but they were soulless and mindless, completely animated by marked *Volkhvy*.

Lev rose to his feet and shifted in one graceful motion. One second he was human; in the next, the earth shook and the white wolf was illuminated in a brilliant flash of ruby light. Madeline had reclaimed her sword. She held Trevor with one arm and the ruby blade with the other. Its light surrounded her and the baby in a scarlet aura. Across the rocky clearing, the white wolf also had an aura of red all around him, and two glittering rubies for eyes.

"How could you all forgive her? She used and abused. She tainted and took. And you bow to her as if she still deserves to be queen?" Aleksandr said.

Madeline could hardly bear to watch him speak. His lank hair was no longer his defining feature. The Ether taint that had made his hair appear heavy with oil was now a streaky black coating all over his skin. But it wasn't a static stain. It flowed like a sentient liquid with his movements. It disappeared and reappeared from his eyes and mouth, from his nose and ears.

The Ether he'd welcomed into his blood and his soul now overflowed the vessel of his body.

"So. You have become Dark *Volkhvy,* and we won't need Anna's bellflower mark to identify you any longer," Vasilisa said. Her hands glowed with violet energy. The power she summoned grew to surround her. Madeline didn't find the queen's power reassuring. She'd never seen her summon the crackling violet aura before.

This Arizona desert plateau had become a battlefield, and she held her babe in her arms.

"I am the chosen vessel of the Ether itself," Aleksandr replied. "And I will rule you all."

He didn't summon typical *Volkhvy* power when he attacked. No gemlike shades of energy erupted from his hands. The oily Ether that coated his skin flowed to his outstretched fingers in a sudden rush, and it was the Ether that exploded from his palms as he aimed them at the queen.

Vasilisa met his attack with a violet arc of energy, but her power was absorbed by the black. Her violet energy merely slowed the attack. The oily black stream

Aleksandr shot from his hands continued to consume Vasilisa's light as it came closer and closer to her.

And then the white wolf broke the stream. He leaped between his queen and Aleksandr. Madeline screamed. The oily Ether splashed against his ruby aura. But as it splashed, it also took hold. It easily penetrated the aura to stain his pristine fur.

"No!" Madeline protested.

But she couldn't leap to Lev's defense, because the zombie wolves and their marked masters attacked her. She was driven up against the rocks surrounding the cave where Vasilisa had hidden.

Trevor was crying now.

As she fought back wolf after wolf, she turned her body sideways to protect her baby. The ruby sword glowed, and its light was suddenly redirected completely toward the aura surrounding her child. Her connection to the blade had subconsciously told the power what to do: protect Trevor at all costs. She was left defenseless except for the sharp blade in her hand. It was all she needed. She slashed and hacked, and the wolves fell.

But they weren't ordinary wolves. They were vessels of Darkness, and their masters caused them to rise again and again.

The white wolf's howl rent the air. Lev's fire and fury was in the wolf. His love for his family was unstoppable. The Ether tried to enter him, but there was nowhere for it to go. He was hard. Impenetrable. Completely filled with purpose. And his wild, savage love was too light for the Darkness to touch.

The oily Ether rode his fur, but it sloughed off, as it couldn't invade his body. It fell in useless puddles on the ground, only to evaporate as black smoke in the hot desert sun.

Lev shielded Vasilisa even as he stalked toward the witch who would take her throne. He had pledged his loyalty to the queen for Madeline and Trevor. Now he protected her in order to protect them. She'd proven that she would stand for his family. The white wolf required nothing more and would accept nothing less.

The Ether Aleksandr sprayed from his hands seemed to come in an endless stream. It didn't matter. The white wolf faced it all, and it splashed off him and fell to evaporate on the ground. The power of the spray was tremendous. He had to press into it and against its force.

But his power was tremendous as well. He refused to back down. He braced his shoulders and his spine and took step after step toward the Dark witch.

Madeline and Trevor were in danger because of Aleksandr. He had to be crushed so they would be safe.

"You will fail!" Aleksandr screamed. His voice was oily and wet as Ether flowed from his lips with his words. But there was something else wrong with Aleksandr's voice. The white wolf's ears were able to detect an echoing quality. When the witch screamed, he screamed with two voices.

"It's the witchblood prince. He's using Aleksandr to try to manifest from the Ether. It's been him the marked witches were channeling all along," Vasilisa warned. "No wonder they were corrupted. He must have ridden the first wave of Ether into Aleksandr, and he's been growing stronger ever since."

"You will fail as you failed before!" the witchblood prince continued to scream. With his own voice and with Aleksandr's.

His words were meaningless to the white wolf. Only

his human form thought he'd failed. His wolf form knew he had been preparing to finish a long battle. What was time to an enchanted wolf? He had all the time in the world.

The black liquid that coated Aleksandr's skin began to form a new face made of oily Ether over Aleksandr's face. The features yielded to high cheekbones, a sharp nose and a lean jaw. When Aleksander screamed, the black liquid face grimaced and opened its mouth wide, too. But the Ether face laughed instead of echoing Aleksandr's scream. The laughter was wet. Black bubbles roiled from the Ether face's lips as the face behind it struggled.

Aleksandr raised his hands to his face, but everywhere his fingers disrupted the Ether face, it liquidly reformed once his fingers passed through. The marked witch couldn't dislodge the entity that used him. He clawed and clawed, but it was too late. Far too late. Wet laughter came louder as Aleksandr screamed in fear and frustration. His utterances had become eerily sibilant as if oily liquid prevented clear elocution. The two faces simultaneously competing for space made the white wolf shake his head to clear the double vision.

"It's him! It's Gregori! The witchblood prince!" Vasilisa shouted.

"I refuse to be banished. I will rule you all and Elena will be mine," the possessed witch swore. "All of the warriors will belong to me. Vasilisa will belong to me."

The white wolf's jaw had been made to destroy witches. Two or twenty. He used it now, crushing the witch that had become nothing but a vessel for the taint of the witchblood prince. Aleksandr fell when Lev opened his mouth to release him. He crumpled in a bloody heap on the ground. His blood was oily and black. The coating that had become another face dissolved into a puddle onto the ground. He'd defeated the witchblood prince before he could fully manifest. Two evil witches with one bite.

"Thank you," Aleksandr said, gurgling as the last of the oily taint flowed from his lips. Once he was empty, he breathed no more.

Lev turned around from the smoking corpse and the puddle that was already being absorbed into the ground, and crossed the clearing. When he had protected Vasilisa from Aleksandr's attack, she had turned her attention to helping Madeline. Trevor was protected by all the ruby's power in an aura of scarlet light, but he was also protected by the queen herself. She stood in front of Madeline's left side and used her glowing violet body as a shield against the zombie wolves' endless attack.

Endless until Lev turned their bodies into pieces that couldn't be reanimated, at any rate.

The marked witches' attack had eased when they witnessed the transformation of their leader. They must have feared that the taint within them might allow the witchblood prince to enter them as new vessels. Their hands came down, and they backed away from the mother and child they'd been terrorizing with the wolves.

Two or twenty. He'd been made to deal with evil witches. Numbers didn't matter. He was tireless. The remaining marked *Volkhvy* fell beneath his crushing bite in the same way that their corrupt leader had fallen. Only then did Madeline lower her sword so that she could comfort her crying child.

He'd saved them. This time he'd saved them. But the baby's fearful cries still pained his sensitive ears. He didn't know how to wage a battle against tears. There was nothing left for him to do. Tireless or not, Lev fell to the ground at the feet of his mate.

Thunder rent the air, and the earth shuddered beneath them as the white wolf shifted back into his human form. Lev immediately acknowledged his exhaustion. Unlike the white wolf, he could admit when he needed to rest. But he reached for Madeline's leg anyway. He grasped her to let her know that he heard Trevor's cry, and he supported her efforts to soothe their baby's tears. He wanted to envelop them both in his arms and protect them forever. At the same time, he knew that wasn't possible.

There was always another threat on the horizon. The white wolf dared a world of evil to face him. Lev wanted to spare his family from the fight.

Vasilisa came forward. She removed the white cloak from her own shoulders and allowed the voluminous material to float down over Lev's back.

"I knew you would come," she said. "I always knew."

Chapter 24

Unlike while in his wolf form, Lev still had reservations about staying with his family. He now knew that the white wolf would never leave them. So there was only one option left to him: disappearing into the Ether. If he chose to make the jump to nothingness, he would take the brash wolf with him into the dark. Only then could he be certain that his family might be able to live a normal life without being chained to a Light *Volkhvy* champion who was determined to fight.

Madeline was covered in black blood on one side. The baby and her left side were completely clean. She had managed to shield him completely from the horrible attack—this time. But she and the baby would always be in danger as long as she wielded the ruby blade.

Long ago, he'd tried to shield her from the battlefield. But she hadn't been safe in Bronwal, either. The ruby warrior was a target. The white wolf could accept that. Lev, in his human form, could not.

As soon as his decision was made, the wolf in his heart began to fight against it. Lev kept the shift at bay the same way he had in the days that he'd traveled with Madeline—with an iron control that severed his connection with her. Even exhausted, he was tireless in his determination to protect her. In that, he and the white wolf were alike.

The ruby sword died.

At first, Madeline was too busy with the baby to notice. For Lev, the sudden silence in his mind and in his blood was deafening. He stumbled through an echoing vacuum of loneliness that was similar to the Ether that would soon welcome him into its icy embrace. He'd been this alone before. He'd endured the ice before. For his family, he would do it again.

Vasilisa brought them all to Krajina. She shielded the baby and her tired warrior with her violet light. No one noticed that the ruby sword was dead. With Vasilisa's power, their time in the Ether was negligible. But it was a reminder to Lev of the nothingness he would endure to protect Madeline from the connection between them.

The island was more beautiful and peaceful than Lev remembered. His fury had disrupted Vasilisa's false atmosphere the day he sensed Madeline waking. The disruption had allowed the true Hebrides' climate to storm in on them with wind and rain. Nature's fury had perfectly mirrored the fury he'd felt that day. He hadn't caused it, but he'd welcomed it. As the rain had lashed his skin and the ocean had crashed onto the rocks below, he'd thought he deserved the pain.

Today, the queen's enchantment held. The air was warm and mild. The ocean was calm. Trevor laughed in his mother's arms as they stepped from the Ether into the light. His son's laughter sealed his decision. Krajina would be the perfect, protected home for them.

They all paused on the cliff overlooking the calm sea. Lev reached to touch his baby's face. Trevor reached up to grasp his hand with a grip more powerful than Lev expected. It was Lev's turn to laugh, even though his joy in his son was bittersweet.

If Madeline noticed his mood, she didn't let on. She smiled in the sun, and her hair gleamed in myriad shades of red, from ruby to copper to scarlet to strawberry blonde. She was shining. She needed a bath, but she was still shining. The black smears of Ether taint did nothing to mar her perfect porcelain skin. Lev tried to memorize the moment. He tried to pretend he could take it with him into the abyss.

Krajina was the place for Madeline and Trevor. Just as it had always been. Except this time, Trevor would grow and Madeline could laugh and sew or sketch to her heart's content. She would never have to wield the sword again. The queen would guard against future invasion. Aleksandr's attack had only prepared her for future possibilities. She would fortify Krajina against them so his family could enjoy their peace.

And he would disappear.

He would protect them the best way he knew how: by removing the white wolf as a threat to their lives.

Lev thought she didn't know. The truth was that she felt the loss as soon as he severed their connection. Her heart echoed with every beat in her abandoned chest— beats that stuttered, as if her heart couldn't quite find the right rhythm.

Madeline continued as if nothing was wrong. She

placed Trevor in a borrowed cradle that Vasilisa provided. The rose-and-thorn motif on its headboard and footboard only caused her a moment's hesitation. She was certain the borrowed cradle was Anna's, and Anna was her friend. There was nothing to fear from Anna's mother. Not anymore. The queen's appearance continued to startle her. She softened by the minute. And her silvery white hair was shot through with strands of silvery gray.

Madeline had stopped crying. The baby was safe. He'd been returned to her arms. They'd survived the attack on their family. Her tears for Lev burned behind her eyes, but she refused to let them fall. Trevor slept the ordinary sleep of a tired baby who'd just been fed. He was back with his family, where he belonged. It was up to her to convince his father that he belonged as well.

She found Lev in the guest room next door. The ocean-facing rooms were barely separated by a latticed wall with an arched opening to the side. Lev stood at the window looking down at a troupe of witches standing guard below.

"They aren't guarding against attack. They're keeping you here. Giving you time to reconsider," Madeline said.

Lev turned from the window to watch her approach. She'd already bathed and changed into clothes that Vasilisa had provided. Her silk gown was loose and flowing, the color of her ruby when it was bright and alive. It matched the color of certain strands of hair on her head and called attention to the deep pale *V* of her cleavage.

She was well aware of how her curves filled out the silk even before Lev's blue eyes tracked the movements of her full breasts and hips beneath the gown. She wore no underclothes. Her body was as bare as she intended her heart to be.

"Reconsider what?" Lev growled. He always growled. And the burr of his hoarse rasp would always cause shivers of erotic response down her spine. The howls that had ravaged his voice over the centuries had all been for her. She wouldn't let them be for nothing. He thought they were saved—he didn't realize that they could only save each other, every day for the rest of their lives, if they stayed together.

"Leaving," Madeline said.

She stopped inches away from his lean, towering frame. Maybe one day he would fill out his big, broad Romanov body, but for now, he was still the runner. Still the starving wolf who had driven himself to the brink of madness to be sure he would be strong enough to save her when the time came.

He had bathed and changed as well. Maybe he hadn't meant to disappear without seeing her first. Maybe he'd always intended to say goodbye, guards or not. He was dressed in truly modern clothes for the first time. A thin, soft marled T-shirt hung softly against his skin, leaving nothing to the imagination. She could see the outline of his pecs and his abdomen, the dusky pebbles of his nipples. With the T-shirt, he wore matching lounge pants. Although they were loose, they clung to his large muscled thighs...and other things.

"You're in danger as long as you're with me. Both of you," Lev said.

"And the white wolf will never leave us," Madeline added. "Though you think you'll take him with you and disappear into the Ether." He wouldn't. Lev would never leave them. The white wolf was his heart. She only had to make him see that. "You won't leave me. Not after all this time. We deserve to spend the rest of our lives together."

"I'm not so savage that I'll put my desire to be with you over your safety. Or Trevor's safety," Lev said.

Madeline stepped closer. Lev didn't step away. She was sure he was more savage than he understood. Because she was more savage than he understood. There was no way she would let him go. Not now that she'd remembered all they'd meant to each other. Not now that they meant more to each other than they had before. The battles they'd fought had only made their love stronger. She didn't need sacrifice. She needed a partner.

"You've always thought you had to protect me, but I'm a warrior, Lev. And I'm meant to be your companion and your partner. We protect each other," Madeline said. "It isn't up to you to decide whether or not I wield the ruby blade. That decision was always mine. It's mine still."

Suddenly, the room was lit by a flash of ruby light as the sword came to life. Madeline had left it in the corner while she fed Trevor. But her hold on it hadn't been broken. She had only allowed Lev to think that it had, until she had time to soothe his concerns.

"There will always be another threat. Another Dark witch waging war against the Light. Or another Light witch hungry for power and ready to rise against Vasilisa," Lev warned.

"If you leave us, you'll leave us to face those threats alone," Madeline said. "I'm not a warrior because of our connection. I'm a warrior…and that's what caused our connection. I will fight the Dark with or without you. But I prefer with."

She pressed her body against his. His heart beat against her breast, meeting and matching the rhythm of her own. He couldn't deny their connection. Neither of them could, although they'd tried.

"But Trevor—" Lev began.

"Has two powerful parents to protect him until he grows into his legacy. He's a Romanov. He'll need both of us to help him learn how to live up to his future," Madeline said. "You were created as savage as you need to be to face the darkness. And I was Called because I can take it. I'm a survivor. Just like you. I'm fierce and tenacious. More than capable of fighting alongside the white wolf…and you. Trevor will grow up to stand against the Dark as well. It's in his heart and his blood."

"I failed you both when I failed to save you from Vasilisa," Lev said.

Madeline slid her hands up the hard plane of her lover's chest. She twined her hands behind his head, threading her fingers into the fall of his wild blond hair.

"The white wolf always had a plan. You thought you had failed, but success only took more time than you allowed yourself. I'm here now. Take me in your arms. Stop resisting our connection. You're punishing yourself when we should be celebrating," Madeline said.

"I've been an exile for a long time. I know how to be wild. I'm not sure I know how to be civilized," Lev confessed.

His erection had risen between them. She pressed his heat between them. Moisture welled between her legs as she remembered that heat stretching and filling her. She could claim the sword's power herself. Just as she claimed their connection. But she wanted him to claim it. And her. Hard. With all the furious passion that time and distance had caused between them. With all the desire that their partnership against evil had kindled. She didn't want peace. She only wanted occasional interludes so they could appreciate their victories between battles.

"You don't have to be civilized with me," she whispered against his neck as she pulled him down to her lips. He didn't resist. He melted into her hot mouth as she tongued his pulse to taste its rapid beat. "I want your wolf heart as much as I want you," Madeline insisted.

Lev swooped to pick her up then. Both of his big arms came around her, and he carried her to the bed. He placed her in the middle of it and then sank down on top of her. Her gown was in the way. His lounge pants and T-shirt were barriers she almost couldn't stand.

But then she realized it didn't matter.

He settled between her legs anyway. His bulging erection was hot against her. Silk and cotton didn't stop her from feeling his urgency or his heat. He thrust his hips, and she lifted hers to meet his thrusts. He dropped his mouth to her left breast to suckle her nipple through the silk of her gown.

"Shhhh," he murmured as she tried to reach for his shirt to pull it over his head. He took her hands and pressed them firmly into the bed on either side of her head. "I need the barrier to slow me down. If this is a celebration, then we need to savor every second of it."

She stilled and stopped, then met his intense gaze. He was taking it all in. Her impatience. Her urgency. Her hunger. Her needs. He gauged her response as he tilted his hips to position his erection against the spot that would bring her the most pleasure. She gasped when he found it. Her hips jerked reflexively. And he laughed, rough and low.

"I'm going to rip this gown from your body before

the night is over. I'm going to tear out of these pants and into you. But not yet. First, I want to watch you come. I want to make you fly," Lev said. "I can feel your heat through the silk. And you're almost more than I can stand like this. You're covered by this ruby gown, but just barely, Maddy. I can see every luscious inch of your pale skin shining through. And I love to anticipate completely baring your skin, inch by beautiful inch."

He illustrated his hunger with a deep kiss, delving with his tongue into the intimate recesses of her mouth. She hungrily met his tongue with hers. She found the moist velvet of his mouth and teased in and out of those vulnerable depths again and again. He groaned into her mouth. Maybe he knew she was showing him what she wanted him to do to her with his cock. She begged wordlessly with her thrusting tongue and undulating hips.

But he moved her hands above her head without letting them go. He placed the back of her left hand in the palm of her right, and then held them together against the pillow with one hand.

"Not until you come for me," he said against her mouth while they kissed.

And then he caressed his free hand down the length of her silk-clad body. She cried out under his gentle, teasing touch, but he ignored her impatience. He softly cupped the neglected breast he hadn't suckled. He moved his lips to that nipple and paid it the attention it so desperately needed.

Then he moved his hand lower.

The silk didn't stop her from feeling the heat of his palm or the firm dexterity of his fingers. Nor did it stop her from aching to know his fingers' final destination.

Her body thought it knew. Her pulse throbbed between her legs as blood rushed to her most sensitive flesh.

"I want to feel how ready you are for me, Maddy. Are you wet? Are you hot? Are you eager to squeeze me deep inside you? Show my fingers what you want to do to me," Lev ordered.

His hand had settled on her mound, and he pressed his palm firmly against her. At the same time, he slid two silk-covered fingers into her wet crevice. The silk prevented his penetration. But it didn't prevent the teasing of her most tender spot. She cried out, and her hips jerked up off the bed. He leaned down to suckle her upper lip and she could taste salt—hers and his—from the perspiration their desires had caused.

"You can't show me, can you? This gown is in our way," Lev said. He still held her hands above her head, but he moved from between her legs. He rolled to the side and used his free hand to grab a fistful of silk. He pulled her gown up her legs as she undulated beneath the teasing sensation of slinky fabric sliding up her bare skin. Cool air finally brushed her sensitized flesh, and Madeline looked up to see Lev staring down at her. "Do you want my fingers, Maddy?"

"Yes," she said, without hesitation. She wanted more. She wanted him. But she knew she had to come first. He'd already laid down the rules of tonight's game. She wanted to be claimed. Giving her pleasure was his way of making her his. And she hoped she'd been right. He wasn't going to leave. His lovemaking had to be his promise to stay.

"Spread your legs for me," Lev ordered.

Madeline complied.

His eyes slid from her face down to the intimate folds she'd revealed, and she was rewarded with heavy eyelids and a softened mouth. He licked his lips as if they'd gone dry. And then he dropped the silk so he could caress his bare fingers up her leg and across her thigh. Madeline watched his face when his hand found her. But then she closed her eyes and threw back her head when he teased a finger just inside her.

"Yes, please," she begged.

"You're supposed to show me, Maddy. Show me what you want me to do to you," Lev said. His voice was raw with emotion. His erection was massive against her hip. She ached for it. So she thrust her hips up to claim his teasing finger. His hand brushed against her as she took his finger. His thumb found where she needed to be touched. And that teasing caused the pace of her hips to increase. "Is that what you want? That hard? That fast?"

Madeline cried out as her body clenched around his big finger. She shuddered with her climax, and suddenly Lev let her go. Her eyes opened as she trembled back down from the peak where she'd been taken. She watched him rip off his shirt and pants and throw them to the side. She was no longer held in place, but she was weak from the strength of her orgasm. She couldn't reach for him. She could only watch as he climbed back onto the bed.

His erection made her tender flesh throb in anticipation. But she was finally able to move. She rose to pull her gown over her head. It settled into a ruby puddle beside them on the bed.

Then she leaned to press kisses on his chest and shoulders. When he tried to reach for her, she held his hands to each side. Their fingers twined. He held her tightly, but he didn't protest as she licked and nibbled her way down to his erection. When she closed her mouth over its tip, he jerked and cried out her name, but she didn't let his hands go. She teased him as mercilessly as he had teased her, licking the tip of him and suckling until his thighs began to tremble with need.

"Get on your hands and knees for me, Maddy. I can't hold back any longer," Lev ordered. His voice was more hoarse than it had ever been. His need was harsh. A thrill coiled deep and low inside her as she remembered what that meant.

Madeline positioned herself in the middle of the bed. She did it slowly; she took her time. She knew every second was killing him because it was also killing her. She curved her back and spread her legs before she looked over her shoulder at Lev. The white wolf was in his eyes. His hair was wild around his face. A shadow had reclaimed the jaw she'd shaved. The sight of the erection she'd just suckled made moisture flood between her legs.

"I can't wait any longer, either," Madeline confessed.

Lev moved to position himself behind her. She watched his beautiful, hard body line up with the sensual offering she displayed for him. He met her eyes just as he spread her cheeks and thrust his erection into her folds. She cried out, but thrust back against him. To take more of him. To increase his tempo. He needed no further encouragement.

With the grace and strength no other man in the world could equal, he rode her pleasure, reacted to her every response. When she tightened, he thrust harder. When she sighed, he teased back to draw out her inner quaking around him. She came again and again, until her knees gave out and she collapsed on her stomach. Only then did he allow his own release. He followed her down to the mattress, but he held his full weight back from crushing her even as he cried out her name and filled her with his hot seed.

They fell asleep bathed in the soft ruby light of Madeline's persistently glowing sword.

Lev woke and disengaged himself from Madeline's embrace. Her lovely nude form sprawled across him and he was sorely tempted to wake her, but he quietly slid from the bed instead. Her breasts were tipped pink from his passionate suckling. Her lips were full and ripe from his kisses. He could feel the sensitized swell of his own lower lip where Madeline had nibbled and suckled until he thought he'd go crazy with need. She'd more than satisfied those needs after. And still, it was hard to leave her.

He had to force himself away from the bed. He dressed quickly before another sigh or the tilt of her smile tempted him back to her arms.

But as he tried to leave the room, he tripped over an object on the floor. He recognized it immediately. In their passion, they had knocked against the table beside the bed, and Madeline's sketchbook had fallen on the floor.

He took it with him out of the bedroom and down the hall. The sun had begun to rise. In an open breezeway between the main house and the guest wing, Lev paused for a moment to open the book. He perused the sketches of the white wolf he'd seen before. This time as he looked at them, he realized she'd drawn the white wolf filtered through Lev's own emotions. He'd hated himself and his failure to save his family from Vasilisa for so long. And that morning when he'd sensed Madeline waking, his loathing for himself had been at its worst.

It was his fear she'd captured. Not her own. She had always been courageous and optimistic. He'd been the one who had become terrified and jaded as the centuries dragged on.

Lev flipped past the wolf sketches that had misled him about Madeline's true feelings until he came to a sketch he hadn't seen. He recognized the moment she'd captured immediately, even if he hardly recognized himself.

He'd already decided that he would never leave her or Trevor. But now the true reason washed over him like an epiphany. Madeline loved him. She loved the man and the white wolf. Lev's face flushed as he looked at the page. The sketch she'd drawn as he'd stood in between man and wolf, fighting one and blaming the other, was idealized. He could never have looked so strong and righteous. He had never been as heroic as he appeared in this sketch. Her love was apparent in every line, every charcoal smudge.

Madeline had always had images in her mind. Before the curse, she'd embroidered her images in giant tapestries with needles and gem-colored threads. There was one self-portrait he remembered. He hoped it still hung at Bronwal so he could see it again. That one had been hyperrealistic. She had captured the beautiful warrior nature he'd fallen in love with from the first moment they met. She'd stood out among all the other women in the castle. Maybe it had been the intense way she seemed to soak up the world around her. She noticed everything, and often recreated what she'd seen on paper or fabric. She still did.

He'd known before he'd seen the tapestry. Once he'd seen the image she'd sewn of herself wielding the ruby sword, he knew that she knew, too. She heard and accepted the sword's Call to be his mate.

Lev closed the book and tucked it under his arm. He might have to hide it. That sketch was her heart on the page. No one else should ever see it. But hiding the sketchbook would have to wait. There was someone he needed to see and something he needed to do before Madeline woke up.

Chapter 25

Madeline's body was tender. She woke with a confused groan that turned into a sensual chuckle as she remembered the night before. Best of all, she remembered *every* night before. Each minute they'd spent together, in bed and out. Her memory had finally returned. Her fully embraced connection to the ruby sword had probably helped, but, as Vasilisa had said, she'd also needed time to heal. Time to recover and find herself again.

The warm glow her memories of lovemaking had created was quickly dispelled when she realized she was waking up alone.

Madeline jumped from the bed with nothing but the sheet to wrap around her. She stumbled into the room next door, only to nearly collapse in relief when she found Trevor kicking happily in his borrowed cradle. A Light *Volkhvy* servant greeted her from the rocking chair in the corner, and there was an empty bottle on the stand.

"The queen advised us to let you rest," the servant said. Madeline's cheeks grew hot when the servant's eyes twinkled in the morning light. Did the entire palace know that she and Lev were enjoying a passionate reunion?

Lev.

Where was Lev?

Madeline leaned over to brush Trevor's strawberry blonde curls from his forehead. He laughed and reached for the heavy locks of her scarlet hair that dangled in his face.

"I have to find your father, but I'll be back and we'll spend the whole day together," Madeline promised.

She forced herself to shower in spite of the worried pounding of her heart. She dried and dressed in a light, short summery dress unlike anything she'd ever owned. Her memories were back, but it would take some time for her to be able to read the variations in the connection they shared. The ruby sword still glowed faintly in the corner of the bedroom. She took solace in that, even though she couldn't quite sense where Lev had gone or what he was up to without her.

He hadn't forgiven the queen.

That thought followed her outside and up the hill to a large gazebo that overlooked the sea. The structure had been built above the rose garden, but Madeline turned her attention away from the roses and toward the ocean. A gentle breeze caused the swings that ringed the gazebo to sway.

Vasilisa was fine. She climbed from a path that led from the shore to the garden. When she saw Madeline, she joined her at the base of the gazebo steps.

She was dressed all in white again. Madeline had been told that Vasilisa had worn violet for mourning in honor of the daughter she'd thought she'd lost. For hundreds of years, she'd worn nothing but shades of purple.

"You told me I couldn't trust him," Madeline said when the queen paused on the stair.

"I was wrong. About Lev and a great many things. He had attacked Anna. He had poisoned her with his bite because of his hatred for *Volkhvy* blood. She almost died. I thought he was lost. Completely feral. But he was only trying to protect his family. He thought she was trying to hurt Soren. He thought she was as guilty as he knew me to be," Vasilisa said. Her story was briefly interrupted by Lev's appearance on the cliff above the sea, where the white wolf had first appeared. They watched him walk down the hill toward them. "I'm sorry I misled you. I was honestly trying to keep you and Trevor safe," Vasilisa continued.

"I can keep us safe," Madeline proclaimed.

"With my help," Lev said as he joined them.

"Where have you been?" Madeline asked.

He came to stand beside her. She noted the way he positioned his large body in between her and the tiny queen. The Light *Volkhvy* queen only smiled.

"You will forever be a wild creature, Lev Romanov. I well remember how skittish you always were around me as a puppy. I suppose I justified that caution in the end," Vasilisa said. The white of her Victorian-style dress gleamed like a truce flag in the sun. "I will leave you two to discuss what Lev has retrieved from Bronwal."

The queen walked away from the stairs rather than climbing them, and headed into the garden on the gravel path.

"You've been to Bronwal?" Madeline asked.

"Ivan has allowed the mirror to be repaired. Elena

insisted," Lev said. "I used the portal to fetch something you may or may not remember."

Lev raised his hand toward her, and Madeline's breath caught in her throat. A bright red gem in his palm had caught the sunlight, and it sparkled in a familiar gold setting. It was the ring he'd given her so long ago. The one that Vasilisa must have removed from her finger as she'd fallen asleep.

"Will you be my wife, Madeline? As we were once upon a time?" Lev asked. He took the ring in his thumb and forefinger and held it up for her inspection. She loved it. She loved him. Of course, her answer would have been yes. Except there was another answer altogether.

"I've always been your wife, Lev. And I will be forever. Even Ether couldn't part us."

Madeline lifted her hand so he could slip the ring on her finger. It felt familiar and fine.

"But I do think a celebration is in order. What would you say to a wedding? I think it's high time the Romanovs reclaimed their former glory, and I have just the place and time in mind," Madeline said.

Lev swept her up into his arms and carried her back toward the palace. They had the whole day and the rest of their lives ahead to plan and play with Trevor.

And with each other.

Epilogue

Straluci was shining in the spring sun. All of its stained-glass windows had been restored, and its copper-tipped towers gleamed. A strong wind whipped brilliantly colored flags above three of the towers, and on each flag the figure of a different wolf had been embroidered in vivid thread outlined in silver—black, red and white, of course. The embroiderer could be forgiven if the white wolf was just a little bit bigger and wilder and more heroic-looking than his brothers. After all, she was his bride.

"I can't stop crying," Patrice chortled. The old loyal housekeeper grinned so widely that no one believed her. "It's been so long since the Romanovs have had such a grand celebration!"

Although Patrice hadn't been asked to serve, she bustled around them all, straightening and arranging as she deemed necessary, often causing more confusion and chaos than relief. No one seemed to mind. Most eyes were damp. Most grins were wide.

But none so wide as Ivan Romanov's.

Madeline's brother-in-law stood on the rampart of the castle facing out to the pass below. Even at this distance, she could see him well. His black tuxedo stood out against the cream of the castle's stone, as did his broad shoulders and tall physique. She had glanced out the open window of her rooms, and his defensive stance had caught her eye. His huge arms were crossed over his barrel chest, and his legs were planted as if it would take an army to move them. He looked as if he dared a group of Dark *Volkhvy* to try.

As she watched, a graceful petite figure approached Ivan, gliding up behind him and taking his arm. Madeline would have known Elena even if the former ballerina hadn't been dressed in sapphire-blue. She would have matched the gem in the hilt of her sword as well as her husband's eyes. But at this distance, all Madeline could see was how her touch softened the big alpha. His shoulders eased and his arms uncrossed, and he turned away from his vigil to take his wife in his arms. As their mouths merged, Madeline stepped back from the window.

Her dress was waiting.

It hung in front of the wardrobe they'd borrowed from Bronwal. All of the furnishings in Straluci had come from the main Romanov castle. Both she and Lev appreciated modern amenities, but they also enjoyed the finer things from a time when craftsmen had created piece by piece with hand tools and extra care. The master bedroom was furnished with rowan pieces that had been hand-carved with a rhododendron design. It had been a gift from Lev to Madeline many years ago.

She reached forward and traced the dips and ridges of the flower petals in appreciation. She remembered her joy in the gift and the way it had commemorated their lovemaking in the rhododendron field below Straluci. They had conceived Trevor in that field. She was glad to have the memories back.

Her wedding dress sparkled against the light finish of the rowan wardrobe. It was ruby-red and a blend of modern and historic designs. Diaphanous chiffon created texture and movement, while layers upon layers gave only enough modesty to cover her breasts and hips. Pale skin would show through at the dips of her waist, the curve of her back and along the tall stretch of her legs as she walked. There was also a deep slit in the bodice from the high neck down to her upper stomach that revealed glimpses of pale chest only when she moved.

The sparkle in the fabric came from ruby chips sewn at the neck like a choker and the high waist like a delicate belt. The sleeves were embroidered satin and bell-shaped. The lower edges of the cuffs extended all the way to the floor. She'd done the embroidered vines herself, and the rhododendron petals had been created with more ruby chips.

There was a scratch at the door, and Madeline crossed to open it. She was expecting her sisters-in-law, and she wasn't disappointed. Elena must have fetched Ivan from the ramparts and then left him to come to her. She and Anna came into the room with Patrice trailing behind.

"Lev is going to love those," Anna said, gesturing toward Madeline's red satin underclothes. They matched the satin on her wedding gown's sleeves.

"I love vintage clothes," Elena said. "Those are from

the 1950s. The high waist of the panty looks amazing with your long legs. And that corset bra slays."

"Better than an actual corset," Anna said. "Believe me. Vasilisa wears them sometimes under those Victorian dresses. I prefer pants."

Madeline fought the moisture that tried to fill her eyes. She blinked rapidly and turned away. She loved having her memories back, but she was also thrilled to have woken to these new sisters. She'd barely known Anna as Bell before the curse had fallen. She'd been one of many castle folk who hadn't played much of a part in a warrior's life. And Elena was fascinating. She'd been born twenty years ago, yet she was strong and wise. The perfect mate for their alpha.

"We thought you might need some help with the finishing touches," Patrice said. She had already walked over to the wardrobe. She reached to take down the dress from its hanger. Anna rushed over to help while Elena grasped Madeline's shoulder. She had to tilt her chin to look up at Madeline, and by then, thankfully, the tears had dried.

"Soren is with Lev, and Ivan is with the children. They are all behaving like angels for the black wolf, but Ivan looks like he might shift and run away at any moment," Elena said. The image of the big alpha outnumbered by his nieces and nephew as well as his own son made Madeline laugh out loud, impending tears momentarily forgotten.

"Anna's twins might prove to be his downfall," Patrice murmured as she prepared the dress to slip over Madeline's head. "He's already grumbling to Soren about future suitors."

"As if the red wolf needs any encouragement to be overprotective," Anna said. She rolled her eyes, but they glimmered with good humor, picking up the green of her silky formal suit. She did wear dresses occasionally, but her clothes, like those of most of Bronwal's denizens, were oddly eclectic, spanning centuries in style, mixing and matching in odd ways.

Patrice wore her ancient apron over a sequined dress that hugged her generous curves. Anna called it a "pageant gown," but seemed secretly pleased that the housekeeper had chosen a shade of blue to honor her former master, who insisted on being called an "employer" now.

"Trevor has shifted twice. That we know of. But I'm sure the alpha can handle a pup," Madeline said.

She lifted her arms, and the ruby gown softly settled over her as the other women exclaimed. Her auburn hair was piled high on her head. There were strands in it that shone almost as brightly red as the wedding dress.

"I remember when I first saw the tapestry. That's when I began to know. I felt a sisterhood to the woman with the ruby sword. To you," Elena said.

"I remember sewing it. The truth was revealed to me, thread by thread. I was already in love with Lev," Madeline said.

"As were half the girls in the castle, if I recall," Patrice grumbled. She straightened the fabric of Madeline's dress with bustling fingers.

"That's true. Everyone was fascinated by the wild one," Anna said thoughtfully.

"Not you. You only ever had eyes for the red," Patrice replied. She looked at the former waif of Bronwal and smiled. Her fingers stilled and dropped from a job even she could acknowledge as perfectly finished.

"I always knew. Even before the emerald sword

Called, I knew he was mine," Anna said. "I just wasn't sure if we would ever be together as we are now."

Elena, Madeline and Anna all looked at each other. It was time to go down for the ceremony, but each seemed to take a moment to appreciate all they'd overcome. Then Elena broke the sudden silence. She reached in one of Patrice's pockets and pulled out a hammered copper circlet. Perfect rubies were spaced at decorative intervals along the band.

"For my sister. The mistress of Straluci. Long may she shine," Elena proclaimed. Tears came again to everyone then, but they were paired with beautiful smiles.

Lev straightened the fur-trimmed vest over his chest for the millionth time. He was dressed in the formal wear of his time. The bell sleeves of his rough silk tunic draped to the floor. With every step he took, he thought he would trip over them and fall. His leggings were new leather to match the body of the vest, but they'd yet to be broken in. They hugged the muscles of his legs uncomfortably close. His beard had been shaved. His hair had been trimmed, and its waves were held down with a hammered copper circlet around his head.

All in all, he looked like a man about to be married.

He couldn't have been more uncomfortable—or more pleased. He would wear anything for Madeline. The excitement in the air of Straluci was long overdue. The halls were filled with laughter and conversation. The kitchens were rattling with celebratory meal preparations.

And he knew for a fact that a reclaimed and polished hip tub was waiting in the dressing room of the master suite.

"So, does that mean you're the Light *Volkhvy* king?"

Lev asked his twin brother. Their gazes met in the mirror, and for one second they remembered a time when they'd both hated all witches. They'd been traumatized by the curse for centuries, and neither of them had known if anyone at Bronwal would survive. Least of all each other. Since then, Lev had revealed to Soren that the white wolf had never been as lost as he'd seemed. He'd merely been preparing in the most extreme ways possible to rescue his mate and his child.

"Technically, I'm a prince consort. Although the Light *Volkhvy* seem intent on referring to me as their queen's champion," Soren said. "Fanfare wherever I go. Food. Adoration. What can I say? You get used to it."

"Not the food. Maybe everything else, but I don't think I'll ever get used to the food," Lev confessed. "My wife isn't a queen, and the food is still sumptuous."

"And the soft beds and hot running water," Soren added.

"How does Anna feel? Is she ready to rule now that Vasilisa has stepped down?" Lev asked. He could finally say the former queen's name without anger. There would always be painful memories, but Madeline had helped him come to grips with the past and prepare to step into a happier future, together.

"Even as a waif, Anna ruled. She took care of us all from the shadows. Everyone seems to think I watched over her for centuries, but I assure you it was the other way around," Soren said.

Soren was dressed in more modern clothes. He was wearing a "tuxedo" that seemed, like Lev's pants, to have been tailored for a smaller man. The cloth conformed to his muscular physique like a second skin. Lev secretly thought their wives enjoyed the Romanov build and occasionally made suggestions to the seam-stresses after fittings.

"She is a fine queen, brother. I promise to serve her well," Lev said. The words carried the weight of the entirety of his former wild rebellion. And he meant every one.

"Can you love a witch, too, Lev?" Soren asked. It was almost time to go down for the ceremony. They had laughed and joked for an hour as they'd prepared. Now they stood side by side at the mirror. So alike, but so different. Together forever, even when they were apart.

"I can and do," Lev promised.

He'd once attacked Anna when he'd thought she was going to hurt Soren. He'd been feral, as far from his human form as it was possible to be. He'd been lost to his obsession of finding his wife and child, eaten alive by grief and loneliness.

Anna had forgiven him. Now Soren did, too. He grasped Lev's upper arms and pulled him into a hug that was almost as fierce as Ivan's. Only the pounding on his back was more tempered than the alpha wolf's, in that it didn't cause him to cough and pull away.

Someone knocked. It was Ivan, standing at the ready when Soren opened the door to him.

"It's time," the alpha wolf proclaimed. No one ar-gued. No one ever would. Well, except maybe for the three children who were held by uniformed nannies be-hind him. Lev walked out and ruffled Trevor's straw-berry blonde curls. His son laughed and the nanny smiled.

"He'll be in the front row, sir," she said.

"No. I think he'll walk with me," Lev replied. He reached for Trevor and placed the toddling boy on the floor. It had been a year since they'd rescued him from the marked *Volkhvy*. Lev adjusted his stride to accommodate Trevor's uncertain steps, but the boy seemed eager to grasp his hand and walk by his side.

The great hall was lined with people. The survivors of Bronwal and the Light *Volkhvy* mingled on both sides. Only Vasilisa was avoided. She sat on a chair placed with honor near the front of the crowd, and there was an obvious space around the powerful witch where humans gave her a wide berth. Soren and Anna's twins felt no such reserve. As their nannies carried them into the hall, they began to reach and beg for their grandmother. Vasilisa welcomed them with open arms, and the little girls sat on her lap and played with her silvery hair.

"Good luck, brother," Lev said to Soren with a chuckle, as his brother walked ahead to stand with Ivan at the front of the hall, where the ceremony would take place. Lev followed with a more measured tread. A witch with a harp played soft music in the distance. A human with a pipe joined in.

In a spur-of-the-moment decision, Lev paused in front of Vasilisa and bowed to the former queen. Trevor copied his father with a giggling laugh. She had cursed them, but she had also saved them. It was important for all of the guests to see that it was time to move on.

When he rose from his bow, Lev saw that Madeline had arrived. She waited for him at the front of the hall. He and Trevor walked together down the aisle. Lev could hardly breathe. His wife was the most beautiful warrior he'd ever seen, and that was saying something in a family filled with lovely, strong women.

Finally, he and Trevor reached Madeline's side, and the entire room erupted in applause. Anna stood, prepared to perform the ceremony. She looked like a queen in her bright green suit. But as the applause continued, she broke into a smile and joined the multitude of guests in their clapping. Trevor pulled his hand free from Lev's and started clapping and dancing as well.

And then, buoyed by the excitement, their rambunctious toddler shifted. There was no thunder and the ground didn't shake. There was only an atmospheric pop, and a large gray puppy took the place of the boy, gamboling at their heels.

Gray just like his grandfather, Vladimir Romanov.

But Trevor would redeem the Romanov name. Lev could hear it in his laughter. Could hear it in his joyful barks.

Ivan quietly said Trevor's name, and the gray puppy went to his alpha's feet. He sat down and fell silent. The crowd also quieted. When the alpha spoke, everyone listened. Lev reached for Madeline's hand as Anna proceeded with their renewal of vows.

The revelry had lasted into the wee hours of the morning. Lev and Madeline had slipped away well before the last keg was tapped. During their last dance, long after Trevor had been taken to the nursery, Lev had leaned close to Madeline's ear and murmured a sensual invitation she couldn't refuse.

"The copper tub is waiting."

Madeline laughed as the guests cheered when her husband swept her up into his arms and carried her out of the hall and up the stairs. Then she moaned when his lips found hers.

They discovered the master bedroom had been transformed into a private retreat, following Lev's instructions. The downy bed had been turned down, and spruce-scented candles filled the air with memories of their most recent first kiss. In front of the fireplace, the copper tub had been filled with steaming water.

"I know we've updated all the bathrooms, but this tub has sentimental value," Lev growled against the sensitive curve of her neck.

Madeline agreed. Especially when Lev placed her feet on the floor to search for the fastenings at the neck of her gown. He groaned his approval when the top of her bodice came free and the ruby chiffon slid off her breasts. The corseted bra cupped the globes of her breasts, as if to raise them toward his lips. He accepted the invitation. Lowering his face to her exposed cleavage, he nipped and nuzzled. Then he took the edge of the satin fabric in his teeth.

She gasped as he tugged, and he looked up at her reaction with the white wolf's eyes.

"Don't stop," Madeline ordered.

Her wolf obeyed.

He bit and pulled the satin, and the delicate silky strings gave way from their hooks. The corset's laces loosened, and the bra came free. Lev released his bite, and the undergarment drifted to the floor. Madeline's breasts peaked in the air beneath Lev's intense gaze. He didn't raise his head. Instead, he closed his mouth over first one nipple and then the other. He suckled until Madeline moaned his name and buried her fingers in his hair. The circlet that bound his hair at the temples was dislodged. It fell with a clang to the floor, but neither of them paused. Madeline rejoiced as his long waves fell free across her bare breasts.

"I'm going to bathe you. I'm going to lather and love every inch of you," Lev promised.

Madeline thrilled at the memories that his promise brought to life. Then she gasped when he reached with impatient hands to pull her loosened dress and her underwear off her body. The satin and chiffon fell in a scarlet puddle around her ankles. Her pale skin was left bare and trembling beneath his perusal.

"Your ruby dress was beautiful, but I think I prefer auburn curls," Lev said. He reached for her mound and cupped it gently to show just which curls he referred to. Madeline leaned into his touch as her knees went weak. And then she reached for his broad shoulders when a questing finger burrowed into the curls to find a more intimate spot.

"Lev," she moaned.

"Yes, Maddy? What do you need, my love?" Lev murmured roughly into her hair. She was leaning against his shoulder now. She'd twined her arms around his neck. Her breasts pressed up against his hard chest, and his free hand had come around to hold her to him.

His other hand was buried in the curls between her legs, and his fingers were doing marvelous things. She throbbed, and his fingers slid with the moisture her excitement created.

Lev chuckled when her hips began to undulate against his hand.

"Is that what you need?" he asked.

"Yes. Please," Madeline begged.

"But I promised you a bath first," Lev replied.

He withdrew his teasing hand and lifted her to place her in the hot water. The heat immediately heightened her arousal. Steam rose up her legs, tickling and enticing. Lev stood back to enjoy the sight of her standing naked in the tub in front of the fire. His eyes were dark in the dancing firelight supplemented only by the scented candles.

"My warrior's need laid bare and beautiful," he murmured. While she watched, he unbuckled and removed his vest. She could see his dusky nipples on the rounded pecs of his muscular chest through the thin rough silk of his white shirt. But not for long. Because he ripped the shirt off his head, ignoring the sound of torn seams in his impatience. His tight leggings rode very low on his lean hips. She could see a hint of gold hair low, beneath his navel. She could also see what her nudity was doing to him. The large swell of his erection bulged out, obvious in the tight pants.

"Bath first," Lev said when he noted the direction of her eyes. He stepped close to the tub and placed a finger under her chin. He lifted until she met his gaze. "Are you hungry for me, Maddy?"

"Always," she replied.

He dipped to kiss her in reward for her raw honesty. The pulse between her thighs increased with the sudden plunge of his tongue between her lips. Their mouths slid together. The tongues twined, and Madeline reached to press against the bulge of his erection with one hand. She weighed and measured his excitement through the leather until he was panting into her lips.

"Still want a bath first?" she asked, questioning his resolve.

"Oh, yes. I've been anticipating this all day," Lev said.

He pulled her hand away from him and raised it up to place a kiss against her heated palm. Then he released her so he could undo the lacings at his waist and pull the leggings off his hips and down his legs. Madeline clamped her thighs together to try to still the ache that arose when she got a glimpse of his massive erection. He was as excited by their play as he meant to make her.

"Lev," she said.

He stepped to her once more. On the way, he stooped to retrieve a sponge from a basket on the hearth. She was in the tub. He was out. But he stood close enough that her breasts brushed his chest. He brought the sponge up to her face and teased it along her jaw.

"Shhhh. I'm here. You're here. We have all night. We have every night. And I have such plans," Lev said.

He leaned to kiss her again, but this time he only gave her a gentle sultry taste and one dip of his tongue into her mouth, and then along her lower lip. She was breathing quickly from his teasing. He raised his face from hers and lowered the sponge. Along her neck, down between her tingling breasts. And lower still. To her stomach, over the curly mound he'd already teased.

Suddenly, Lev crouched to dampen the sponge in the hot water. He reached in the basket for a bar of soap, but as he lathered it, he looked up at Madeline. His head was even with her knees, very close to the core of her that throbbed from his earlier touch. As if he knew what she was thinking, Lev leaned closer to her legs and kissed the inside of her knee.

Madeline reached for his hair and buried her fingers in his blond waves. She squeezed and he chuckled. This time he didn't say "bath first," but she knew he thought it because he brought the soapy sponge up and washed the knee he'd just kissed. Then he lathered her higher, trailing the massaging motions upward, and her blood flow seemed to follow until her core pulsed with need and her head grew light.

"Your curls look so inviting when they're damp for me," Lev said.

"You make me wet," Madeline confessed. "No tub necessary at all."

Lev dropped the sponge and replaced it with the

palm of his hand. His fingers glided on the soap. He
brought up his other hand, and suddenly both of his big,
powerful hands were massaging her soapy thighs. He'd
dropped to his knees beside the tub. Water and soap
trailed down his muscled arms to dampen his chest.

And then both of his thumbs met at the crux of her
mound. They gently penetrated to tease and slide and
open her. She threw back her head, overwhelmed by
the sight of her wolf on his knees in front of her. Then
he speared the bud he'd revealed with his tongue.

Madeline cried out. Her body jerked as a sudden ex-
plosive orgasm rocked her. Lev moved his hands around
to cup her cheeks as he continued to thrust his tongue
along the tender crevice he'd found. He heightened and
extended her pleasure until her knees gave out and only
his strong arms wrapped around her kept her on her feet.

"Is the bath finished?" Madeline gasped when she
could speak again. Lev stood. His erection jutted out
in front of his hips. She pressed against him and his
steely hardness. She throbbed for more than his tongue.

"Definitely," Lev replied. He moaned and rocked
against the warm press of her body. She wound her
arms around his neck, and he raised her up by stiffen-
ing his spine so that her toes came up off the bottom of
the tub, and her curly mound teased against his erection. She joined her legs around his waist, and the teasing grew more serious. He penetrated her with just the
tip of his hard shaft, and it was her turn to rock against
him. He chuckled against her lips as she hungrily sought
his kisses, with frustrated murmurs and whines as the
deep penetration she craved eluded her.

She panted as the teasing inch of stimulation drove
her crazy with need. Her body was now moist inside
and out. She was damp from the bath, and perspiration,

and need. She soaked his shaft, and he slipped a little farther inside in spite of his supreme control. But Lev only relented when her whines became more urgent. He lifted her into his arms and cradled her to his chest. She tightened her arms to hold on. The scent of spruce was now joined by the scent of musky sweet excitement.

"I never know who I'm teasing the most when we play," Lev said. He backed away from the tub toward the bed.

"Tell me what you want," Madeline murmured into his hot neck.

"I want to bury myself inside you. Forever," Lev said. "And you?"

"I want to make you howl," Madeline said.

Lev took her with him as he fell back on the bed. She landed across his chest, but in moments, she had rearranged herself so that she straddled his stomach. His erection was hot against her bottom, and she wiggled against him to tease his swollen shaft, and also to tease herself against the golden trail of curls that led to his groin.

"I will, Maddy. I'll howl for you. Always," Lev promised.

She loved his promises.

Especially when she helped him fulfill them.

Madeline rose and slid back to position herself above his erection. He reached to place his thick shaft against her opening. She undulated her hips to tease her moisture against him. He cried out her name, and then shouted in pleasure when she lowered herself back down to engulf him.

"Howl for me," she ordered against his lips. She matched the thrusting of her hips with the thrusting of her tongue. Lev growled against her deep kisses and grabbed her hips. He pumped up into her and aided her movements with his strength, until the rapid friction caused her to tense and clench as she began to orgasm around him.

Her tightness slowed him down, but he didn't seem to mind. He only lifted his hips more insistently to drive into her tightness. Madeline rode him, just as she had done when he ran through the woods with her on his back. She followed his movements; she reacted to his every groan and sigh. This time they were as one. Joined. Connected. Never to be broken apart again. The bounce of his thrusting stimulated her nipples, and she peaked again. As she clenched and shook, his whole body went rigid, as hard as it was possible for a human to be, and then he did howl for her. He threw back his head and howled his release, long and loud and not caring if the whole world witnessed their connection.

Ruby light glowed from their eyes as they collapsed in each other's arms.

A long time later, after they had drifted lazily in the candlelight and the afterglow of their connection, Madeline rose on her elbow. She looked down at the big wolf she'd married. He looked rumpled and loved, but still wild. Lev Romanov would never be tamed.

Lev opened his eyes and caught her stare. A large smile curved his full lower lip. As always, it softened his lean, hard face. He reached for her hand and raised her ring to his lips. He held her gaze as he kissed the ruby.

"You knew you could shift when you carried me through the forest on your back. But you didn't. You almost ran yourself to death as a man to carry me away from the wolves," Madeline said.

"You would have refused to ride on the white wolf's back. I offered you a man's back instead," Lev said.

"I wouldn't refuse now. I love you. All of you. And I'm not afraid," Madeline said.

"Would you like to see the rhododendron field in the moonlight, Maddy?" Lev asked. He had risen on his knees. His hair was a tangled riot around his handsome, scarred face.

"Yes. I would," Madeline replied.

Lev leaped off the bed, and in the next moment, thunder crashed and the earth shook. The giant white wolf stood beside the bed. Its eyes glowed softly with her ruby's light. Madeline rose and dressed. She pulled her wedding clothes back on. As she fastened the neck of her dress, she knew she would embroider this scene. The mirror across the room captured the image for her as the white wolf kneeled down and she climbed onto his snowy back.

She wasn't afraid, not of the white wolf or of her capabilities. She had proven to herself and to the world that she would always remember how to wield the ruby blade and how to wed a legendary beast.

Lev jumped from the bedroom window. He used various architectural elements that jutted from the castle to leap from level to level until they reached the ground below. And Madeline easily held on.

I offer this back to you.

Her legendary husband had given her his back, his heart and his always. Most of all, he'd trusted her to make her own decision about the ruby sword. Their connection had helped all her memories to return, and now their past stretched out, clear, behind them, and their future stretched out ahead.

There would be more battles against the Dark

Volkhvy, but with a strong triumvirate of three legendary brothers and their warrior wives to stand against evil, the Darkness didn't stand a chance.

But for now, they enjoyed the interlude they both deserved. Lev's fur was soft and warm beneath her. She held on to his ruff with tight fists as his powerful body effortlessly carried her away.

They left Straluci to their guests and raced through the forest toward a field of rhododendron blooming in the moonlight…a warrior and her wolf, reunited forever.

* * * * *

COMING SOON!

We really hope you enjoyed reading this book. If you're looking for more romance, be sure to head to the shops when new books are available on

Thursday
18th October

To see which titles are coming soon, please visit
millsandboon.co.uk

LET'S TALK
Romance

For exclusive extracts, competitions
and special offers, find us online:

 facebook.com/millsandboon

@millsandboonuk

@millsandboon

Or get in touch on 0844 844 1351*

For all the latest titles coming soon, visit
millsandboon.co.uk/nextmonth